MW00881784

THE PAINTING BOX

A Novel

JULIA R. COOPER

Julia R. Cooper
United States of America
www.mylittlefrenchfarm.com

Publisher's Note: This is a work of fiction. Names, characters, places, and incidents are a product of the author's imagination. Locales and public names are sometimes used for atmospheric purposes. Any resemblance to actual people, living or dead, or to businesses, companies, events, institutions, or locales is completely coincidental.

The Painting Box/ Julia R. Cooper. -- 1st ed.

To my family, those who've gone on and those who remain, you mean the world to me.

Midway, Kentucky

Her breath turned to frost on the glass of the kitchen door. She pulled the dish towel from the pocket of her apron to wipe it away. It had been decades since Kentucky had seen such a crippling snow. In the glow of the security light, the snow fell heavy and wet, silencing the night air and every sound with it. The farm had never felt so still.

The boys were finally asleep in their bunk beds after a long day begrudgingly spent indoors. They'd fought over toys, argued over sports, and wrestled in the floor over absolutely nothing at all. She sighed, remembering, as she walked through the house picking up a basketful of their toys.

Her husband, too, had gone to bed earlier than usual out of sheer boredom. Hard working farmers do not like to be sidelined by the weather. But the deep and drifted snow, accompanied by subzero temperatures and blizzard force winds, had forced him inside. She rolled up his scattered newspaper sections and stuffed them into the kindling box.

She took her time finishing the daily chores, dreading what may come. Dishes washed, laundry folded, fire stoked, she treaded lightly down the hallway and listened at the door. When she heard her husband snoring, she opened the hallway closet, careful to avoid the squeak, to retrieve the video camera.

After having a houseful of discontented people in foul moods at her heels all day, she sat down in the rocking chair and closed her eyes. All was finally quiet inside the hundred-year-old farmhouse, save the crackling fire and whistling wind. She breathed in the stillness while she waited.

Every night for the last week and a half, she'd waited like this. Video camera at her side, power on, she'd waited. Night after night, she prayed she would not have to use it. Night after night, she prayed that it would never happen again and that she could forget that it ever had.

But tonight, it was not to be. She was startled out of her prayers. It was happening again. She knew she needed help, but first she would need proof. She grabbed the camera and hurried down the hallway. She paused before entering to clear the blurring tears from her eyes then took a steadying breath and pressed the record button.

1

Jules
Lexington, Kentucky

The late September sun peered around the curtain into the bedroom warning her she'd slept late. Jules Merritt lay motionless in her bed, trying her best to pull herself out of the hangover she felt from last night's adrenaline rush and subsequent crash. Like always, she'd lain awake for hours wanting only to drift off into nothingness. After all this time, Jules was tired of thinking about it, tired of trying to figure it out. She certainly did not want to talk about it this afternoon with Dr. Gray.

The sound of the shower curtain slinging open pulled Jules out of her dread. Will was already back from his morning run. Hearing her husband sing his happy morning tune lured her from the security of the blankets. Jules shuffled barefoot into the bathroom and hugged her husband from behind as he shaved. With his free hand, Will reached around and swatted her backside. Jules returned the favor before turning on the shower.

When she'd finished, alone in the bathroom, she ran a wide toothed comb through her unruly mess of hair then gave it a good shake. This was the extent of Jules' primping. She rarely wore makeup, self-consciously not wanting to draw attention to her eyes.

Jules knew she was a stark contrast to the women Will worked with. He'd once told her that there seemed to be an unspoken competition among them. He was one of only three male teachers in the school, far younger than the others. He'd told her that some days he felt as if he were the prize.

In the kitchen, Will peeled a banana, laid half on each plate, then sat down to eat his bowl of granola. "Are you sure you don't want me to meet you at Dr. Gray's office?"

"No, that's okay. You can't be in the room with me." Jules didn't want to have to be there herself. She certainly did not need Will there expecting her to have some kind of breakthrough.

"I feel responsible for encouraging you to do this."

Jules considered her words then said only, "I'll be fine." She draped the leather satchel across her chest and grabbed her coffee-filled Yeti cup. Without telling him about last night, she was out the door.

Will sighed as he poured her granola back into the box and tossed the uneaten banana into the trash.

***

Jules sat at her desk in the windowless office, checking off a couple of the easiest items on her to-do list, but her mind kept finding its way back to the dream. For as long as she could remember, she had been abruptly jarred from sleep.

As a small child, she remembered waking up feeling shaken and scared. Her parents would chalk it up to too much sugar, then her mother would calm her and tuck her back into bed.

As a young teen, just as she was drifting toward sleep, a feeling of dread would overwhelm her. Despite knowing her mother would shrug it off and send her back to her room, Jules still went to her. She knew her mother cared, but wondered why she'd always swept it under the rug.

Back to work, she scolded herself.

Jules taught French 101 and 201 at the University of Kentucky. She loved her job and was respected by her colleagues. Since she and Will did not have children, she was singularly devoted to her career, spending many unpaid hours helping struggling students or assisting others in the department. Chloe Wright, who taught English as a Second Language as an adjunct professor, was one of those she mentored. Jules never minded helping her, as the two had become friends.

Chloe knuckled a knock on the open office door. "How about lunch today? I'm buying," she asked as she helped herself to a piece of candy from the bowl on Jules' desk.

"I'll have to take a rain check. I have to leave early for an appointment this afternoon."

"Not a problem. How's my favorite fourth grade teacher?" Chloe picked up a picture of Will from the corner of Jules' desk.

"Sweet as ever. Annoying as heck." Jules looked up from the stack of tests just long enough to smirk at her friend.

"Well, I'd trade you in a heartbeat."

Though the women had similar personalities, their men were from different worlds.

Chloe's boyfriend was a project manager for a large commercial construction company. Josh was a manly man who worked hard and spent his off time with the guys. He enjoyed happy hour with his co-workers several days a week. On the weekends, Chloe would find herself alone again as there always seemed to be a playoff game in one sport, then another.

Jules wondered why Chloe stayed with Josh. She was accomplished for her thirty years. She spoke four languages and was working toward her doctorate. She took obvious care in the way she presented herself. Chloe had a way of pairing form fitting slacks and high heels with her signature boho style shirts, making her look professional, while still showing her youth. Most days, she wore her long dark hair in a chignon at the base of her neck, pulled away from her painstakingly, yet moderately made-up face. Jules doubted that Josh noticed the attention to detail, much less appreciated Chloe's efforts.

She had once confessed that she was not-so-secretly jealous of the friendship between Will and Jules.

Chloe grabbed another piece of candy and was all the way at the end of the hallway when Jules heard her sing, "Maybe next time."

***

A single lamp cast long shadows about the room. Jules lay on her back, stuck to the leather sofa from a nervous sweat. Her eyes, veiled in thought, saw neither the ceiling nor the shadows, as she contemplated how her life had come to this.

She pulled the birthstone ring on her right hand back and forth across her knuckle, trying to decide if she should stay or bolt. She thought back to the day her mother had surprised her with the ring. She had been shocked to receive a gift so out of the ordinary. Money always seemed scarce on the farm, so an opal ring set in a gold band certainly seemed frivolous, even to a fourteen-year-old. Thinking about it now, Jules questioned her mother's motives. *Was it to assuage her own guilt or was it to take my mind off what happened?* Whatever the reason, Jules knew her mother would never approve of what she was about to do.

On the other hand, she began to twirl her wedding band. *But I promised Will that I would follow through this time. He has been so patient with me. I can do this for him, just this once.*

It had been Will who suggested that she see the doctor. Though he had known about Jules' troubles since before they were married, his optimistic attitude led him to believe that if he could just make her happy, it would all simply fade away. For most of their fifteen-year marriage, that seemed to be true. However, recently her anxiety and phobias had intensified, and worst of all, the night terror was back.

Will had learned about the doctor through the experience of one of his students who had been traumatized by seeing his grandfather struck by lightning. Though the grandfather had survived, the boy panicked at simply the forecast of an approaching storm. His parents explained how Dr. Gray had helped their nine-year-old son through trance therapy, a lighter form of hypnosis. After witnessing dramatic improvement in the boy's behavior at school, Will had cautiously approached the subject with his wife, hoping she would understand his loving intention.

She did not. It hurt her that someone whom she confided in, someone she thought understood her, could injure her in her most vulnerable place. Once Jules had gotten over the initial shock of his suggestion, she was able to admit to herself that anything was worth a try. Trusting Will, she agreed to see the therapist.

In the background, a soothing voice set against monotonal music sought to coerce Jules into a state of calm, but the voices in her head drowned it out completely.

Again, she pulled the opal ring off her finger as the negative thoughts kept coming. *I cannot believe I ever agreed to this.* Jules forcefully slid the ring back into place and arched her back to release herself from the grip of the couch and from her promise to try this in the first place.

Dr. Gray entered the room quietly, expecting to see her patient relaxed on the sofa but nearly bumped into Jules, who was preparing to leave. "Is something wrong?"

Jules opened her mouth to explain but blew out her breath and walked back across the room, giving in. *After all*, she told herself, *this has been planned for weeks. It has been discussed at length. What do I have to lose?* Jules lay back on the sofa, placed her head on the pillow and followed the instructions coming from the recording.

Monitoring her patient's breathing, Dr. Gray stopped the recording and softly began. "I would like for us to take a walk back through your memories. I want you to recall only pleasant moments in your life." Since Jules' troubles had been with her for as long as she could remember, Dr. Gray felt the key to success was to spend time on her early years.

She planned to use this first session to access the limits of her patient's conscious and perhaps, subconscious memory, in the most benign way.

"Let's begin with last week. Tell me something that made you happy. Was there an accomplishment at work that you were particularly proud of or a special evening spent with your husband?"

"Will surprised me by signing up for Netflix."

Watching movies together was a constant in their relationship. They would sometimes spend an entire Sunday locked in their bedroom under the covers, watching one movie after the other, stopping only to snack or to enjoy one another's company.

"He chose the DVD service by mail, instead of the streaming option, because of its extensive library of vintage foreign films, which he knows are my favorite. He spent the entire afternoon filling our queue with them."

Dr. Gray continued, "Now, let's walk a little further back to your time in college. Tell me, what was your most enjoyable year?"

"Junior year, meeting Will in art class," Jules said immediately.

"Can you picture where you were when you first laid eyes on him? Did he notice you, too? Allow yourself to be there, on that day, in that classroom." Dr. Gray was silent as her patient remembered.

Jules was consciously aware but felt herself transported. She felt as though she was actually there, seeing Will as he bounced into the room, late for class but not a bit ashamed. He'd addressed the class with an unapologetic, 'Morning, all.'

Will was 5' 11", an average height, but that was the only average thing about him. Jules would never forget that moment. He had the whitest teeth and a big smile that dared you not to smile back. His shaggy blonde hair made his blue eyes sparkle. He'd worn a button-down shirt, half tucked into khaki shorts that showed just enough of his tanned legs to make her look all the way down to his sockless loafers.

Dr. Gray began again, "Staying with pleasant thoughts today, can you tell me how it felt to get your driver's license?"

"Like a bird let out of its cage," Jules responded.

"Be there in the car, the first time you drove alone. What was the weather like? Where did you drive?"

A pleasant look took over Jules' face as she thought back to that day.

It wasn't surprising that her father had let her take the truck out. She'd been practicing driving the stick shift around the farm since she was old enough to reach the pedals.

"When I got to the end of the driveway, I realized I had nowhere to go. So, I rolled down the windows and drove down the country roads, along all the horse farms. I even stopped a few times to pet them if they were close enough to the fence. It was a freedom I'd never known." The smile lingered on her lips, but she said nothing more.

Dr. Gray wrote a note on her pad questioning why Jules didn't have any place to go and why she hadn't shared this milestone with friends.

"A little further still," the doctor continued. "Talk to me about your high school years."

Dr. Gray watched Jules' smile fade while a look of sickness took over her face.

"There are no happy memories there, or middle school either," Jules said bluntly.

"Moving on then," Dr. Gray quickly redirected Jules' unpleasant thought while penciling another note.

"Now, let's go back to life on the farm. As a little girl, what fun things did you do? What brought you joy there?"

"The barn. I spent most of my time there when I was a teenager, grooming Honey after a long ride. But even before I had my horse, I was always up in the loft playing with dolls or reading a book." Jules pictured herself lying on a quilt, spread over a soft cushion of hay. It had been her place of refuge. Solitude was rare in their small farmhouse, so Jules had appreciated a secluded place of her own.

"When you were younger, where did you play outside?"

"The swing," she replied in a near whisper. Jules had spent her childhood daydreaming in that swing.

"Allow yourself to stay there and swing for a moment."

Jules took a deep breath, her eyes still closed. She remembered leaning back, stretching her legs out as far as she could as she soared forward, trying to reach the lowest branch of the tree.

Dr. Gray turned her head to see Jules pointing her toes.

"Now tell me about one of your favorite Christmas memories."

"We always cut our own tree." Jules pictured it vividly in her mind, piling on layers, going out into the cold with her father and brothers to the back of the farm where a grove of evergreen trees encircled the pond. Jules could smell the intense aroma of the pine.

Dr. Gray asked, "Do you remember a favorite present?"

Jules remembered the Christmas she'd received an orange Barbie camper. She could see the drawn-on scenes inside it. She could hear the snap of the rigid plastic side door. Lying there, Jules felt the excitement of being a kid again.

"You mentioned in our initial meeting that you loved being rocked as a child. Can you see the rocker in your bedroom?" Jules slightly shook her head. "It was in the living room."

"Can you feel the warmth of your mother as she held you and rocked you to sleep?"

Jules placed herself in that familiar place, turning her head to the side. She had serene memories of being rocked.

"Did she sing to you?"

"She hummed," Jules whispered fondly.

Her mother had been happy to accommodate her request, even after she was far too old to be rocked to sleep. Jules replayed the creak that the cane bottom rocker made on the hickory floor. She could feel the quickening pace of her mother's rocking that threatened to put her to sleep right there in the therapist's office.

"Now, Jules, let's walk back further still. Can you place yourself in your room, in your crib, awake and listening to the sounds of the farmhouse? What do you hear?"

Jules took her time, letting her mind find its way there. "My brothers playing in another room, the farm report on the radio in the kitchen."

"Can you picture your mother picking you up?"

Surprisingly, she could place herself in the crib. She could smell the comforting aromas of coffee and bacon, imagined or remembered. But it was her father she saw, leaning over the crib, smiling as he reached for her.

Dr. Gray pushed a little further, taking care not to lead her patient, "Very good, is there anything else?" She looked for a long moment at her patient. Jules' face muscles were completely relaxed. Her arms and legs were limp like dead weight. She had only ever seen Jules fully present and in control.

Jules, being completely relaxed, gave in and let her subconscious mind have the moment. *Floating weightlessly backward into calm darkness…dead silence…drifting…* Then abruptly, *a jolt…chaos…panic!*

Suddenly, Jules' peaceful smile faded. Her muscles began to tense. Dr. Gray witnessed Jules' brow sharpen as a terrified look took over her face. Her arms began to flail as she arched her back upward off the couch. Then Jules let out a terrified scream.

Dr. Gray dropped her notebook and moved to her patient. She gently pulled Jules' arms to her side. Speaking quickly but calmly, the doctor guided her patient back to the present.

Jules opened her eyes. Her heart was racing, and she could not catch her breath. Her eyes darted back and forth as she searched her mind. *What in the world just happened?*

Then Jules saw the wide-eyed look of shock on Dr. Gray's face, as if the doctor were asking herself, "What have I unlocked?"

2

Joëlle
Bordeaux, France 1685

The summer sun made its way over the city row houses of Bordeaux, pushing light down the narrow and cobbled streets into windows and door cracks, announcing the morning house by house.

Eleven-year-old Joëlle Violette Reynaud awoke to the clattering of porcelain plates being stacked and the low rumble of chairs scooted across the wood floor in the kitchen. She lay still, momentarily confused by the unfamiliar hum of busied conversation. Then her eyes widened, and a smile took over her face when she realized the day. She tossed off the covers and hurried to get dressed, eager to help with the preparations already underway a floor below.

"Henri, get up." She rapped on her brother's curtained doorframe. "Today's the day!"

Her brother was only three years younger than Joëlle but was still a baby in many ways. Henri was quiet, the opposite of his sister's *joie de vivre*. He was gentle, whereas Joëlle had no time for minced words.

"Not yet, JoVee," he whimpered, rolling onto his stomach.

Though the siblings had differing personalities, the two were the best of friends. Joëlle was Henri's guardian, his protector. His mild manner left him an easy target for the older boys in their Catholic school. Once, when Joëlle had been released early from the girl's nunnery school, she'd witnessed the bullying and retaliated against a boy two years her senior in her brother's defense. From that day forward, Henri began calling her his victor, Joëlle la Victrice, which soon became shortened to 'JoVee.' Their parents believed it to be short for Joëlle Violette, so they allowed it, but only in the privacy of their home.

Joëlle and Henri were the privileged children of Guy Reynaud, the owner of a successful cooperage in the heart of Bordeaux during a period of historic growth in the wine shipping industry. Guy, however, was the not-so-privileged son of Louis, a craftsman barrel maker from Baran, a little-known hamlet set deep in the Dordogne countryside.

Their mother, Marguerite, was the only child of Pierre and Emilienne De la Croix, of the high-born gentry class. Their fortunes were such that Marguerite had grown up the beneficiary of the art and culture of the day.

With a hardworking, successful father and a refined, cultured mother, Joëlle and Henri were blessed to live a picturesque life, at least for a while.

"Whatever you wish, but I'm not going to miss out on one more minute of this day," Joëlle said, giving up on her brother.

She scampered down the curved staircase and smelled fresh bread being pulled from the wood-fired oven by Clarise, her mother's occasional helper. "Mmmm, that smells good," Joëlle smiled with hopeful eyes.

"*Je suis désolée*, Mademoiselle, the bread is for this evening. Your mother has set breakfast for you," Clarise pointed to the small round table in the corner of the kitchen.

"Merci, Clarise." Joëlle thanked her but snarled her nose at the plate then skipped off to find her mother giving instructions to the gentlemen who were moving the twelve-foot dining room table from the center of the dining hall to make room for dancing that would take place at the party.

"Bonjour, Maman. What job can I do?"

"Bonjour, ma chèrie," Marguerite welcomed her daughter to the day with a kiss on both cheeks. "First eat, then I shall put you to work." At that, Marguerite spun around and was back to orchestrating the activities of the morning.

As Joëlle ate yesterday's leftover bread with butter and jam, she watched her mother move about in the next room, clearly in her element. Joëlle was never prouder of her mother than she was on party days. It was Maman's day to shine.

Marguerite was the envy of the who's who in all of Bordeaux. She was a creative soul who put her lifelong experience with art and culture to use when planning the themed parties she hosted twice a year.

In her youth, private tutors had come into the De la Croix home to teach Marguerite reading, writing and the basics of mathematics. Others taught her philosophy and dancing. Artists were brought in to educate her in the finer arts of painting, sculpting and music. She was assisted in her bath and helped into fine clothes. Her hair was even brushed in the evenings by someone else, but Marguerite was unaffected by all this lavishing. It was not who she was and certainly not who she would become.

For her parties, Marguerite called on those who had taught her music lessons to perform during dinner. Those who had taught her to dance were hired to genteelly assist those that might need lessons on the spot. Her art teachers were commissioned to paint murals on canvas that were to be displayed and sold during her parties, with the funds being used in her charity work. It was no wonder that Marguerite was a friend to many, the wealthy, the working class, and the poor alike.

The annual summer celebration was Joëlle's favorite because it marked the end of the school term which meant she would soon leave to spend the summer months in the country with her paternal grandparents. She longed for the days of bare feet, swimming in nearby rivers, and dinners eaten outdoors.

Just as Joëlle finished eating breakfast, Henri dragged himself into the room. She pushed her chair away from the table and stood to butter her brother's bread while he stared sleepily into space. "Here," she laid the breakfast on his plate. "Eat quickly so you can help." Then she disappeared from the room, eager to receive the first assignment from her mother. Henri yawned once more then began eating his tartine.

Joëlle was thrilled to be tasked with setting the formal dining table. This was the first time she had been trusted to handle the family's finery. A stack of delicate plates, rows of gleaming crystal goblets, and a mound of freshly polished silver flatware awaited her on the ten-foot walnut worktable in the kitchen.

"Be very careful," her mother instructed as she watched Joëlle attempt to balance the stack of wobbling plates.

"I will, Maman. Do not worry." Joëlle would not allow herself to disappoint her mother.

For the next half hour, she diligently placed each setting, taking care to adjust each piece again and again. Once she was satisfied that it was perfect, she sought her mother's approval.

"Très jolie, Joëlle, très jolie!" Marguerite praised her daughter as they both stood admiring the table.

"What shall I do next?" Joëlle was eager to impress her mother once more.

"I have an important job for you. It would be a great help if you would play with your brother outside to keep him occupied until time to get dressed."

Joëlle was disappointed that she was not asked to do more inside the house but knew that she would be helping her mother by keeping Henri from being underfoot.

"Allez, Henri." She motioned for him to follow her as she opened the glass door to the back stoop. She hopped down the steps, one at a time, humming a happy tune. Henri followed her silently as they ran the familiar route through the back garden, weaving around bushes and statues and along the flowered borders that were in full bloom. They climbed the rock wall lined with a myriad of rose varieties, all exploding in vibrant color. "Smell that, Henri? That's the smell of summer."

Marguerite smiled as she passed the kitchen window at seeing her children climbing rocks with her roses.

When the children reached the back of the garden, they took turns pushing each other on the wooden tree swing that had been made by their grandfather Reynaud. He had hung it from a branch so tall that the swing glided out past the fence at the edge of the property. The danger made it that much more thrilling, and Joëlle and Henri never tired of it. Hours passed before they knew it.

When Marguerite called them inside to get dressed, Joëlle, whose turn it was to push, ran as fast as her feet would carry her toward the house, leaving Henri to sit in the swing until it slowed enough for him to jump off.

"Wait for me," he called, but his sister was already hopping up the steps.

After climbing the back staircase, Joëlle found Clarise waiting in her bedroom to assist in getting her into the clothes that her mother had laid out for her. Joëlle happily allowed Clarise to pull and tug the dress into place over her undergarments, then again to yank and pin her curls here and there. She left a few dark tendrils to set off Joëlle's azure eyes.

When Clarise finished, she took a calming breath and wiped the sweat from her face.

"Merci, Clarise." Joëlle pinched up the floor length dress and sauntered into her mother's room to view herself in the looking glass. She was surprised to see how grown up she looked in the new blue and yellow printed silk dress that her mother had special-ordered from Lyon for just this occasion.

While she stood admiring her reflection, Joëlle could hear Henri protesting from his room that Maman was taking too long to fasten his waistcoat, which had buttons from the high collar all the way down to his knickers. "Must I wear this? It is too tight."

"It is only for a little while. You will forget all about it when your friends arrive."

Joëlle walked into the room and watched her mother yank at the hem of Henri's coat, then stand, hands on hips, to admire her handsome son.

Henri was a beautiful boy and was told so by everyone who met him. Like Joëlle, he had his father's dark curly locks and his mother's blue eyes.

Marguerite smiled at her son, pulling him out of his mood.

He smiled back with his wide, partially toothless smile. "Ok, Maman. Je suis désolé." Henri also wanted to please his mother.

She patted him on the back and scooted him out of the room, then turned her attention to Joëlle.

"I love the dress, Maman. Merci."

"You look as lovely as I knew you would. I chose the colors to match your eyes." Joëlle had unusually colored eyes, sea-colored irises with a rare starburst of yellow bordering her pupils. Her mother always told her that she had been born with those eyes because she was meant to bring sunshine to the world. Joëlle took those words to heart and did her best to make them so.

Joëlle concentrated on stretching her frame tall and holding her head high, trying to walk like the lady she had seen in the glass. As she glided down the stairs, she heard musicians tuning their instruments and smelled the scent of herbs that simmered on the cook's fire.

When Joëlle made the turn into the dining hall, she gasped upon seeing her mother's sketches had come to life. She looked around the space in awe. The velvet drapes had been drawn and the wall sconces lit to create an ambiance, though the sun still shone outside.

Three ceiling to floor murals of scarlet poppies ablaze in fields of spring green had been hung on the interior wall for the candle auction that was to be held during the party.

A multitude of tiered candles stood in each corner, lighting the room. The wood floor, bare of its rugs, gleamed in their light and awaited dancing feet. Joëlle smiled at how lovely her table setting looked, now adorned with flowers and dozens of dripping table candles that made the plates and glassware sparkle. Once again, her mother had designed and executed a lovely stage.

Joëlle and Henri stood with their parents inside the front door to greet the appreciative guests upon their arrival. Joëlle craned her neck to watch the faces of each one as they turned to see the dining hall. She could not wait to tell her friends that she had been the one to set the table.

After everyone was seated, Guy stood and raised his glass, "We are pleased to be with you this evening. As usual, Marguerite has made sure that we will all have a good time." He nodded to his wife.

Marguerite stood and walked to the table beside the muraled canvases.

Guy began again, "Once my lovely wife lights the candle, the bidding shall begin. You will have until the flame goes out to outbid each other throughout the evening by writing your bid down on the paper provided. Once the candle goes out, the highest bidder will receive the lovely canvases. Marguerite?"

She lit the candle on the bidding stand from the flame of one of the tiered candles, placed it back into its holder then took a dramatic bow. The crowd applauded her theatrics.

During the hours-long dinner, guests devoured each carefully planned course and chatted happily while their wine glasses were filled again and again. Joëlle watched them *ooh* and *aah* from the children's table in the corner of the kitchen as each new course was delivered to the table. She thought she might burst from pride when a jovial applause broke out at the sight of the multi-tiered dessert cart being rolled in, carrying a variety of layered cakes, honeyed fruit tarts and sugared nuts.

After dinner, the children played in the corners of the room while the adults danced in the center. Joëlle watched her mother glide across the floor with a look of utter joy glowing from her face. She anxiously awaited the day that she could join them. She had begged her mother for lessons and was promised they would begin when they arrived home after the summer away. Joëlle determined in her mind that she would be dancing with the adults at Christmas.

Moments before the flame went out, Marguerite's father, Pierre, placed the final bid, doubling the previous high bid, just as he had done in all the years past.

Shortly after announcing the winner, a flurry of commotion waved through the crowd as the women and children began being ushered out by the menfolk. The party was ending abruptly and much earlier than usual. Even the musicians seemed confused. Joëlle looked at Henri with a questioning look on her face, then shrugged her shoulders, feeling reassured upon seeing her mother saying jovial goodbyes to each family.

In her room, Joëlle lay in bed reliving the scenes of the night then turned her focus to the warm days ahead that she would soon spend in the countryside.

Shortly after she had fallen asleep, Joëlle was awakened by the sound of men's voices. She sat up in bed and stilled herself to listen. She could hear the seriousness in their tone, so she tiptoed from her bed and peered through the curtain into the hallway. Though their voices grew louder, she still could not make out their conversation. She made her way to the staircase just in time to hear her father slam his fist onto his desk and shout, "No!"

Other men, whose voices she could not distinguish, chimed in, "Guy, you must be reasonable." and "This may happen whether you want it to or not."

Suddenly, the study door flew open and slammed the wall behind. Then she heard her normally mild-mannered father demand, "Out of my house, all of you. Now!"

Joëlle gasped before her hand could reach her mouth.

Her father whirled around, looking up. His eyes met hers. Then for the first time in her life, her father shouted directly at her, "Joëlle, to bed!"

She ran back to her room, threw herself onto the bed and cried herself to sleep.

3

Jules
Lexington, Kentucky

When Jules walked through the waiting area, clearly out of sorts and wanting to get out of there as quickly as possible, she heard her name from across the room.

"Jules?" Will called.

Her stomach tightened. *Why is he here? I told him not to come.* She shot Will a look that said, *Don't ask.* The fact that she forgot her sweater and made a beeline for the exit spoke even louder.

Will nodded a goodbye to the receptionist who pointed to Jules' sweater. He took it from the hook then hurried to catch up to his wife, but she had already closed the door and put the Bronco into reverse.

Jules drove faster than she should have on the drive, hoping to beat Will home. She pulled into the driveway and was gathering her things when Will pulled in behind her.

He rolled down the window and called again to her, "Are you okay? What happened with Dr. Gray?"

Jules did not look at Will. She blamed him for suggesting this type of therapy in the first place. Not only was it not helpful, but it had made things worse, adding a new layer of anxiety and questioning.

In the house, Jules was still not speaking. She slumped down on the sofa and closed her eyes. Will placed the monogrammed throw they had received as a wedding gift along her curled-up body. He stood looking curiously at her for a long minute before turning toward the kitchen to come up with something to cook. He had planned to surprise her with dinner out after the session.

It was their usual weekday routine that Will had dinner prepared for Jules when she arrived home in the evening. He taught elementary school and was free in the afternoon, hours before Jules finished teaching her last class at the university. In addition to their work schedules, Will was by far the better cook.

While Jules slept, Will chopped fresh basil and vine-ripened tomatoes, then added them to the canned sauce. He tossed in extra seasonings and his secret ingredient, a pinch of sugar. He emptied a bag of romaine salad mix into a wooden bowl, then topped it with a sliced hardboiled egg and a few crispy pieces of bacon. Next, he sliced French bread down the middle, brushed it with olive oil, then placed a layer of shaved Parmesan cheese and red pepper flakes on top. He shoved the bread into the oven, tossed the noodles into the pot and went to gently wake his wife.

As Jules sat down to the lovingly prepared dinner, she noticed Will's attention to every detail. Straight-faced and without speaking a word, she raised her glass of white wine in toast to her thoughtful husband. With a coy look in his eye, Will attempted to break her spell by clinking his glass hard on hers, then proceeded to down the entire glass of wine. The last gulp ended up spewing from his mouth and running down his chin. They both burst into laughter, her funk instantly replaced. Jules followed suit so Will emptied the bottle into their glasses.

The Merritts did not stand on ceremony when it came to mealtime in their house. They dunked bread in the extra sauce and crunched their salads loudly. They twirled pasta on their forks while they took turns telling stories of their workdays, each of them genuinely interested in the descriptive words coming out of the other's mouth while delicious food was being shoved into their own. As they finished the main course, their enthusiasm came to an awkward end when it came time to discuss the session.

Jules knew Will was anxious to hear what had happened, so she palmed her glass with one hand and led him to the couch with the other.

Jules' described in detail her happy trip down memory lane, guided by Dr. Gray, but her mind raced to come up with an explanation that would explain to Will what had happened to turn her mood.

Though Dr. Gray had told Jules that she would remember everything that happened during the session, she was still unsure herself what had transpired at the end. She simply told Will that when they got to her early childhood, she had come abruptly out of her trance state, "For some odd reason and that was that--the session and the memories were over."

Having seen her state of mind following the session, he raised an eyebrow, questioning her *that was that* statement.

Jules responded with a quick, "What? That's it. Let's watch a movie."

Will reached across her, sneaking a kiss, to pick up the Netflix movie that had arrived in the mail. He popped it into the player and snuggled under the throw with his wife.

Jules felt guilty about not telling Will the full story of what happened at the end of the session, but first she would need to figure it out for herself.

4

Joëlle
Bordeaux, France 1685

The next morning, Joëlle should have been excited about packing for the trip to Baran. Instead, she found herself fearful about going down to breakfast. She worried that she would be scolded for being out of her bed last night and far worse, for eavesdropping on an adult conversation. She took a deep breath and walked timidly down the stairs, hoping her father was already out of the house.

"Bonjour, ma fille," came his deep voice before she made the turn into the kitchen.

Her stomach tightened, but she turned to find him smiling at her. "Bonjour, Maman, Père." She directed her eyes to her plate and slumped into her chair. She was unusually quiet this morning, taking care not to ruffle any feathers. Though Joëlle was still curious about what the men had been so passionately discussing and what could have driven her kind father to ask his friends and colleagues to leave his house, she knew her place and would never speak of it. At least, not to her father. Joëlle was not one to let things go unanswered.

"After breakfast, your mother is going shopping for goods to take to your grandparent's house. I want you both to go along to help carry the packages. Do as you are told, and she will purchase some clothes, more appropriate for the country, for both of you. Can I count on you to be helpful?"

"Oui, Bien sûr." Joëlle knew this was his way of letting her know that he was not upset at her curiosity last evening and that it was, in his own way, an apology. "Thank you, PaPa."

After breakfast, when Joëlle reached the top of the stairs, she overheard her father say to her mother, "I told you. It is just business. I will hear nothing more of it."

Joëlle and Henri trailed behind their mother walking the city streets. Joëlle was chatting to her brother about this and that, as she always did, but still she noticed people looking at her mother, smiling at her, then whispering to each other after her mother passed by. She could tell that they were not speaking ill of her. They seemed pleased that she knew them. "I bet they're hoping for an invitation to the next party," she told her brother. Joëlle and Henri stood a little taller, happy to carry their mother's purchases along the way.

Marguerite picked out fabrics and buttons for her mother-in-law. She purchased the food and other staples from the list her husband had prepared. Guy had unusually requested that she make large purchases of salt, vinegar, pots, and jars that were to be delivered to their house later in the day.

Back at home in the afternoon, Joëlle was sent to her room to pack for the entire summer in one allotted bag. Marguerite packed bags for herself and Henri. Guy loaded them onto the heavily burdened wagon, full of barrels to be delivered en route.

Once everything was strapped down, the family walked together to the cathedral. Though Guy had been raised Protestant, and still considered himself to be, he had converted to Catholicism, on paper only, to be able to marry Marguerite. While in Bordeaux, the family attended weekly Mass. But when they visited his parents in the country, they attended the Protestant church. No one was there to know the difference. Guy was one of the few men who was able to blur the lines when it came to religion.

The Reynauds arrived at Mass at the same time as Marguerite's parents. They greeted each other with kisses on cheeks. Just before entering the cathedral, Grand-mère De la Croix straightened Joëlle's hair bow and Henri's back.

After the Mass ended, Joëlle and Henri went to say goodbye to their friends while the adults visited. As usual, Joëlle did most of the talking. She rattled on and on about how excited she was to be leaving for the country the next day.

Vivienne, Joëlle's lifelong friend, questioned her excitement, "I do not understand why you are looking forward to that. My father says the countryside is filled with dirty houses, dirty air and mostly, dirty people."

Joëlle drew in her breath at the offense being thrown at her, "I cannot say where your father has been, but the houses I have been to are charming and are filled with love. The air smells of fresh grass and sweet flowers. And most importantly, the people there are..." She paused for effect, then raised her eyebrow, "Kind." She gave a 'hmph' and spun around and marched off with her arm around her brother's shoulder. Joëlle loved her friends but would not hesitate to put them in their place if needed.

Walking together to her grandparents' house, Joëlle whispered to her mother, "Must we go to dinner this week?" Joëlle and Henri loved their grandparents but did not enjoy formal dinners where they were expected to sit quietly and remember which utensil to use at the appropriate time.

"Yes, chérie. We need to enjoy dinner with them because we will be away for quite some time. Tomorrow will come soon enough."

"Of course, Maman. I'm sorry." Joëlle blushed and made a conscious effort to spend quality time with her family.

After dinner, Pierre led Guy into his office and closed the door behind him as the women and children settled in the salon. Almost immediately the men's voices began to rise, then her grandfather said in a loud voice, "You cannot afford to be stubborn. You are out of time!"

Marguerite moved over to the piano and quickly began playing a lively tune, but before she had finished the song,

Guy came in to announce their departure. No one, not even Joëlle, spoke a word on the short walk home.

Once inside, the family went straight to the study for their nightly Bible reading. Some nights there was also a poetry reading. Other nights, their mother led them in a psalm singing, but not tonight.

Joëlle did not like it when routines changed. Thankfully one thing that never changed was that every evening ended with the family holding hands while Guy led them in prayer.

"I'll miss this, PaPa. I wish you could stay all summer with us."

"Me, too," Henri chimed in.

"As will I, but your grandfather will lead your nightly prayers in my stead. Now, get some sleep. Tomorrow will be a long day."

5

Jules
Lexington, Kentucky

The moon hung heavy and low. It was as if the world itself felt what she felt. With no energy left to cry, her tears simply glided into her ratted hair. Wanting respite, she turned to her side on the frost-covered moss and placed her arm as a pillow to support her weary head.

In the fog between wake and sleep, she felt someone pull her shirt collar, forcing her up. Their eyes met in silence then the running began again. She prayed not to snap a fallen limb as she kept her eyes fixed in the darkness on the skirt zigzagging in front of her.

Abruptly, the running stopped. The skirt twirled upwards as the woman in front of her spun around. Wide-eyed, they listened. The sound they heard was the confirmation they feared. Though no words were spoken, she knew the woman's pointed finger meant… hide!

Jolted from sleep, Jules sat up and bit her lips to suppress a scream. Realizing it was the dream again, she dropped her shoulders and released her breath, then slipped from the covers, careful not to wake her husband.

In the kitchen, Jules turned on the tap and bent over the edge of the sink to take a sip while searching her mind for any new details of her dream. As always, she just felt an unreasonable fear, her rapid heartbeat as proof. She questioned why she'd had the dream again but remembered her next session with Dr. Gray was scheduled for that afternoon. Jules made up her mind then and there that she would never allow herself to be that vulnerable again.

When she stood, water ran down her chin and fell between her breasts. Cold and somehow fitting, she didn't bother to wipe it away.

Back in the darkened bedroom, Jules wiggled into the Will-warmed covers. He always made things better, even in his sleep.

***

Jules arrived at her appointment to find Dr. Gray waiting for her, already seated in the recliner beside the couch.

"I see you're anxious to get started."

"Good afternoon, Jules. Yes, in fact, I am. I have slightly changed my plan for going forward, given what happened, and would like to discuss it with you before we start today's session."

Jules interrupted the doctor, "Before you go any further, I want to let you know that I have decided not to continue with hypnosis or trance work or whatever you want to call it. Since last week's session, things have only gotten worse. I have had anxiety through the roof, and last night I even had the dream again. I don't see how another round of it is going be helpful." Her tone was unyielding.

"I see. And do you attribute last *night's* dream to last *week's* session? I understood your increasingly frequent nightmares to be one of the reasons for our appointments.

"You told me in our consultation that as a teenager, you felt anxiety before going to sleep for fear that you would wake up in a state of terror. Perhaps that is what you are feeling now. Sometimes to get beyond a problem, you must go through it, but you do not need to face it alone. We can go through it together. If you prefer not to do that through trance work, we can simply talk about it. Would you like to do that today?"

"Sure, ok." Jules was still skeptical that any kind of therapy was going to help her.

"Can you tell me a little about your evening before you went to bed? Did you have wine? Did you watch a movie? Did you argue with Will?" Dr. Gray's pen sat perched on her notepad.

"No, no and no. It was a typical evening. We had dinner, then watched a little television. That's it."

"Please lie in the position you were in when you woke up."

Jules humored the doctor, turning onto her side.

"What time did the dream wake you up?"

"I'd barely been asleep, like always."

"Please tell me what you remember."

While Jules searched her memory, Dr. Gray remained silent.

"There was a full moon. The ground was cold and wet. Then the woman grabbed me and pulled me up," the words spilled half-heartedly from her lips.

Me? Pulled me up? Dr. Gray wrote then underlined the word "me" in her notebook. Jules was placing herself in the dream. She was not watching this happen to someone else.

"We started to run. I was following her, then I saw her spin around. We were scared. I think we were being chased by someone because she told me to hide. That's all I remember. Same as always. I guess that's when I woke up."

"Was the woman your mother?"

"*My* mother? No, I don't know who it is."

"Can you describe her?"

"Not really, her hair was up in a top knot kind of thing. She looked older. She had on a long skirt."

Dr. Gray continued making notes while asking, "Is there anything else you can tell me? Do you recognize the place? Do you remember hearing anything?"

"I only recognize it from my dreams. It's always the same place." Jules paused to remember. "Wait, I do remember something else. We heard dogs barking in the distance. That's what made us think we should hide." Jules surprised herself. She had never remembered that detail before.

"And you have no conscious memory of anything like this ever happening to you?"

"No. Of course not. I have certainly never been chased in the middle of the night."

"Have you considered that this could be a scene from a movie? You said that you and Will watch a lot of movies."

"No, it definitely isn't. I have had this same dream as far back as I can remember, and I wasn't allowed to watch movies when I was young."

Dr. Gray paused in thought, "Since this isn't something you have personally experienced and since it isn't something that you've seen in a movie, what do you think the explanation could be?"

"I don't know. Isn't that why I'm here? Short of me remembering a past life, I have no idea." Jules mocked in frustration.

"Do you believe reincarnation to be a possibility?" Dr. Gray cut her eyes sideways from her notepad to gauge Jules' reaction.

"No, of course not!" Jules was surprised that Dr. Gray had taken her seriously.

"I am simply following up on your comment. Some people believe in reincarnation. Therapy is a place of no judgments. We are simply exploring all the possibilities."

This is exactly the kind of thing my mother said would happen if I ever saw a shrink, Jules thought. "No," she said again.

As Dr. Gray continued making notes, Jules interrupted, "I need to be on my way."

"There's still quite a bit of time left in our session." Dr. Gray countered.

In the hours leading up to the appointment, Jules' anxiety had grown steadily and for good reason. She always felt panicked discussing the dream and just wanted to get out of there as quickly as possible. "I promised Will I'd be home early," she lied while gathering her belongings and, once again, she bolted out the door.

Outside the building, Jules wrapped her sweater around herself and cinched the belt. It felt as if the temperature had dropped ten degrees while she had been inside. While she waited for her 1979 Bronco to warm up, she questioned what she was even doing here. This session was just as unsettling as the last and had ended in even more confusion. *Reincarnation?* She scoffed.

Jules had been brought up to think that simply considering such a thing might be a sin. *When one dies, their soul is either rewarded with Heaven or punished in Hell. Those are the only two options. Period. The end.* "Amen," she said aloud in her car. She laughed out loud at herself then manually moved the gear shift into reverse.

***

Jules looked again at her watch, wondering what was keeping Will. She had stopped for groceries and had dinner prepared when he finally walked in the door. "What kept you? I was beginning to worry."

"Oh, uh, this week's faculty meeting went longer than expected. I'm sorry." Will pulled off his jacket and hung it in the back corner of the hallway closet, taking care that Jules did not see.

Will could feel his face blushing, so he excused himself and closed the door of the hallway bathroom. He turned on the faucet and splashed his face with cold water, then looked at himself in the mirror. He thought back to the morning when he had been preparing for the children to arrive. He had seen

Laura, his teaching partner, in the doorway. "Come in," he had warmly welcomed her.

"Hey, Will. Would you have some time after the meeting this afternoon? I need to talk to you."

He noticed her lip quivering and moved toward her to give her a hug but stopped when he heard the children approaching. "Of course, my room or yours?" he'd joked, trying to lighten the mood.

"Can we go somewhere private?"

Will splashed his face again and flushed the unused toilet then walked back to the kitchen to see Jules filling a plate for him from the stovetop.

When Jules sat down to eat, she looked at her husband. She could see on his face that something was bothering him.

"What is it, Will? Is something wrong?" she asked, genuinely concerned.

"No, no, not at all. Looks good, let's eat," he replied, redirecting the conversation.

Jules did most of the talking during dinner. Will was usually the one who carried the conversation. "Will, are you feeling all right? You seem distracted and you never even asked me about my session."

"I completely forgot. I'm sorry. How did the hypnosis go today?"

"Well, it was interesting, to say the least." She chose to leave out the fact that there was no hypnosis. "I had the dream again last night, so that was our focus today."

"Wow, you didn't mention it this morning. Was Dr. Gray able to help you remember any details during hypnosis?"

Again, Jules did not correct him, "Well, the dream was mostly the same as always, but I did remember one new detail. There were dogs barking, and that's why we hid."

Will looked up from his plate, "We?"

"Yes, we. I think I have always known but was not willing to admit that I am the one in the dream."

"What does it mean? What did Dr. Gray say?"

"Funny story, she actually mentioned reincarnation. Can you believe that?" Jules smirked.

"What? Why?"

"The reason she mentioned it was because I haven't seen anything like it in a movie, and it has obviously never happened to me. But the kicker was the way that I described the woman."

"How did you describe her?"

"She was wearing a long, heavy skirt and had her hair up in an old lady bun. I guess she seemed to look like someone from the past." Jules stood and took his dinner plate.

"Wait, I'm not finished. What did you say to her?" He forked the last bite and handed the plate back to her.

"Nothing really. Just that I don't believe in things like that because it doesn't fit with my religious beliefs." She surprised herself by mentioning it. Religion was a subject they rarely talked about.

"I agree, reincarnation is not worth discussing. It is interesting, though, to think about how people lived in the past. I wish I could have known my grandparents. I never even got to meet them. You've got to think that they were a lot like us. I mean, my mother's parents raised her with certain values, and I am sure my grandparents were raised in a similar way. The same for your family. Your grandparents taught your father, who taught you and so on."

And so on. Those words hung in the air. In that moment, they both realized that it ended with them. All the family traits, stories and traditions ended with them. Thinking quickly on his feet, Will continued, "I wonder if my family has ever done a genealogy. That could be fun to look into. Do you know if anyone in your family has done any research?"

"I heard my dad say that Uncle David had. I have no idea if he has much information. But yes, I agree it would be interesting to learn more about them and the way they lived. I'll email him to see what he has, and we can look at yours when we go to your parents' house for Thanksgiving. Who knows, we might be cousins." Jules rattled on, eager to keep off the subject of their ended family line.

For the rest of the evening, they made small talk, each aware of the secrets between them.

6

Joëlle
Bordeaux, France 1685

Joëlle found her mother standing at her easel in the garden, putting the finishing touch of morning light onto the flowers of her landscape painting.

"It's lovely, Maman."

"Merci, ma chèrie. It's for Grand-mère. This way she can enjoy them all year long."

Joëlle smiled at her mother's thoughtfulness.

Marguerite removed the canvas and placed her painting on the rock wall then began to disassemble the easel. "JoVee, will you pick a few of the prettiest flowers? I thought we could make bouquets during our travels to give to the vineyard owners on our stops."

"Bien sûr, I'd love to help and besides, I'm sure father will not even notice they're gone."

"No, I don't imagine he will." Marguerite smiled, carrying her painting toward the house.

***

Marguerite and Guy were quiet on the first leg of the trip, content to listen to their children chat on and on about the adventures they had planned for the summer.

After a rough morning ride, wagon wheels bumping in uneven dirt grooves and grassy paths, the family stopped for an early *déjeuner* beside a river. They sat together on the riverbank and ate the bread, cheese, and fruit that Maman had packed for them. They drank water from the river in a shared cup.

When they finished eating, PaPa slipped off his boots, "I'd like to cool off a bit before we continue. Would anyone like to join me?"

"Moi!" Joëlle and Henri said in unison, happy to see their father starting to relax as they moved closer to his childhood home.

Marguerite smiled, watching her husband toss their joyful children around in the water while she packed away their lunch.

By late afternoon, they reached the first vineyard stop at Château Richarde. Guy had written months earlier to ask if his family could spend the night in one of the vineyard barns again this year.

The Richarde children, Gilles and Renée, ran to greet them as they entered through the large iron gate. Monsieur Richarde came out of the barn, dusting himself off before greeting Guy and Marguerite with kisses on both cheeks.

"We have made a comfortable place in the barn for the children to sleep since they are older this year, if that is suitable to you. My children are looking forward to sleeping outdoors. We have prepared a room for you and your wife in the château."

"That is most kind of you. Merci beaucoup."

"It is good to see your family again. My wife and her staff have prepared dinner which will be ready in a couple of hours. I am sure you would like some time to rest after riding all day."

"Again, that is most gracious of you. We thank you," Guy looked toward his family as they all showed their appreciation.

Gilles and Renée lead Joëlle and Henri to their chambre in the barn. Joëlle smiled when she saw the blankets and pillows laid out on a soft bed of hay. "This shall do quite nicely."

M. Richarde called to his children, "Come now, let our guests rest for a bit. Gilles and Renée left the barn to give their friends time to settle in. "We will be back before dinner."

Joëlle lay on her back in the makeshift bed with her hands behind her head and her legs crossed at her ankles. Henri followed suit. "Grand-mère De la Croix would be appalled by this. I love it."

After a casual supper of ratatouille and fresh-baked baguettes, the children played on the garden lawn while the adults sat around a fire. Joëlle stopped playing to take a long look at her parents. She watched them enjoying the house wine and noticed that they were laughing unrestrained as friends do, not at all like business associates. She wondered again what had been happening at home to cause her father so much stress that he had become cross with not only his friends but also his father-in-law. She decided then and there that she would keep up her snooping whenever it was called for. Then she whirled around and became a kid again.

The second day's journey included stops at several vineyards along the way to deliver barrels before spending the night under the stars along a riverbank.

On the morning of the third day, they came to a meadow filled with red poppies. Her father halted the horses and pointed to the large cross that sat on a rock wall just across the meadow. Joëlle recognized it immediately. "Henri, we're here!" Everyone smiled, happy to see the familiar sight, but Joëlle was not one to hold back. "Hurry, PaPa. Can you make the horses run?"

"No, I am afraid not. They are still pulling quite a load. Be patient. We are almost there."

The tiny hamlet of Baran sat in a shallow bowl on top of a flattened hillside. It was a steep haul to the top. Guy instructed his wife and children to gather what they could easily carry and sent them ahead to retrieve his father with another team of horses.

When they reached the top, Joëlle spotted the much beloved ochre-colored stone house. She ran as fast as she could, without considering her mother and brother.

"Wait for Henri," Marguerite called, but it was too late. Joëlle had already burst through the half-opened Dutch door, jingling the string of doorbells along the way.

"Grand-mère, Grand-père, we're here!"

Her grandmother wiped her hands on her apron then wrapped Joëlle up in her arms. "Bonjour, my child, bonjour! It has been far too long."

"Six months!" Joëlle had been counting the days.

Marguerite sat the bags she was carrying on the ground beside the two stone steps and smiled, noticing the stone sink draining water down onto the potted flowers underneath. She wiped her brow then followed Henri through the door.

While Grand-mère greeted Marguerite and Henri, Joëlle turned to her grandfather who did not care for hugs, but she gave him one anyway. "PaPa wants you to bring the horses down to help pull the wagonload up. I will go with you."

"Wait, Joëlle. I think the men can manage that." Her grandmother redirected her, "And besides, there are four new kittens in the barn waiting to meet you." Without another word spoken, Joëlle and Henri flew out the back door.

"It's good to see you all." Odette kissed her daughter-in-law.

"We are happy to be here. I can't believe how much the grapevine has grown since last summer. It's all the way across the house."

"It is. We are hoping for enough grapes to juice this year. I'm glad you've decided to stay here with the children this summer."

"It was Guy who insisted that I do, but honestly, I am glad to be away from the city for a while. Things seem to be growing more tense there by the day."

"Are there problems with the business?"

"I don't know. He keeps me in the dark about such matters." Changing the subject, Marguerite said, "We've brought all the food preserving supplies you requested."

"Merci, but it was not I that requested it. We always have plenty, but Guy wrote to us back in the winter, saying that we should double the garden this year."

"He did not mention that to me. Did he explain why?"

"He said it would be a good idea because the kids are growing and that we never know who might need our help."

"Seems my husband has been quite the orchestrator of late," Marguerite furrowed her brow, in thought. But before she had time to further question her husband's motives, Joëlle and Henri backed through the door with their hands full of yellow-striped kittens.

Supper under the barn's covered porch was just as dreamy as Joëlle remembered. Kittens rubbed at her ankles while the family ate a feast of sauteed chicken and aspereges du Blayais. Joëlle watched the chickens pecking the grounds in the flower beds and wondered if her dinner had been pecking around with the others just a day ago.

Thankfully Grand-mère interrupted her disturbing thought, "It is wonderful to have you all home with us. I am full up in every way." Joëlle loved the phrases her country grandmother used.

When the sun had set on the farmer's field behind the barn, Joëlle and Henri scurried up the stone steps to their bedroom. They took turns changing into their night clothes behind the curtain under the eave then hung their clothes over the low ceiling beams. Joëlle opened the windows on each end to let out the heat before climbing onto the horse hair-stuffed cot.

"I am sorry that PaPa will have to go back to Bordeaux tomorrow, but I am ready for summer to begin. Goodnight, Henri."

"Night, JoVee." Joëlle could barely make out his words through his yawn. Henri was already half asleep. Joëlle blew out the candle but lay there for hours, too excited to sleep.

7

Jules

Lexington, Kentucky

Several weeks had passed since her last therapy session. Each week, Jules had found a reason to reschedule without telling Will. Some weeks, he had asked about it, but she had wiggled her way out of answering. He had taken that as a cue that she did not want to talk about it. Other weeks, he didn't bother to ask.

An unspoken distance had been growing between them. Will was staying at work longer and Jules found herself going to bed earlier. Whenever the dreams started up again, she always withdrew into herself. In the past, Will would always find a way to bring her out of her moods. Jules wondered if he had grown tired of her issues or if there could be something more. It troubled her enough that she decided to keep this week's session with Dr. Gray.

"Jules, hello. It is good to see you. I have missed our sessions."

"Well, yes. I..."

"No need to explain. Let's get right to it."

Jules started to recline.

"You may sit if you prefer. I would like to talk more about the history of your family relationships today. Let's begin with your relationship with your siblings."

"I have two brothers. Jasper is four years older, and James six, so we didn't really play together. From the time I was old enough to remember, they were always helping Dad on the farm."

"Are you close to them now?"

"I guess. We call each other on birthdays and see each other during the holidays. Will and I always attend their children's birthday parties. So, yes, I guess that means we're close." She had nothing to compare it to since Will was an only child.

"What about your father?" The doctor moved on.

"You might say that I always wanted to be a daddy's girl. He and the boys were always out in the barn or working with the crops. He would sometimes let me ride on the tractor, but my mother did not like that. She didn't want me to be a tomboy."

"You spent your days with your mother then?"

"No, I wouldn't say that either. She was always busy in the kitchen. She would occasionally let me help her bake cookies or brownies. I wanted to learn more about how to cook, but she would just tell me that I would do plenty of cooking in my life then send me off to play."

"What type of things did you play by yourself?"

"I mentioned during the last session that I spent a lot of time in the swing. I loved to make up songs while I swung. I remember one day being so excited to sing a song I had written for my mother. She didn't even look up from the stove. She told me she was busy and to *scat*. I never made up another song again. Creative things seem frivolous to my parents. Joseph and Lillie Laurent are practical folks."

"What type of socializing did your family do?"

"None that I remember, unless you count church."

"Did your family attend regularly?"

"Without fail. We never missed a Sunday service unless one of us was sick. Even then, the others would go. My dad would not even miss when there were crops that needed tending. He would work well into the night afterwards. He said it was a sin to miss church and that God had always blessed his efforts."

"Do you and Will attend church?"

"We don't, much to the dismay of my parents. It especially bothers my mother. At least, she is the one who always mentions it to me. I mean, we have nothing against it. It just is not something that we ever started. Sundays are our rest and fun days. Will did not grow up going to church except for Christmas and Easter. We believe in God, though." She paused, "At least, I know I do."

"That may be something that you could explore on your own before our next session, how religion has shaped your life. If you would like, we could discuss it next week."

Jules quietly doubted that conversation would ever happen. Though she believed there is a God, her experience with church did not seem like something that could help her.

***

When she arrived home, Will was already preparing the dishes to take to his parents' house. Will's family did not have a traditional Thanksgiving dinner. Each year, his parents would choose the main course, then Jules and Will would come up with a new take on the accompanying dishes. This year they had decided on a baked apple with Brussels sprouts dish and scalloped potatoes, made with heavy cream and Gruyère cheese to have with Ina Garten's recipe for roast chicken. Though Jules enjoyed Will's unique family tradition, she would miss the typical turkey and dressing meal served with southern side dishes. She would have to wait until next year when Thanksgiving would be with her family.

Jules pulled an apron over her head and was tying it when she noticed a large box by the door. "What's that?"

Will glanced up from chopping the sprouts, "It's the food for the kids' backpacks for next week."

For years, Will had been placing snacks in the backpacks of his underprivileged students so they would have something to eat in the evenings and on weekends in case they needed it.

"I may have gotten a few extras since the holidays are here," he winked at her. "Oh, I forgot to tell you that the package from your uncle came today. It's on the table by the sofa." He pointed with his knife.

She could not imagine that this lumpy overstuffed envelope could be the genealogy. When she opened it, papers fell out and scattered everywhere. There were lengthy computer printouts and copies of black and white photographs with names written in fancy cursive underneath. Nothing was in any kind of order. This was not something that was going to be gone through quickly, so she picked up the papers that had scattered and stuffed them back into the package as best she could, leaving some of them sticking out of the top.

"That is a project for a rainy day, certainly not today," she said as she walked toward the kitchen. Together, they prepared the casseroles and placed them in the refrigerator to be baked the following morning.

***

The Merritts drove through sunshine and falling leaves, arriving early at Will's childhood home, a modest but well-kept brick home in a traditional family neighborhood. Will grew up in a family and a place that resembled a 1950's television show.

Every year, Will's parents volunteered at their church's Caring Means Sharing events. Held on Thanksgiving, Christmas, and Easter, businesses donated money and volunteers prepared a meal and provided fun and games for struggling families. Will had always gone with his parents, even after he and Jules had gotten married. For the first few years, they invited Jules to go along. Will's mother would always encourage her, "It doesn't matter how late we eat. It's just more time we will get to spend together." But Jules preferred to let them have their family time, at least that's what she had always told herself. She preferred to stay at the house to have their meal ready for them rather than being in a crowd of strangers. Over the years, they had given up and stopped asking.

Hoping Will would see it as a gesture toward improving their relationship, Jules surprised them all this year by volunteering to go with them. She broke their stunned silence, "It doesn't matter how late we eat. It's just more time we will get to spend together." Will's mom helped Jules into her sweater with a happy smile across her face.

At the church, Jules assisted Will in serving the children. He set up a small table and sat on a child-sized chair so he could speak to them at their level as he handed them their drinks. During dinner, she helped Will walk refills to their tables.

Will's parents had always been extraordinarily kind to Jules, but she had assumed that it was because of Will. But watching her in-laws serving the adults in the line, greeting each of them with a smile, genuinely curious about their lives, she realized why Will was such a giving person. After all these years, her respect for his parents grew even more.

Back at home, Jules set the food on the sideboard, appreciating Will's parents' casual but classic style. The walnut table was set with cream-colored dinner plates, topped with linen napkins, and decorated with a simple floral arrangement in muted fall colors.

During their dinner conversation, Will's parents had only good things to say about whatever or about whomever they were talking. *It is no wonder Will is such a positive person. That is all he knew. Until he met me.*

Over dessert, Will asked his parents, "Has anyone in our family ever researched our genealogy?"

"Not that I am aware of but, we will be happy to find out for you. I am sure we would both love to learn about our ancestors," Will's father responded, looking at his wife.

Will and Jules left that evening with hearts as full as their stomachs. In the car, Jules reached for Will's hand and braved an unfamiliar conversation.

"Dr. Gray brought up the role that religion played in my upbringing. She asked me to think about it this week so we can discuss it during my next session."

"How do you feel about it?"

"I don't really know. Going to church was something my family felt obligated to do every Sunday. At least, that's how it seemed to me. I never saw my parents read the Bible at home. We didn't pray before meals. God wasn't talked about in our home unless He was used to keep us in line."

"We always went to services on Christmas and Easter. Whenever the church was doing any community outreach, my parents would show up to help. Even though we didn't attend services that often, my parents always stressed to me that we show God's goodness to friends and neighbors, and even strangers. In our family, weekly attendance was not representative of our faith."

"I love that about your parents. We went every Sunday, but never attended any of the activities of the church. In fact, we were always the first family out the doors as soon as the last 'amen' was said."

Though church may have seemed to be more of an obligation to her parents, Jules' thoughts of church were happy ones. "I loved the a cappella singing. I could always hear my mother singing over everyone else. She told me once that she came from a musical family and had always wanted to become a professional singer but when she married Dad, she became a farmer's wife and put that part of her life behind her. I told her I thought that was sad, and I will never forget what she said, 'Sometimes in life, you choose to give up one thing for another. You must accept your choice, then don't stew on what might have been.'

"Speaking of moving on, now that Thanksgiving is behind us…" She reached into the glove box and pulled out her favorite Christmas CD, *The Carpenters' Christmas*. She slipped it into the player and turned up the volume.

8

Jules
Lexington, Kentucky

Off and on after Thanksgiving, Jules recalled the doctor's orders to reflect on how her religious upbringing had shaped her and the way she sees the world. But with all the work involved in Christmas, Jules had, again, canceled one appointment after another. Finally, Will suggested that she keep the final session of the year.

"But it's scheduled for Christmas Eve."

"It's fine. I will have everything ready to go when you get home," Will promised.

***

"Should we pick up with our discussion of religion?" Dr. Gray asked while Jules was getting seated.

"I'd like to wait on that."

"Not a problem. Let's move on then. During our last session, we talked about your relationships with your brothers and your father. Today, I would like to discuss your relationship with your mother."

I need to lie down for this, Jules thought, already reclining. "First of all, I want to say that I had a happy early childhood. I loved life. In fact, sometimes I think I may have loved it a little too much. My family always said that I lived in the clouds. My father and brothers were always working outside, and my mother was busy inside. I was left on my own most of the time. I was always making up plays and wanting to perform them for my mom. She was a busy woman, and I think I drove her nuts with them."

Jules watched Dr. Gray make a note.

"Her world was practical. Mine was fantasy. She and I are exact opposites. She told me on more than one occasion that I was literally born different."

"Did she explain what she meant?"

"Apparently, I screamed for hours after my birth. I guess it caused quite a scene in the hospital. It was so troubling that she said the nurses were talking about it and that other patients had inquired if everything was okay."

Jules searched her memory and then continued, "She said that just moments after I was born, I glared into her eyes intently, without blinking, like I was trying to figure out who she was. She said it made her so uncomfortable, she had to look away from me."

"And do you remember how it made you feel to hear your mother say these things to you?" Dr. Gray asked, waiting to write down her response.

"It wasn't just my mother. My brothers were constantly telling stories about what a strange kid I was. Apparently from the time I was just a year old, every time we would start to cross the low water ford near our farm, I would scream hysterically and try to crawl up my mother. My father said it was the strangest thing to see a baby act that way, since I was far too young to comprehend what drowning was. To this day, I have to close my eyes when we cross a bridge over a large body of water. I cannot tell you the panic that I experience.

"When I was in the fifth grade, another crazy thing happened. I was riding my horse in the field along the road. A truck driver coming from behind us decided to honk his loud horn at us and it spooked Honey and she reared up and took off running. I wasn't prepared for it either and fell off backward. I hit my head on a rock and became unconscious.

The truck driver witnessed what happened and pulled over to help. I was taken by ambulance to the hospital and was there for several days. My brothers told me later that I was talking out of my head about being in a boat full of sick people and that I was crying because they were throwing dead people overboard into the ocean. I assume it was the heavy medications, in addition to the head injury. I was a little girl and we rarely watched television, much less a movie where I would have seen something like that. They have teased me about that my whole life.

"As I got older, I started to do even stranger things. I have always hated the smell of something burning, whether it was something on the stove or a campfire. I will never forget when I was around eleven or twelve, there was a drought, and everything was incredibly dry. One windy day, a tree line between our fields caught fire. It spread quickly and there was no way to put it out. It was too late to save the wheat crop. My parents started frantically hosing water around the house so it wouldn't burn. My brothers were helping to attach all our water hoses together. They were all screaming at me to help, but all I could do was violently throw up. The smell of smoke still sickens me."

Dr. Gray looked up, obviously intrigued, "Can you think of any explanation?"

"There is no explanation for that or any of the other issues I have. These things were running jokes in our family. They all constantly teased that I was switched at birth."

"And how did that make you feel?"

Jules put up a wall. "I didn't take offense to it. Growing up with only brothers, I was constantly teased about one thing or another. None of it was mean spirited. When you add it all up, I was different. I am different. But when my anxiety started and caused so much drama in our family, that is when I could see that they all started to look at me differently, especially my mother. But still, we had a good relationship…until middle school."

"What happened then?" Dr. Gray asked.

"Only everything," Jules responded, feeling a punch to her gut.

***

After the emotional session, Jules' hands were shaking, and the tears would not stop. She was relieved to have some time to collect herself while the Bronco warmed up. She wondered why today, of all days, Dr. Gray would bring up the worst time in her life but then realized that the doctor could not have known how deeply she had suppressed this memory. She did not know that Jules had never allowed herself to honestly think about what had happened back then. And now, on Christmas Eve, the full weight of it, all of it, was trying to come to the surface.

Jules noticed the time, forced her feelings down and dried her tears. She made a conscious decision not to let her session ruin this day. Celebrating Christmas at the farm was her favorite time of the year.

***

Will had checked the weather and was loading the car when Jules returned from her appointment. "They are calling for snow. We'd better get on the road."

"A white Christmas? Maybe this Christmas won't be so bad after all."

Will stopped loading the packages and looked at Jules. "What do you mean *after all?*"

"Nothing, I don't know why I said that."

She helped Will load the last of the presents into the trunk. "I hope they like their gifts." Jules loved shopping for her nieces and nephews. "I can't wait to watch their faces when they open them."

Will tuned the radio to a station that played classic Christmas songs. Jules tried to sing along, hoping it would take her mind off what Dr. Gray had forced her to relive, but her hope was not enough. To keep her emotions at bay, Jules bit her lip and stared out the window, counting the posts on the miles of plank fencing along the route to her childhood home. Will was singing a duet of *Blue Christmas* with Elvis and didn't notice.

***

Pulling onto the gravel lane at the farm, Jules pointed to the short Christmas tree on a table in the front window, lit with large colorful lights, a popcorn garland and finished with silver tinsel. "This never changes." Then she saw her father walk out onto the front porch. Her father's warm hug was just what she needed to convince herself that she was finally ready to celebrate Christmas.

Joseph held the aluminum storm door open while Will walked through, balancing the stack of presents, each wrapped in brown craft paper and labeled with a hand painted name tag.

Nieces and nephews came running and surrounded them, hugging their waists and thighs. Four-year-old Caroline practically jumped into Jules' arms. James' eight-year-old twin boys, David and James Jr. picked at the packages, searching the tags for their names. James' only daughter, Ivy, had just turned twelve and had become a young woman since they had last seen her. Ivy was shy and stood back until the boys ran off. Jules held a special place in her heart for Ivy. She reminded her of herself at that age. Ivy was a girl surrounded by boys, living on a farm. Jules knew the loneliness that can bring.

Jules sat Caroline at her feet and hugged Ivy. "I cannot believe how much you have changed in the last few months. You are all grown up now."

Ivy smiled at her favorite aunt, "You really think so?"

"I do! We should get together more often. Before we know it, you will be off to college." Jules and Will lived in Lexington, only twenty minutes from the farm in Midway, but other than special occasions, they rarely got together. In that moment, Jules made a silent promise to do better.

"I would love that." Ivy put her arm in Jules' and walked with her into the living room where Will was placing the presents under the tree.

"Welcome to the madness," Jasper's wife, Nichole, joked.

James and his wife, Scarlette, stopped herding their running twins just long enough to say hello before running toward the crash they'd just heard in the next room.

"I wouldn't have it any other way. Where are your boys?" Jules asked, referring to Jasper and Nichole's teenage boys, Matt and Nick.

"Out in the barn. No doubt up to no good." Jules felt Jasper helping her out of her coat and turned to see him dressed in his Sunday clothes. It was nice to see her brothers in something other than their everyday overalls.

Jules took their coats into her parents' bedroom and laid them on the same chenille bedspread that she had napped on as a child. She touched her cheek and remembered waking up with the pattern of the cotton knots on her face. She could not wait to curl up on it and take a nap between Christmas lunch and leftover dinner.

Her mother had not come out to greet them, so Jules went to find her in the kitchen. Ivy trailed behind, quiet and listening. Caroline was on her tiptoes, stretching to reach a plate of red and green sprinkled sugar cookies. Ivy pushed it out of reach.

Lillie was concentrating on her cooking and barely looked up. "Merry Christmas, I'm glad you're home," she said as she stirred a pot on the stove.

"It looks like you have cooked for days. What can I do to help?"

"That's okay, I just have to get this last dish into the oven and then we can open presents."

"Okay, but I insist on helping with the dishes."

"I insist, as well," her mother finally looked at her and winked.

"You look very pretty today, Mother." Jules always loved how her mother dressed. Even in daily farm life, she wore pretty, handmade dresses, usually in a floral lightweight cotton. Today, she wore one Jules had never seen before, but her grandmother's pearl necklace was not new. Her mother wore it on all special occasions.

After Lillie slid the last dish into the oven, she joined the rest of the family as they sat in a circle in the living room, adults on the furniture and kids on the floor.

Sitting beside her father, watching the children so excitedly opening their gifts, Jules thought back to one of her favorite Christmases. She had opened a box with a horse bridle inside with a note attached that read, "Go look in the barn." She hadn't asked for a horse, and they had never had one on the farm before. Inside the barn, Jules had fallen instantly in love with a tan-colored colt that she named Honey. Jules smiled at her father, remembering his thoughtfulness. He could not have known what a lifeline that horse would become.

Jules' gift from her mother this year was a handmade apron, sewn from one of the sundresses she had worn in high school. It was another unexpected but perfect gift.

"Hey, I do most of the cooking. Where's mine?" Will joked and the family howled.

After all the presents had been opened, the happy family squeezed in around the long farmhouse table. Jasper surprised everyone this year by volunteering to bless the food. Jules felt proud of her brother.

After the blessing, they passed around the dishes. Jules loved that her mother always served their fancy Christmas dinner on her wedding china. Joseph sliced the honeyed ham to the sounds of 'oohs' and 'aahs'. Instead of marshmallows on the sweet potatoes, she had topped them with a coated pecan crumble. She baked homemade sourdough dinner rolls instead of everyday cornbread. Dessert was always a traditional red velvet cake with snowy white coconut icing, garnished with green rosemary leaves and sugared cranberries. Coffee and homemade chocolate covered cherries, a secret recipe handed down through the generations, were saved for later.

The dinner conversation was spirited and upbeat. The subjects ranged from sports to jobs and all things in between. Will liked to tease his nieces and nephews by asking them questions about their recent marriages and other such silly things. The children always protested, but they loved how Will always made their family gatherings fun.

Just as Lillie was clearing the dinner plates to make room on the table for dessert, James asked, "So what's new with the city folk?"

Will responded, "Nothing new really. We are both staying busy with our jobs. Well, there is one new thing. Jules and I have been researching reincarnation."

It was not true. He only said it to make them laugh, and they all did, except for Lillie.

"What in the world?" Lillie spouted.

The laughter stopped and the room fell silent.

Will's face turned the color of Lillie's red velvet cake. He tried to fix it but dug in deeper. "I'm sorry. It was just a joke… sort of. Her therapist just suggested that we look into it."

Lillie looked at Jules, and while trying to conceal her surprise, she asked, "Therapist?"

Before Jules could respond, Lillie turned and walked the armful of plates into the kitchen.

"Who's ready for dessert?" Joseph acted as if nothing was amiss. He gathered up a few more plates and hurried to do damage control. He saw his wife standing over the dirty dish filled sink, staring out the window. Though Lillie tried to appear unruffled, it was clear that what Will said had upset her.

Jules excused herself from the table to reign in her anger at Will. In the bathroom, which shared a common wall with the kitchen, she could faintly hear her parents' conversation. She stilled herself to listen.

"Lillie, come back to the table. You've made Will feel bad."

"*I've* made *him* feel bad? I cannot believe he said that in front of the children and why is she doing that? I don't even know how to respond."

"You don't have to. Just come back to the table and don't mention it. It's Christmas, for heaven's sake."

"For heaven's sake? I hardly think so. Reincarnation? That is downright sacrilegious. She is searching for answers that won't be found in that kind of foolishness. Jules has always been a little quirky, to put it nicely. But therapists and reincarnation? This is all my fault. Joseph, what did I do wrong?"

Jules felt like she had been stabbed with a knife.

Do wrong? Did she just say do wrong? Jules instantly felt weak in the knees. Her breathing stopped. She was sure her heart had stopped too.

All her life, she had been teased and had acted as if those little daggers weren't making her bleed. But she had always reassured herself that they were just words, not sticks and stones, or blades. *Wrong…do wrong* replayed in her head. Today, there could be no reassurance. She had just heard her own mother, the person who was supposed to love her more than anyone else in the world, say that something was wrong with her.

Jules put her hands over her heart, feeling the sting of those daggers, hundreds of them, all at once. She was going to bleed to death if she did not get out of this place and quick. The damage was done. Christmas was over.

She tried to calm herself by taking deep breaths before walking through the dining room to announce that she was not feeling well and that she needed to go home.

"But Jules…," Will pleaded.

"No, Will. I mean it. We are leaving," she demanded, as she went to retrieve their coats.

Still in the kitchen, Lillie agreed to let it go for everyone's sake. "I don't want to ruin Christmas for the children."

Joseph left her there to compose herself. He walked into the emptied dining room and went to find the others helping Jules and Will get their things to the car. He ran back into the house just in time to see his wife enter the dining room, proudly carrying the red velvet cake. Her insincere smile quickly faded when she saw the vacant room.

"Hurry, make a to-go box. They are leaving," Joseph urged.

Just as Jules and Will were pulling out of the driveway, they saw Joseph running through the yard with tins of Christmas goodies. While Jules was hugging her father, she saw Lillie watching the snowy scene through the branches of the Christmas tree in the front window, holding the apron she had made for her daughter. When the children turned and ran toward the house, Jules saw Lillie wipe tears from her face then turn back toward the kitchen.

In the car, Will apologized. Jules did not answer. She sat stone faced, holding her breath. Then Will said the second thing he would regret, "Jules, this is all my fault. You should not be mad at your mother."

The dam broke. Jules could no longer hold it in. She had been on the verge of a meltdown since the therapy session but had held it back, hoping to enjoy Christmas. Her sobs burst out. She was crying so hard that Will could barely make out what she was saying.

"I shouldn't be mad at *her*? You have no idea what she has done to me, Will. And I am not just talking about today. You don't know. You don't know."

Will had never seen Jules cry like this. He knew better than to say anything else. He reached for her hand, but she jerked it away, turning her back to him.

***

Christmas Day was just another day. There were no gifts to exchange as they had agreed to renovate the guest room into an office instead. Jules stayed in the bedroom most of the day. Will packed away all signs of Christmas.

9

Joëlle
Baran, France 1685

Joëlle woke to the crows of a dozen roosters in the village and slipped out of bed, careful not to wake Henri. She listened for the sounds of Maman and Grand-mère downstairs, but the kitchen was still quiet. Wide awake and ready to start the day, Joëlle took the bedside candle and stooped down to look under the bed for Grand-mère's box that held their toys from years past. Happy it was still there, she dusted off the top of the metal box and unlatched the ornate lock. The sight of the stack of homemade paper dolls made her want to squeal. Joëlle desperately wanted to grow up, but the little girl in her was still in control. She seated herself on the stone window ledge that overlooked the barn. By the light of the candle, she pulled out each of the dolls and laid them on the flat ledge then began choosing from the stack of tabbed clothes that Grand-mère had made for them.

A few minutes later, she noticed the lantern hanging in the workshop end of the barn and saw Grand-père move about, getting an early start to the day. She left the dolls unclothed and rushed quietly down the steps without bothering to get dressed herself and slipped ever so quietly out the back door.

"*Ma choue*! What are you doing outside so early? And in your nightgown, no less!"

"Bonjour, Grand-père. I did not want to wake the others by rousing about. What is that you are working on?"

"Bonjour, Joëlle. I am making some special barrels for your father."

"What kind of special barrels? What for?"

Louis grimaced then changed the subject, "I have already heard the kittens this morning. Perhaps you could play with them until we see the candle in the kitchen."

Joëlle climbed up the plank ladder to the still-darkened loft.

Louis smiled when he heard her squeal. But it wasn't more than a minute before he heard her backing down the steps, her hiked up gown full of fluff.

Joëlle found a lighted corner to sit and play with the kittens while watching Grand-père attach a metal ring to the staves of a barrel.

"How do you know how to build them?"

"It's in my bones, I suppose. I was taught by my father, Henri, who had been taught by his father, Guy, and so on, back as many generations as anyone can remember, Guy, Louis, Henri, Guy, Louis, Henri… Through the generations, we have perfected our technique and I'm proud to say that Reynaud barrels are known to be the best in the south of France. But it wasn't until your father came along that the business moved off this very farm."

"Why did he do that? I cannot imagine ever wanting to leave here?" A kitten stood on her shoulder, pulling at her hair.

"Your PaPa has always been good with people, so when he was around fourteen, I trusted him to go alone on the routes and deliver the orders to our customers. He liked them and they liked him. He grew the family business by venturing further and further along the route, and by the time he was seventeen, he had expanded our territory into the city of Bordeaux."

"Really?" The kitten was now biting at her ear, so she pulled it down and placed it in her lap.

"This company would not be what it is today without him. I would have been perfectly content to stay in Baran and make one of a kind, custom barrels."

Just as he finished the story, Joëlle saw the candlelight in the kitchen, so she replaced the kittens in the loft.

On her way out the door, she glanced sideways at the custom barrel. She had not forgotten about it and the fact that Grand-père did not want to talk about it made her even more curious. She made a plan to come back and check it out when Grand-père was away from the barn.

On the farm, everyone had designated daily chores. Joëlle gathered the eggs from the hen house. Henri fed the chickens and since PaPa had not left yet, he fed the livestock while Grand-père milked the cow and the goat. All this was accomplished before the family gathered for breakfast.

"We wish you could stay a few more days, Guy," Odette said to her son as she sat the loaf, fresh out of the outdoor bread oven, on the table.

"As do I, but I am afraid there is much to do with the business that only I can handle. I will visit again in a few weeks as soon as I can get away." Guy responded as a table full of solemn faces looked on.

Grand-père chimed in to end the somber mood, "Since the vegetables are not ready for harvest for another week or two, I thought we could take a ride to the market in Saint-Cyprien today."

"That's a wonderful idea," Guy looked around the table with a big smile on his face, forcing each one to smile back.

After they said their goodbyes, Guy rode off in one direction and the rest of the family loaded onto Grand-père's horse and buggy headed off in the other. They made the trek down the hill, crossing a shallow creek, then up the neighboring hill to Saint-Cyprien.

The market was packed with shoppers purchasing their neighbors' early harvest. Joëlle was pleased to see that one of the vendors had late strawberries for sale. She and Henri darted over while the adults picked over olives. Henri innocently picked up a strawberry from a wooden crate and popped it into his mouth.

The lady in the booth saw him and raised her voice to get the attention of whoever's child this was. "Madame! Child took a strawberry!" her wrinkled face glancing this way and that.

Joëlle quickly pushed Henri behind her and apologized, "Sorry," taking the blame on herself. Joëlle protected Henri not only from bullies but also from himself. He mumbled a *merci* to his sister, with strawberry juice running down his chin.

Marguerite witnessed the scene and stepped over to purchase the crate. "One can always use more jam," she said curtly to the woman, then directed her children away from the booth.

When they arrived home, Joëlle and her brother played with the other children in the hamlet, chasing chickens and each other around the olive tree in the center of the circular graveled courtyard. The tree was protected by a half-wall that surrounded it, which made it a perfect place to sit and visit with their friends from summers past.

In the late afternoon, a light rain began to fall, so dinner was eaten inside the kitchen with an early Bible reading and evening prayers. Joëlle was happy for an early bedtime after the active first full day of summer. She fell asleep easily, listening to the rain strike the tiled roof.

10

Jules
Lexington, Kentucky

In the week that followed, Lillie's calls to her daughter went unanswered. What happened at Christmas weighed heavily on her. Though she was unaware that Jules had overheard her, she knew that her reaction to Will's comment about a therapist had ruined Jules' Christmas. Lillie wanted to apologize to her for that, but it was not the only thing troubling her. Will's revelation that Jules had been seeing a therapist made Lillie realize that her daughter's troubles had not ended when she had left home. She had wanted to believe that when Jules moved away for college, things had gotten better for her. Jules had never mentioned any problems, and since Lillie had not been with her to witness any, she let herself believe that Jules had outgrown the troubles that plagued her youth.

Lillie always hoped that she would never have to reveal what she knew, but when she learned that Jules was still suffering, she knew she had to do it. This had gone on for far too long and Lillie felt responsible. Since Jules would not take her calls, Lillie decided to put it in a letter. Her daughter deserved to know the truth, no matter how many decades had passed.

***

Though Jules and Will had gone about their normal routines between the holidays, the pretense between them was obvious. Will busied himself by tearing out the carpet and installing an engineered wood floor in the new office. Jules kept herself busy refinishing an oak desk they had purchased together on one of their weekend antiquing trips.

Will and Jules had spent every New Year's Eve at home, waiting for the ball to drop in New York City on television, though they rarely stayed awake until it did. Following tradition, homemade pizza and champagne was on the menu again this year.

Together, they chopped vegetables and tossed them onto the ready-made crust. While the pizza cooked, they discussed the details of the work they hoped to accomplish in the office on New Year's Day. When the oven timer let them know dinner was ready, Will rolled the pizza slicer while Jules carried their drinks into the living room on a wooden tray they had picked up at a local thrift shop. They had intended to use it in their bedroom but found that it worked perfectly between them on the couch, holding their nightly popcorn and drinks.

When Will delivered the pizza, Jules was already sitting cross-legged on the couch facing the tray. He picked up the remote and turned up the volume, so it did not feel like they were celebrating alone. Will sat on the other side of the tray and picked up a slice of pizza, "So, do you have a New Year's resolution this year?" He took a bite, stringing cheese from the tray to his mouth.

"Well, let's see. Do you mean other than the generic ones, like exercising more and eating better?" With that, she shoved a hunk of cheesy crust into her mouth. She laughed at her own joke and got a little choked. "But seriously, you know I never do. Why, did you?" she asked with her mouth full.

He smiled. "Yes, actually I did this year. Well, it's not as much a resolution as it is a goal. I have been thinking a lot about it, and I really want us to take a long trip. I think we need it, Jules. It could be our long-awaited honeymoon since we never got to take one. Somewhere far, somewhere romantic, during our summer breaks. What do you say?"

"Yes. I would love that. I agree it could be good for us." She was intrigued. "Where to?"

"I don't have a place in mind. I thought I would let you choose."

"Ok. Planning it will be half the fun."

After dinner, Will carried the tray into the kitchen and emptied it into the sink while rehearsing his next move in his head.

Early in their marriage, they had the baby discussion around the first of every year. "Not yet," was Jules' answer for the first few years. "I just don't know when," came next. Then eventually, she realized it was time to quit fooling herself and to quit lying to Will. "I don't think I am ever going to want to have children. I'm sorry, Will. I just can't," she had said a few years back. "Please don't ask me again."

The champagne bubbles danced in the glasses as Will nervously walked toward Jules. As he handed her the stem, he took a reassuring breath. 'I've been wanting to have this conversation with you for a while now."

Instantly, she knew. Her smile faded. She stopped breathing and turned her gaze away from his.

He went on, "We haven't talked about it for a while now, but I've still hoped that you would change your mind about having a child. Time is running out, Jules. I couldn't let the new year pass without asking one more time for you to reconsider."

She could feel her face getting hot. *Why is he doing this again?* It had been years since he had mentioned a baby. She thought he understood that she would never change her mind.

He saw her reaction but continued. "Jules, I know you're scared, but everything will be fine. I will be an overly involved father. I will help with everything, even breastfeeding, if that will help convince you." He smiled.

She did not. When she finally looked back at him, he saw the dejectedness in her eyes. Though she did not give a response, at least verbally, he clearly saw her answer. She gently placed her flute on the coffee table and walked back to their bedroom. Will followed. He wanted to continue the conversation, but she closed the door behind herself, unaware.

Will stood with the closed door in his face, knowing that this was a defining moment in their lives. Jules was never going to change her mind. This was a door that would forever remain closed. Will now knew that he would never be a father. He felt sick to his stomach. He walked back into the living room, again rejected and increasingly resentful. He snapped off the television. When he was putting the leftover pizza away, he noticed the invitation to a New Year's Eve party from one of his fraternity brothers hanging on the refrigerator. He yanked it down and threw it into the trash bin.

Will fell asleep on the couch. The ball would drop without them watching again this year.

***

When Jules woke the next morning, Will was already in the new office preparing to paint. He had laid out the drop cloths and was setting up the ladder when Jules passed the room without saying anything. Will called out to her, "I cut a grapefruit for you. It's in a bowl in the fridge."

She was relieved. She knew that this was Will's way of letting her know that last night's discussion had been a mistake and would not be spoken of today. After pouring a cup of coffee, she walked back to the room and leaned her back against the door facing. "If you'll wait, I'll help you."

"It's fine. Go eat. You can help when you're finished."

Back in the kitchen, she ate her grapefruit, hopeful about the new year ahead. Will climbed the ladder, feeling anything but hopeful.

11

Jules
Lexington, Kentucky

Will worked hard to finish his part of the renovation before having to go back to teaching on the fourth of January. He had painted the walls and installed new wood blinds. Before he left for work, he moved the desk into the center of the office, not knowing where his wife would want it placed.

Jules was happy to finally have some time to herself to think about Will's pleading on New Year's Eve. Though she and Will pretended as if nothing had happened, it obviously had bothered them both, as the tension and awkwardness had not gone away. Decorating the new office would be a good opportunity for her to sort through the implications.

She tore open the package of curtains and saw that they were too wrinkled to hang. The mindless task of ironing would allow her plenty of time to think. She set the iron setting to steam and retrieved a can of spray starch.

With each pass of the hot iron, her mind wandered back to that night. Though she felt sad for Will, she convinced herself that his recent disappointment was born from his refusal to understand her fear of having children.

Pssst, a foamy mist fell on the bone-colored linen. She had never misled him on this subject, she reasoned. He had hurt himself, expecting her to change her mind.

She hit the steam button and watched the iron do its magic. She had always been honest with Will about her mental health issues and the fear she had of inflicting them on an innocent child. Though Jules had learned to manage her symptoms, they were always there under the surface.

With each new panel, she continued her introspection. Her mother was the other reason for not wanting children, though she had never confessed that to Will. She played it over in her mind. *It was my mother who caused me to lose all my friends.* She could feel the deep wound even now. *It was my mother who forced me to become an introvert.* Jules had wanted friends. She loved to have fun. *It is no wonder I am so screwed up. It was my mother who…*

Jules finished ironing just in time to stop herself from getting burned. She laid each of the ironed panels on the floor to cool, then put on some music and turned the volume up loud enough to drown out her thoughts while she hung the freshly starched curtains.

Now for the walls. She went to shop for artwork in the garage, which had become more of a storage shed over the years. Filled wall-to-wall with their treasures, there was no longer room to park their cars.

Besides antiquing and thrifting, the Merritts had become experts at attending auctions. Will would pack their lunch while Jules filled a large backpack, covering every contingency: bug spray, Chapstick, sunscreen, an umbrella and most importantly, a measuring tape. They would always arrive early to get their auction card, scope out items they wanted to bid on, and to get a seat up front. Jules would make a list in her notebook of all the items they wanted to bid on. Then together, they would decide how high they were willing to bid on each piece. They had learned a costly lesson at their first auction; how easy it was to raise the paddle but how hard it was to write the check. More times than not, they would go home with a trunk full.

Jules chose a couple of framed maps from their collection to hang behind the desk and a landscape scene that Will had painted for the window wall. After hanging them, she unrolled the new rug she had ordered, then placed the desk just over the edge. She stood in the doorway to see what else the room needed. "I know just the thing," she remarked aloud. She went back to the garage to retrieve the old Barrister bookshelf with chipping paint, just the way she liked it. She knocked off all the loose paint and gave it a good cleaning. After dragging it to the office, she filled it with favorite books and a few trinkets. All that was left was to place the comfortable side chair that she stole from the bedroom.

Just as she'd hoped, she let the process of doing something she loved bury what troubled her.

***

Will was happy to see his students after the long winter break. He let each of them share a story of their holiday. He knew he would not be able to teach them anything until it was out of their system. He instinctively understood children and knew he would have been a wonderful father.

Will had recognized his connection with kids as a teen when he helped his parents in their volunteer work. He developed a bond with them at the church's events. His kindness and enthusiasm drew them to him. He realized even then that teaching was his calling.

Will had taught at the same elementary school for fourteen years. He'd taught all grades from kindergarten through fifth grade but found that fourth grade was his favorite. Laura Harris had only been teaching for a few years but had been on Will's teaching team from the beginning. He had taken her under his wing, as he had always done with other first-time teachers, and the two had become fast friends.

During lunch, he was looking at Laura, thinking back on their time together before Christmas, when she caught him staring. He gave her a caring look and a half-smile. She quickly looked down at her feet and walked away, hoping no one had noticed his concerned face.

***

It was mid-January when Jules returned to the university. Before unlocking her office door, she went to see if her friend was already on campus. Since Chloe did not have an office of her own, Jules found her in a conference room and motioned her colleague to her private office.

The friends were eager to catch up, having been away from campus for a month.

"Need I ask how Christmas was with Prince Charming?" Chloe asked as she rubbed her hand over the top of his picture, then propped her feet up on the desk.

"You'd be surprised if you did." Jules popped in a coffee pod.

"You mean to tell me that snow wasn't falling on your picket fence as Will gifted you with a diamond necklace?"

Jules laughed at the contradiction of the scene Chloe had just painted with the reality of her actual Christmas, or lack thereof. "Well, let me tell you a sad little tale of the Christmas that wasn't," Jules said, handing her friend a steaming mug.

Chloe looked surprised, "Do tell."

Jules described how much she had looked forward to Christmas on the farm. She told her friend how she enjoyed the peaceful adult conversation of Will's family's Thanksgiving holiday, but much preferred the chaos of her large family gathering. She described in detail how good it felt to be home on the farm, enjoying the familiarity of their traditions. "Until all hell broke loose."

Chloe sipped her coffee and raised a curious eyebrow.

Jules realized she could not go any further without telling Chloe that she had been seeing a psychiatrist but reasoned that she needed someone to talk to other than Will at this point. In the past, Jules had never allowed herself to get too close to anyone who tried to befriend her. "How much time do you have?' Jules asked.

"Well, class doesn't start for two days."

"Hopefully, it won't take quite two days."

Jules began with how she had felt as a child, like she didn't belong in the family she was raised in. She told her about how they joked that she must have been switched at birth. "Honestly, it wouldn't surprise me, either." She told Chloe how she was a dreamer, but her family was pragmatic. She explained all the strange things they had told her she had done as a child.

"They are, in fact, strange. I can't explain them myself. Nevertheless," she said, "It was never a real problem in my life until middle school. That's when I started to wake up remembering a recurring, disturbing dream, which in turn, caused me to fear going to sleep and that led to the onset of my anxiety. All this started when I was in middle school."

Jules stopped again to think. *Should I go any further? Is this enough to explain what happened at Christmas or should I finally speak the thing that changed my life?*

"Jules? Where'd you go?" Chloe interrupted her friend's internal dilemma.

"Other than my therapist, I've never told anyone this in my entire life, not even Will, but something happened during my eighth-grade year that changed everything for me."

Chloe removed her feet from the desk and moved in closer. "You can trust me, Jules."

"I know I can."

Dr. Mary Benning, the department head, rapped on the doorframe, "Excuse me, ladies. I trust you both had a nice holiday. Good to see you back at work a few days early." She walked toward Jules' desk. Chloe was perturbed at the interruption.

"I received something in the mail over the holiday break and thought of you. Look at it, and if it is something that interests you, get back to me and we can go from there." She handed Jules an opened envelope, then made her way out the door, "I will let you get back to work. Have a good day."

Jules pulled the paper out of the envelope and began to read it.

"Hey, get back to your story." Chloe was obviously more interested in what her friend was about to tell her than she was in today's mail.

"What's this?" Jules ignored her and kept reading. "Well now, this *is* interesting."

"What is it?"

"Oh, nothing. Just a job offer in Paris."

"Paris? As in Paris, France?"

"It is, indeed. It's for the summer term, teaching English. Wouldn't that be a dream?" she swooned, lightening the mood.

"I know how you love anything French. You should go for it."

Jules thought back to her senior year when she first discovered her love of the French language. Since she didn't hang out with friends, she had found herself renting one movie after the other from a local video rental store that carried an extensive collection of foreign films. After seeing Jules there on a weekly basis, the owner began to recommend movies for her, especially old French films. Through them, she discovered her love of France and the smooth melody of the French language.

"It's a three-month commitment. I couldn't leave Will for that long. It's for someone single, I guess."

"I'd gladly break up with Josh and go find myself a rich Frenchman," Chloe said, only half-joking.

"Guess it'll have to be someone else's dream," she sighed, tossing the letter into the trash.

"Now, where were we?" Chloe asked. "Come on, Jules, you can't stop there."

Jules took a deep breath and told Chloe what had happened in her eighth-grade year, when her life took a drastic turn.

After listening to the story, Chloe got up and gave her friend a hug. "I don't know what to say, Jules. I am so sorry. That must have been devastating."

Jules pulled uncomfortably out of the hug. "It's fine. That was a long time ago. We really should get to work."

"I don't have a lot to do. I have plenty of time to talk more about it if you want."

"I don't." Jules said while walking her friend to the door. She was already sorry she'd shared it. She did not need pity.

Chloe walked away, wiping tears.

Jules pulled the envelope out of the trash can and stuffed it into her desk drawer.

12

Jules
Lexington, Kentucky

It had been a bitterly cold January, but February was trying to compete and appeared to be winning. The heating system in the building was ancient and could not keep up. Mrs. Merritt and her students had to wear their coats and hats in class. As she was teaching French terminology used in shopping, a loud boom caused her to jump and squeal. She had always been easily startled. The students laughed until the smoke alarm started blaring. Mrs. Merritt calmly instructed them to gather their things and make their way out the exterior door of the classroom.

Outside, Chloe saw the plume of smoke rising from the building and the crowd of students gathering outside. Having recently learned about Jules' aversion to fire and smoke, Chloe hurried to find her friend.

"Where is Mrs. Merritt?"

One of the students pointed in the direction of the parking lot, where Chloe saw Jules bent over the drainage grate, heaving. She picked up her friend's bag and stack of books and placed them on the nearest car. She was beginning to realize that Jules' seemingly ideal life was anything but perfect.

***

As Jules drove to her afternoon session, she reflected on Dr. Gray's suggestion that she spend the week between sessions focusing on her relationship with Will. Little did the doctor know that it was all Jules had been thinking about for months. Things had been steadily going downhill since Christmas. There were still moments of laughter between them, but also more spats over insignificant things. Will spent his evenings in the office pretending to be busy, while Jules daydreamed about the application she had secretly mailed to France a month earlier.

***

"I know you said you met in a college class. Please tell me more." Dr. Gray wasted no time with small talk, knowing her patient was prone to bolting out of their sessions.

"Yes, we met in Intro to Painting. Will is a natural artist, mostly in oil landscapes. I was jealous of his talent from the moment I first saw his paintings. I'd always wanted to be able to paint. I could see the scenes so clearly in my mind, but somehow, they didn't translate onto the canvas. He saw I was struggling in class and came to help me. I was my own worst critic, but Will assured me that it was art, *my* art. It wasn't supposed to look like anyone else's.

"That's just the kind of man he is, always building people up. Will loves life and people and it's contagious. I only had a couple of friends when I met him, so I felt so privileged to be included in his circle of friends. They accepted me because Will accepted me, but I'm sure they must have questioned what he saw in me. He was always so happy, and I was somewhat of a downer. I wanted to have fun, but my phobias stopped me from even wanting to try."

"Would you care to expand on that?"

"I remember the first time Will asked me to go with him to a fraternity event, a bonfire. In the back of my mind, I knew better. I knew what the smell of smoke does to me but since

I'd been with Will, my troubles had all seemed to go away. I let myself be hopeful, but instead, it ended in embarrassment for Will and absolute humiliation for me."

"Please tell me what happened."

"Will didn't know about my phobia or he would have never put me in that position. But I decided to put my fear aside for him. I planned to stay as far from the actual bonfire as possible. When the day came, I began to second guess my decision. My anxiety rose steadily throughout the afternoon. By the time he came to pick me up, I was a nervous wreck. I tried to back out of it by making excuses, but Will's charms won me over and I gave in. When Will pulled me toward the fire, I felt my blood pressure rising. Still, I kept trying to keep it together for him. But eventually, when I felt the heat from the fire, I couldn't handle it.

"I started sweating and having trouble breathing. I tried to quietly get Will's attention, but he was preoccupied, talking to his friends. I felt like I was going to be sick, so I blurted out loudly to him that I needed to leave which made everyone turn to look at me. I turned around to run but it was too late. I got violently ill all over a couple of his friends who had been standing behind us. All the fraternity brothers, who had been drinking, laughed and gagged. It was so humiliating. I felt embarrassed for Will. He, of course, agreed to take me home. I didn't answer his calls for days."

"Did you blame him?"

"No, I just couldn't face him. I was beginning to realize that we didn't belong together. But, of course, he convinced me otherwise."

"Is that the only time anything like that ever happened?"

"That following spring, the fraternity had rented a cabin on the lake for the weekend. Will really wanted us to go. He loves to water ski. Knowing my uneasiness around water, and considering what happened at the bonfire, there was no way I was going to put myself in the position of being on a boat. Finally, I broke down and told him about my phobias and of course, Will being Will, he decided to stay home with me instead of hanging out with his friends. I've always felt guilty about holding him back."

"Is that how Will sees it?"

"No. At least, he never makes me feel that way. But I see how, even now, he sacrifices his outgoing social life to be at home with me."

"How long did you date before getting married?"

"Almost two years. We got married right after we graduated. Neither of us wanted a big wedding, so we got married at his parents' house, with just our immediate families present. We didn't have jobs yet, so we didn't have money for a honeymoon. His parents offered to pay for one, but neither of us wanted them to have to do that. So, Will planned a surprise for me. He and his friends decorated our apartment with string lights and candles. They put our mattress in the center of the living area and hung sheets from the ceiling around it to make it cozy. He called it our 'homeymoon'. I loved that. We stayed in our tent bed, watching movies and drinking wine. It was very romantic."

"That sounds lovely. So, you've been married for several years then. And what about children?" Dr. Gray treaded lightly.

"Well, I guess that is a part of why I'm here. Will really wants children and I do not."

"May I ask why you feel that way?"

"Well for starters, I wouldn't want a child to inherit my phobias and end up like me in a place like this. No offense, of course."

"Of course." Dr. Gray was familiar with the stigma. "Talk more about that. How has this conflict played out in your marriage?"

"Will has always thought I would change my mind or that he could convince me. In fact, he tried again on New Year's Eve."

"Did you argue?"

"No, he could see that I hadn't changed my mind. Anyway, things are back to normal now. It didn't last long. He'll be fine with it. It's just the new year thing."

"The new year thing?"

"On New Year's Eve, we always talk about our plans for the new year ahead and most years, Will would bring up having a baby."

Dr. Gray paused, then said, "You haven't changed the way you feel about having children. Have you considered the fact that he may not be fine with it? That he may never be fine with it?"

Jules defensively looked away from her and sat silent. She didn't like hearing Dr. Gray say what she knew deep down to be true. Jules wanted Will to be fine with it. She needed him to be fine with it.

Dr. Gray continued, "How does it make you feel when he tries to talk you into having a baby?"

"I understand that he wants children, but I've never misled him on the subject. I have always been honest with him about it. I think he thought that teaching children would be enough for him. He isn't wrong for wanting kids, but I'm not wrong for the way I feel either." A voice rose from somewhere deep within her. *Am I?*

"Have the two of you ever considered adoption?"

"He's brought it up before, but my phobias aren't the only reason I don't want to have children. I'd never want to hurt a child the way my mother…" Jules twirled the ring on her right hand and stopped herself from voicing the words she'd thought for years.

***

After dinner, Jules walked into the office to find Will setting up their new speakers. "Can we talk?"

"Sure, what's up?"

"I wanted to let you know that I've decided not to continue with therapy."

Will spun around in his office chair to face her. "What? Why?"

"We are paying her a lot of money just to pry into my life. I feel like all she ever does is ask personal questions, never offering a bit of advice. I am forced to think about every dreadful thing that has ever happened in my life and it's making everything worse. Not only for me, Will, but also between us. I think it's time we were honest with each other. Since I've been seeing her, things haven't gotten better. They've gotten worse."

Will took a deep breath then blew it out slowly through his mouth, "Jules, I've tried to understand how hard this is for you. I love you for who you are but—"

"But?" she interrupted.

He continued, "I've always had a vision of what our life would be, what it could be. It isn't just about what you want." He could not stop himself. "What will our life look like in the future if it's just the two of us?"

"Exactly like it does now, like it always has. Is that so bad? I've always been honest with you about the fact that I can't even consider having children, and you've always accepted it." Her voice grew stronger. "Why can't you accept it now?"

Silence filled the space between them as they each contemplated their impasse.

"Because, Jules, I want more," he said, looking her in the eye.

A knife went through her heart. "You are just like them. I was never enough for them and I'm not enough for you." She felt the tears building and rushed out of the room.

"Jules." He tried to call her back to the office but heard her pick up the car keys then slam the door.

***

By the time Jules had driven out her emotions, Will had already gone to bed. She found a note on the counter, apologizing to her. Of course, he took all the blame on himself and reassured her that she was enough. She knew it was a lie. *Why does he always have to be so nice?* The postscript read, "Your mother called again."

***

The next morning, Jules was abruptly awakened when Will stormed into the bedroom, holding a piece of mail. He tossed it on the bed. She sat up, rubbing her eyes and tried to focus on what had him so upset.

"When were you going to tell me?" He condemned her.

She picked up the paper and saw that it was a letter from the university in Paris officially offering her the three-month teaching position. She could hardly believe her eyes and tried to pretend that it was not good news. "Chloe and I were curious about it. I just filled out the application to see what would happen. I certainly never thought I would get offered the job."

She had never seen him pacing like this. "So, let me get this straight. They hired you for a job in Paris, France, from just an application alone?"

"Well, no. There was a Zoom interview," she spilled awkwardly, her cheeks growing redder by the second.

He stopped pacing and turned to look at his wife. "I see."

"Of course, I'm not going to take it."

Will turned to walk out of the room and threw up his hands. Defeated, he mumbled, "Maybe you should."

Maybe I will.

13

Jules
Lexington, Kentucky

Jules announced that she would be spending the day in the office as she walked out the door. Will didn't bother to respond. She phoned Chloe from her car to ask if she would meet her at the university. Jules assumed she'd be free, guessing that Josh would be off watching college basketball somewhere.

Chloe was standing by the door with two lattes in hand when Jules arrived. "What's this all about? Of course, I don't mind. I was looking for a reason to get out of the apartment. Josh is going to a friend's house to watch basketball."

So predictable, Jules thought. "I'm glad," she said out loud as she unlocked her door. They complained about the weather while pulling off their coats and making themselves comfortable.

"So, what are your plans for June?" Jules peered over the cup while taking a sip of her latte.

"June? No clue, why do you ask?"

"I was thinking we could do some things together, away from campus. We could visit a museum or take a cooking class together."

"I think that would be fun. I'm pretty sure they offer classes at the community center. I'll be happy to check into it for us."

"No, I was thinking somewhere out of town," Jules teased.

"A road trip? Yes, that's a great idea!" Chloe was still oblivious. "Josh will protest, but I don't care."

"More like a plane trip. Do you have a passport?" Jules watched the light bulb finally go on in her friend's head.

"Are you saying what I think you're saying?" Chloe asked, leaning in.

"I got the job in Paris, Chloe. And I'm going to take it." Jules couldn't believe the words coming out of her own mouth.

"Wait. I saw you throw the application away. What about Will? Is he going to stay with you for the entire summer?"

"I don't think he's going at all." Jules' demeanor saddened.

Jules explained to Chloe how her marriage had been slowly unraveling in the last few months and that some time apart might be good for them.

"Oh, Jules. I had no idea. I am so sorry. If your marriage can't make it…" she stopped herself from finishing the sentence. "Of course, you and Will are going to work things out."

"I hope so, Chloe, but at this point, I don't see how. We want different things."

Jules spent the rest of the day finding things to do in her office, dreading going home.

***

The house smelled delicious when Jules stepped inside the door. She hung up her coat, put away her bag, and went into the kitchen to find Will, in his apron, finishing up dinner. He had set the table. There were no candles burning, no romantic music, but there *was* a Valentine's Day card beside her plate.

She felt her stomach knotting. She had forgotten and Chloe hadn't mentioned it either. She didn't know what to say so she stood by the table staring at the card.

"It's ok. I had forgotten, too. But when I saw all the men buying flowers at the grocery store, I just picked up a card. And besides, we never make a big deal of it anyway. Were you able to get things caught up at work?" Will sat a basket of bread on the table.

"Mhmm. Thanks for making dinner. How about you?" the words slipped half-heartedly from her lips.

"Since it was too cold to be out, I decided to go through the envelope of your family history from your uncle. It took all day to sort through his unorganized documents and piece it all together but finally, I was able to trace your lineage back to when your ancestors first arrived in America. I found out something you're going to love to hear."

"What's that?" Jules asked, confused by his mood change since this morning.

They each filled their plates from the stove top.

"You're not going to believe this, but I discovered that your ancestors came here from France. I knew you'd like to hear that you have a little French blood running through your veins." He poured their glasses full.

"I've always wondered about that, with the last name Laurent." She took a bite of peppered asparagus and smiled.

He did most of the talking while she ate. "I've done a lot of thinking today about the opportunity you've been given, and I think you should take the job. It's just for a few months. While you're there, you can do further research on your ancestry. I think you'd really enjoy that. And more importantly, you can have some time to yourself before I get there."

Get there? She took a drink of iced tea to hide her surprise.

Will went on, "I was thinking that once school is out, I can get a few things done around the house and when you're ready, I'll come to Paris. We can spend some time together away from the stresses of home and have that fresh start we've talked about. What do you say?"

Jules didn't tell him she'd already made up her mind to go and wondered if guilt showed on her face. She had expected Will to be furious with her. But once again, she had underestimated her husband. "We don't have to decide this tonight."

I do not deserve him, she thought as she took a bite of filet mignon.

14

Joëlle
Baran, France 1685

After the rain moved past, the summer sun came out hot and bright, ripening the vegetables day by day. Joëlle and Henri spent those days reconnecting with old friends, playing in barns and swimming in the creek at the bottom of the hill. They knew their time was limited because the garden would be ready for the first harvest soon and there would be less time to spend with them.

Sunday in Baran was Joëlle's favorite day of the week. The Protestant church believed it to be a day that was set aside for only worship, fellowship, and rest. Joëlle knew that Grand-père would not be working in the shop today. She excused herself from breakfast, "Maman, may I go play with the kittens until time to leave for church?"

"Of course, but only for a few minutes and do not dirty your good clothes."

"I won't. I promise." Joëlle skipped out the door before Henri could ask to join her.

When she got inside the barn, she looked back toward the house through the slats in the barnwood to see if the coast was clear. The special barrel was no longer on the worktable. She looked around at the dozens of barrels sitting here and there.

"How will I tell which one is the special barrel?" she asked herself. She walked through them, looking them over, spinning them around and trying desperately to find one that seemed different. She was about to give up when she spotted a tarp covering something in the far corner of the shop. Once more, she peeked outside and didn't see anyone heading her way. She pulled the tarp aside to uncover a half dozen barrels. They looked like the others on the outside, so she lifted one of the lids and saw that it contained a large compartment in its center.

"Wonder what that could be for." she whispered.

"I don't believe the kittens are in there," her grandfather said sternly.

Joëlle jumped and squealed. "Oh, uh, I didn't know you were here, Grand-père." She couldn't bring herself to look at him.

"I can see that. Now, take yourself to the house. The shop is no place for a young lady to be without an adult. Do I make myself perfectly clear?"

Joëlle knew she was being scolded. "Yes, Grand-père. Perfectly." She rushed past him and darted out of the barn, disappointed with herself that she hadn't been more careful.

The family walked together under dappled sunlight as they made their way through the woods toward the church, appropriately named L'église de la Forêt. Grand-père led the horse, pulling a cart with the picnic lunch that the women had prepared the day before. Joëlle walked behind everyone, wanting to stay as far away from Grand-père as possible.

When they came out of the trees, Joëlle saw the cross they'd seen when they had arrived a few days earlier. The tall, yellowed cross had been built on a large stone post and seemed to be out of place, sitting at the edge of a meadow, but to those who knew its purpose, it served as a marker to the entrance into the woods on the other side of the meadow. The church sat far inside the forest with no road leading in. Grand-mère always said, "This church is set apart from the world, making it truly divine." Joëlle would never forget those words as she knew them to be true.

The ancient church was made of golden stones, with three large windows in the front. The only entrance to the chapel was in the back, so that when one entered, the focus was solely on the light streaming in from the three windows, landing directly onto the altar. To Joëlle, it seemed as if God himself was leading his parishioners to worship. The Catholic church they attended in Bordeaux was enormous, with thirty feet tall ceilings and beautiful stained-glass windows, but in Joëlle's eyes, there was no comparison to the feeling she felt inside this modest 'home of God,' she called it.

Joëlle remembered her grandmother saying that the local people, even people that don't attend, write their prayers on paper and stick them in the cracks between the stones. She'd said that when their prayers were answered, they would remove the paper and sometimes have a marble plaque made that simply read, 'Merci'. The side wall of the church was full, from floor to ceiling with them. Joëlle liked to imagine God walking through the chapel after everyone left, pulling the written prayers from their hiding places, and reading them, one by one.

Joëlle loved the metrical psalm singing of the Protestant church, as witnessed by those sitting near her, hearing the sincerity in her sweet voice, seeing her raised palms and head turned Heavenward. Henri watched her and tried his best to mimic his sister though not with quite the sincerity.

Thanks to her father's nightly scripture readings, Joëlle knew most of the verses being read and silently mouthed the words. During the homily, however, she found her thoughts wandering from this to that…*Who is that girl I've never seen before…I sure hope someone brought a cherry tarte…If no one gets baptized, I bet they will let us play in the cold creek…* From time to time, she would scold herself back to the lesson, though it never held her attention for long. But when the congregation had communion together and took up a collection for the poor, she again paid close attention. Those things interested her.

After the benediction, Joëlle noticed Henri crossing his heart as he did in the Catholic church. She quickly pulled his hands down, hoping no one else had seen him. Though she wasn't sure the reason, PaPa had told her that it was especially important now to keep the two separate and not to discuss their unique situation with anyone in Baran or Bordeaux. Joëlle was not one to keep a secret, but it was made clear to her that this was a line she was not to cross.

While the women of the congregation were setting the food out on a wagon bed under a plane tree, Joëlle asked her mother, "Maman, may we play in the cold creek after lunch? It doesn't look like anyone is getting baptized today," Joëlle said, clearly pleased.

"Joëlle!" her mother gently scolded while suppressing a smile.

"I'm sorry. I didn't mean to *sound* so happy about that."

Marguerite giggled at her daughter's honesty then agreed to let Joëlle and Henri wade in the water with the other children until it was time for the afternoon singing.

As the children walked the narrow path along the cliff down to the creek, Joëlle instinctively pulled Henri to the inside edge and traded places with him, putting herself in danger of falling down the steep hillside.

Henri protested, "I'm a big boy, JoVee."

Joëlle, in her big sister way, put her brother in his place, "Big boys don't say things like that."

Henri didn't respond. Joëlle knew he secretly cherished her protection.

After the midday singing, Marguerite called her children to the wagon.

"May I have just one more minute, please. I forgot something in the church." Joëlle sprinted to the back door and looked around to make sure she was alone. When she saw that she was, she walked to the altar. "God, I hope you can hear me. I don't have a paper to write my prayer on, but will you please be with PaPa while we are away since Maman will not be there to look after him?" She listened for a moment, hoping for an answer, then rushed toward the door, where she found her grandmother smiling with a tear running down her cheek.

After a full day, the family arrived home just before nightfall. Joëlle was worn out from giving her heart and soul to worship and fellowship with her friends. Most nights, she talked on and on to Henri about whatever thoughts that were running through her mind. But not tonight. Her only words were, "I am full up in every possible way."

15

Jules
Lexington, Kentucky

It was not unusual for Lillie and Jules to go a month or two without talking to one another, especially in the early months of the year, when there were no family birthdays to celebrate. But this was the longest they had ever gone without speaking. Lillie had tried to call her daughter every couple of weeks, but Jules refused to return the calls.

Lillie considered mailing the letter but decided that their relationship needed to be in a better place before she added to Jules' confusion. Lillie convinced herself that it had remained unknown for decades and that she should wait until the time was right for Jules. Though neither of them had planned for this much time to pass, the weeks had turned into months, and the months were adding up.

***

Jules knew that she should call her mother before leaving for France, but wondered how she would attempt to explain what she was about to do? Jules knew exactly what her mother would say. *You're doing what? You mean to tell me that you are leaving your husband for months, to run off to a foreign country, alone?* Jules could not bear to have her mother misunderstand her again, not after Christmas. Jules would never forget those words, *What did I do wrong?*

***

By mid-May, winter had finally given way to spring. Flowers were beginning to bloom, and hope was in the air. Whether it was the anticipation that comes with spring or new possibilities on the horizon, Jules and Will found themselves in a better place. They had spent the last couple of months planning the home projects for Will to complete before joining Jules in France. Together, they had decided on the paint color for the exterior of the house. They designed the new deck and shopped for the supplies together. Jules spent the rest of her free time going over the curriculum, researching the attractions of Paris, and boning up on conversational French.

***

Weeks of planning and preparations behind them, finally, the day arrived. Will drove Jules to the airport for her midnight flight. She'd intentionally chosen the red eye so she wouldn't be able to see the Atlantic Ocean through the window of the plane.

Will hauled her luggage to the departures counter, his heart heavier than her bags. He stayed with her until she had signed in and her luggage was checked, then walked with her to security.

Will turned to face his wife, "I can't believe this is really happening. You're quiet. Are you ok? Are you anxious about the flight?"

"I think I'm just numb. It doesn't feel real. It'll probably hit me when I get off the plane, not knowing what's going to happen next."

That was exactly what Will was afraid of, what was going to happen next, but instead of voicing his concern, he reassured her.

They held each other for a long time, both with thoughts they couldn't find words for. Will handed her the carry-ons and looked his wife in the eye, "I hope this is everything you want it to be."

"Thank you, Will. I promise I'll email every day since we might not be able to always talk due to the time difference. You, too. Promise?"

"I promise." Then Will kissed Jules and watched her walk away from him. Once she cleared security, she turned around for one last look. Through tearful smiles, they waved their final goodbyes.

As Will drove home, he wondered if he'd done the right thing by letting her go. Not only was he worried about her safety, but he was also hurt that she could even consider being away from him for that long. The truth be told, he was beginning to feel a little angry. *Why am I always the one to sacrifice in our relationship?* He had wanted their lives to include friends and socializing, but she had been too afraid her phobias would surface. Though she had told him on many occasions that he was free to go without her, it wasn't in his character to leave his wife home alone. But the sacrifice that hurt him most was that he would never be a father. He wanted children, but she was the one who inevitably got to make the decision for him. Though Will was trying to protect his heart by being frustrated with Jules, when he pulled up to the darkened house, he could not hold back his tears.

***

Jules found her gate and took a seat for the hour-long wait before boarding. The lobby was full of young men in personalized wheelchairs, darting here and there. She tried not to stare, but their exuberance constantly caught her attention. They shook hands and laughed heartily while catching up with each other. They were clearly excited about whatever adventure they were heading toward. It was obvious to Jules that even though life had chosen their altered conditions for them, they were joyful. *Why can't I accept my obstacles and be as happy as they are?* Occasionally one of the men would catch her looking and smile at her. There was something about them that made her not want to turn away. Instead, she almost wished she could join their conversation. Just then, one of the men wheeled past and Jules noticed a bumper sticker attached to one of his carry-ons that read, "Paralyzed Veterans Racing." In that moment, she realized that life had not chosen this fate for these men. They had chosen it for themselves, voluntarily and at all possible costs. What an inspiration they were, however unwitting.

On the flight to Baltimore, Jules thought about Will's questions. *Should I be afraid?* She wasn't. She was eager to manage things on her own for the first time in her life. *Should I feel sad?* She didn't. In fact, she felt an excitement she had never known. *Should I feel guilty?* She did not. Will had given her the green light. *At least, I should feel guilty about not feeling guilty?* She scoffed at her own ridiculousness, then settled into her seat. Instead of the in-flight movie, she watched the Veterans on their way to D.C.

After Jules successfully made her connecting flight in Baltimore and was seated on the international flight, she swallowed a sleeping pill. With the moon above and the sea below, she slept her way through the skies to Paris.

***

She arrived at the Charles de Gaulle airport in the early afternoon, Paris time. Her joints were stiff from the long flight, and she was still groggy from the sleeping pill, but Jules was excited to finally be in France. Once she had retrieved her luggage, she scanned the names on the handwritten signs pointed toward her until she saw her own. An undergraduate from the university met her there to take her to the apartment they had secured for her in the seventh arrondissement close to campus. When her eyes met his, she smiled at the young man holding the sign. He acknowledged her but did not smile back.

"Bonjour, madame," he said in French. "Welcome," he added in English, graciously allowing Jules to choose the language they would speak going forward.

Ever since she'd agreed to take the position, she had thought about whether to speak English whenever possible. She knew that most Parisians could effortlessly speak her language, and it would be the easier choice. On the other hand, she considered that by choosing to converse solely in French, she would not only improve her skill, but it would also give her the experience of *being* someone else, someone French.

"Bonjour," she chose. "Je suis Jules Merritt. Et-vous? Comment vous appelez-vous?" A deep satisfaction began to set in.

"Je suis Claude Dumont. Enchanté. On y va." At that, he turned on his heels and walked briskly through the sea of people. She struggled to keep up, pulling her heavy luggage behind her.

Following him under the *Sortie* sign, she stepped outside the airport to a line of people waiting for a taxi. She was impressed by the speed at which the crowd and cars moved. One after the other, a taxi pulled up with an abrupt tap of the brakes. An airport employee would swiftly open the car door for the curbside passenger to plunge into while he threw their luggage into the awaiting opened trunk. No sooner than the lid slammed shut, the taxi would lunge forward into traffic. It was quite the dance, obviously perfected over time.

"I've never seen anything quite like this," she remarked in French. Claude either did not hear her or had chosen not to respond. Jules second guessed herself, replaying the sentence in her mind, but felt confident she'd made no mistake. His non-response reminded her that understanding cultural differences is just as important as knowing the language.

Following Claude's lead, she stepped onto the curb. She pulled her luggage close, with the handles turned outward, ready and waiting to be manhandled. It went off without a hitch. Jules felt proud of herself. But then, as the taxi bullied into the traffic, she drew in her breath. Cars, buses, mopeds, and taxis all rallied for their position on the road with an, *I dare you* attitude. Her eyes met with the driver's whose moped was in a T-bone position to her taxi. His first reaction was to throw his neck forward and his hands up. Then seeing the wide-eyed look of fear on her face, he realized this was her first experience with Parisian drivers then threw his head back and laughed. Not sure if he was laughing at her or with her, she lowered her sky-high eyebrows and smiled back. Then they were off again. This was going to be the ride of her life. She knew the taxi was only the beginning.

After arriving at the apartment, Claude held the taxi long enough to get Jules into the secured building. He pulled her luggage to the elevator then handed her the keys to the apartment. "Fourth floor, room 48," he said, unknowingly breaking the, *all French, all the time* rule she had arbitrarily made.

"Merci, Monsieur Dumont." She tried to thank him, but he was already making his way outside. She heard the screech of the taxi speeding off just as the old elevator bell dinged. Jules backed inside then rolled her suitcases in tight around her. The tiny glass elevator was barely big enough to hold her and her luggage. It overlooked a neglected, but nonetheless pretty interior courtyard. The elevator moved at a snail's pace, allowing her time to take in her new surroundings. The building was a square of apartments all with a view into the unkempt garden. When the elevator jolted to a stop, Jules pulled her luggage into the hallway, confused about which way to turn. In that moment, she was glad that Claude had left it up to her to figure it out on her own. After all, she was a different person here, a confident one. She winced trying to convince herself of it.

She put her key into the old lock, curious as to what she would find on the other side of the ten-foot wooden door. She jiggled. It rattled. She tried the handle, but it was still locked. She piled all her bags on top of her luggage and used both hands to forcibly turn the key. She heard the loud clack of the metal latch moving aside, allowing entry into her new life. The symbolism did not escape her.

When she opened the door, the first thing she noticed were the herringbone oak floors. Being more than a little worn made them beautiful in her eyes. The apartment was surprisingly small, but her eyes were drawn upward to the trim work in the soaring ceiling. The unit came furnished, but she almost wished it hadn't. In place of a sofa, a lumpy looking daybed faced an ancient cabinet-style television. A tattered side chair was pulled up to a short desk near the front window. An apartment sized refrigerator and stove were shoved together on the opposite wall. Next to them was a standalone cabinet stocked with the bare minimum of cookware and a few mismatched dishes. A small bistro table and chairs completed the makeshift kitchen.

Jules scanned the room, looking for the entrance to the bedroom. Seeing a curtain, she walked through and slammed her knee into the toilet. "Ouch!" She caught herself from falling into it on the tiniest sink she had ever seen. The shower stall touched the sink that touched the toilet. The bathroom was barely big enough to turn around in. A small oval mirror hung above the sink so low that she had to bend over to see her hair. When she was looking at her grimacing reflection, it hit her, there was no bedroom. That uncomfortable looking daybed *was* the bedroom.

She limped over to what she thought was a large front window and pulled back tall curtains to reveal double doors that opened out onto a small balcony with a typical Parisian scrollwork railing. She sat down on the rusty balcony chair, rubbed her bruised knee, and looked down into the overcrowded street. "Perfect."

Jules hobbled back inside to email Will to let him know that she had arrived safely in Paris. She was happy to see that he had already emailed her.

J,
I miss you already. Seriously, the house feels so empty, and I don't know what to do. I guess I'll get started on those projects to distract myself. But first, I'm going out for dinner and drinks after work tonight with some of the old college guys. It will be fun to catch up. Can't wait to hear all about your trip.
Much love,
W

"Well, that didn't take long," Jules smiled before typing her reply.

W,
I made it. I'm in Paris! Can you believe it? The flights were fine, but long. The sleeping pill worked great. I never even knew when I was flying over the ocean.
The apartment is small but wonderful, right in the heart of everything. I'm tired and hungry so I'll write more tomorrow. I just wanted to let you know that I'm here and getting settled.
By the way, there's no need to rent a car when you get here. The driving is madness!
Love you,
J

Her stomach growled, reminding her that she had not eaten in over twenty-four hours. She had been too nervous to eat before leaving for the airport and had slept through the snack served on the overnight flight. Jules decided to unpack her luggage then venture out to find something to eat.

She pulled the curriculum that she had received from the university out of her carry-on and laid it on the desk. Jules wanted it out in plain view as a reminder to review when she returned to the apartment from her sightseeing adventures over the next few days.

As she was stuffing her clothes into the insufficient chest of drawers, she became light-headed. The room started to spin. She decided to lie down on the daybed to rest for a bit. Just as she got comfortable, a puny sounding car horn and a man yelling in French shocked her eyes open. She jumped up and closed the double doors, careful to turn the lock even though she was on the fourth floor.

When she woke up hours later, she noticed the darkness and looked at her cell phone to check the time. It was eleven p.m. in Paris. She would not be eating dinner tonight, so she rummaged through her purse for a protein bar. *So much for my first meal in France.* She undressed and went easily back to sleep on the lumpy daybed, jetlagged and still slightly under the influence of the sleeping pill.

As morning came and she awoke in her new setting, Jules felt genuinely happy. She pulled on her robe and opened the curtain to the back window which overlooked the garden she had seen from the glass elevator. She rubbed her hand across the dead flowers in the basket that was attached to the Juliette balcony. She looked around and saw that all the apartments had the same metal flower container on their window balconies. None of them held even one live flower. She wondered why, given her preconceived notion that the French people love all things floral.

Movement across the courtyard refocused her attention to a wrinkled lady in the apartment directly across from hers. The woman instantly reminded Jules of the character Estelle from *Friends*. In the series, Estelle was a chain smoker, who was never without a cigarette in hand. "Bonjour," Jules said timidly as their eyes met. The lady quickly looked away, put out her cigarette, and turned back into her apartment.

Jules watched as she pulled the curtains closed. The woman's coldness stung, but Jules would not let it ruin her first day.

The cool, gray weather and the sound of scurrying Parisians called her out into the bustling city. She showered in the tiny bathroom and hurried to get dressed. Tossing the skeleton key into her shoulder bag, she began her temporary life as a Parisian.

16

Jules
Paris, France

Jules stepped outside her apartment building and smelled heaven. When she rounded the corner, she nearly ran into a line of groggy Parisians waiting for their morning espresso at the boulangerie next door. She took her place in line and while she waited, she shopped the wall-sized window filled with puff pastries and tall standing baguettes. The smell of freshly baked croissants taunted her senses, making her stomach rumble. Jules realized that she needed something more substantial, so she left the line in search of a breakfast bistro, no matter how delicious the pastries smelled.

She passed a flower shop with buckets overflowing beautifully onto the sidewalk and decided to purchase a bouquet for the apartment upon her return. As she walked, she noticed something strange. Not only were there unwrapped baguettes in the bakery window, but also in the street windows of a camera shop, the pharmacy, and even a real estate office. She smiled, questioning if this was a mirage that arose from her near starvation.

Keeping pace with the crowd, she came to an intersection where she heard rattling dishes and the hum of conversation coming from the street to her right. She rose to her tiptoes to peer over a well-dressed gentleman and saw a restaurant aflutter with activity. Since all the outdoor tables were full, she walked inside and was promptly seated by the window. She was pleased to have a front row seat to study how true Parisians take their breakfast. Men sat with crossed legs, scanning the morning paper, while women chatted and sipped foaming coffees. She noticed men and women alike had turned their chairs to face the street to do their own people watching.

After ordering an Americano coffee and a bacon and egg croissant, Jules was served fresh-squeezed orange juice and a roll that she had not ordered. She noticed that the other tables were all served the same items. Though she was not familiar with the practice, she was thankful and began eating the bread right away.

Jules pulled a small notebook from her bag and noted the two turns she'd made so far. She planned to add to the list throughout the day so she wouldn't get lost on her first day. On the second page, she made a note to stop for flowers on her way home. *Home*, she thought as she scribbled her note. *I like the sound of that.*

The waitress dropped her hot breakfast and quickly hurried past. Jules sunk her teeth into the crunchy crusted, soft-centered croissant, smiling before she could swallow. She savored every bite, including the crumbs.

Before leaving the states, Jules purchased the *Michelin Green Guide to Paris* from a local travel agency. She had studied it thoroughly and had mapped out the places she wanted to visit each day prior to starting her teaching position at the university.

Of course, La Tour Eiffel was at the top of the list. It was several blocks from her apartment, and she was grateful that the travel agent had suggested purchasing comfortable walking shoes. After paying the bill, she left only the loose change on the table, having learned that from the agent, as well.

There would be no need to use her Michelin Guide to locate the first adventure. The sky-high structure was clearly visible as soon as she exited the bistro. As the base came into view, she was surprised by the long line of tourists that weaved back and forth in the enormous lot. She made a rough calculation that it would take hours just to reach the ticket window and clear security. She pulled out her notebook and jotted a reminder to research a better time to visit. Then she would brave the elevator to the top, perhaps at night once Will arrived. She snapped a few pictures, having to step far away just to get a portion of it in the frame. Walking away, she tried her best to dodge the many people harassing her to buy "Made in China" Eiffel Tower key chains.

The second attraction on her list was the Louvre Museum. Walking her way from the Eiffel Tower, she passed a vintage carousel drenched in gold with elaborately decorated white horses dancing to a classic Parisian song played on the accordion. She stopped for a few minutes to soak it in. Somehow her senses were awakened here, the colors brighter, the smells stronger, the tastes more intense.

She continued the long walk along the Seine to the museum, taking in one unfamiliar sight after the other.

Before crossing the walking bridge over the Seine, Jules paused for a moment to look at the river. *It's a wide bridge. I can do this.* She even bravely stopped in the middle to take a selfie, taking care not to get too close to the edge.

The size of the Louvre stopped Jules in her tracks as she scanned the enormous u-shaped building. She quickly sped up her pace to get into the growing crowd of people waiting to enter the museum through the glass pyramid.

Through her research, Jules knew the first place she wanted to visit was the Sully wing. The Histoire du Louvre is filled with paintings that document the storied history of the museum. She passed a class of students sitting cross-legged on the floor, making sketches of the paintings that lined the hallway. The oil paintings, in varying sizes, were hung in stacked rows, with the upper paintings leaning out at the top. Jules wondered if that was done for ease of viewing or to accommodate the barrel ceiling. Many of the paintings depicted people in period clothing, viewing older paintings throughout the centuries. Men in top hats and coattails, double-breasted vests with upturned collars, wore poofy pants tucked into shining boots. Women in empire dresses that skimmed the floor had their hair stacked high with feathers sticking out even higher. Little boys wore ruffled shirts paired with high-waisted knickers, and little girls had their hair in tight ringlets flowing onto lace dresses that fell to the tops of their heavy boots. Jules thought about the people in these paintings who had also visited the Louvre and had gazed upon some of the very same pieces of art that the students were sketching. The realization stirred her mind. *What a visual documentation of how fleeting life is and that even though people come and go, pieces of them, images of them, and things they create, remain.*

She took her time meandering through the rooms, paying attention to the details in each painting. *Will would absolutely love this place.* For the first time since she had arrived, a tinge of guilt and sadness hit her. Jules fidgeted with her wedding rings, wishing he was there with her. She decided the Louvre would be the first place she would take him when he arrived then noted it in her book.

Hours later, after Jules had seen all the paintings in the Histoire du Louvre, she decided to have lunch in the museum café. While she ate a bagel sandwich, she took notice of the French women's hairstyles, their manicured nails, and their stylish shoes. Jules knew that she probably stood out to them. She looked around and didn't see a single person wearing jeans. *Isn't this the country that started the fad?* Jules recalled learning that the word denim was derived from d'Nimes. *But it was the Americans that took hold of it and never let go.* She smiled at the thought.

Jules had never cared about the way she looked or dressed. Sitting in the Louvre Museum, in Paris, France, she wondered now if it was because of her insecurities that she didn't want to stand out, or even to be seen at all. Away from home, Jules was already seeing herself from a new perspective.

After she had finished eating lunch and comparing herself to others, she continued her tour of endless hallways, lined with painted works of art, including *The Coronation of Napoleon*, *The Wedding at Cana*, and of course, *The Mona Lisa*. Though she wanted to stay longer, her feet were beginning to complain, even though she was wearing her expensive and unattractive walking shoes.

As she passed the ticket counter on her way out, she made a mental note to purchase a Paris Museums Pass. She was learning that the Louvre, one of Paris' many museums, had far more to offer than she could experience in one summer.

***

Jules entered the bistro, La Pluie, eager to get off her feet and have her first real French meal. The hostess seated her in the back at a candlelit table for two with mismatched chairs. Jules chose the gilded chair that faced the room. She looked over the menu and quickly made her choice. She wanted to signal the waitress but thought better of it, not wanting to offend with her American fast-food mentality. The waitress, having served her share of *Américains affamés impatients* was watching and promptly took her order of *magret de canard, gratin dauphinois* and *carottes glacées*. It was only after ordering that Jules allowed herself to take in the scene playing out in front of her.

The *salle à manger* was dimly lit, yet her senses were flooded to overflowing. The walls, a cozy red, were lined with dark oil portraits, framed in varying patinas from old gold leaf to modern day rust. String lights hung in sparkling strands in the windows from ceiling to floor making it feel as if it were raining inside. *Hence the name*, she noticed.

The clanging of forks on china plates and the clinking of glasses raised in celebration made Jules feel that she was not alone. The smell of a newly lit cigarette coming from the kitchen mingled with the aroma of someone's espresso. She wondered why cigarette smoke had never bothered her. She closed her eyes, took in a slow breath, soaking in the hum of French conversation that surrounded her. Edith Piaf sang through crackling speakers. *So cliché*, she thought. *So lovely.*

"Madame?" broke Jules' train of thought. The waitress artfully filled the stem from her carafe of sparkling water. Before Jules could offer her *merci*, the waitress was on to the next empty glass. She took a lukewarm sip then returned her focus to the room. While she waited for her dinner, she rebelliously propped her elbows on the table and viewed the scene as if it were a movie and thought, *I might just smoke my first cigarette.*

17

Jules
Paris, France

The alarm on Jules' phone rang, but she was already awake. It was impossible to sleep knowing that there was an open-air market setting up just a block away.

As excited as she was, a sinking feeling hit her. She wished Will was there to go with her. Together, they had frequented the markets in and around Lexington, looking for old pieces that they could find new ways to use. They had even dreamed aloud about shopping for European antiques together some day. She made a mental note to share every detail with Will in today's email.

She slipped into her nicest jeans, paired them with a graphic t-shirt, then completed the look with a light chambray shirt. Though this may have been an appropriate ensemble for antiquing in Kentucky, she knew she would stand out as an American in Paris, but today but she didn't care. She slapped on her sunglasses and headed straight into her dream world.

***

As she neared the market, she noticed that all the early morning shoppers had brought their own baskets, so her first purchase was an open-weaved market basket lined with a light floral fabric that reminded her of one of her mother's dresses. She began filling it with rosy apples, purple skinned grapes, and colorful vegetables. It was a unique experience to be able to purchase food directly from the growers along the city streets of Paris. Most of the farmers displayed their produce in old crates, labeled with handwritten prices on tiny chalkboards. As a bonus, they were eager to share their knowledge about their products. Booth after booth, she found this to be true.

At a booth selling cooking oils, Jules purchased a tin of walnut oil. She chose to purchase items that were not sold in the chain grocery stores back home. The vendor recommended that she season with the oil instead of cooking with it, 'as heat can destroy its vast health benefits, as well as the taste.' She wrote his suggestion in her notebook. Jules found the French people to be surprisingly helpful and she was learning a lot.

Further along, she came to an enormous booth lined with tables, stacked high with rounds of cheese in more varieties than she ever knew existed. The apron-clad, sun-wrinkled couple behind the stacks was busy cutting wedges, weighing and wrapping them, all the while responding to customers' demands for samples. Jules waited patiently for her turn and with the help of the woman, she chose a wedge each of Gruyère, Beaufort, and Parmesan. When she picked up a small log of Chèvre cheese, the old man recommended serving it on crackers with fig jam. She made another note. At this pace, her pocket-sized notebook was going to be full in no time.

The fruit and vegetable stands were intermingled with clothes, antiques, and art. As she was choosing which booth to go to next, Jules heard women chattering across the aisle. They held up dresses and slacks, looking at themselves in full-length mirrors that were propped up against the back of the booth. When one of the women moved aside, Jules caught her own reflection in the mirror. After looking at stylish Parisians for just a couple of days, she realized that her boring hair and her basic clothes did cause her to stand out here in Paris. *If I'm ever going to make a change in my personal appearance, this would be the time and place to do it.*

Jules followed the ladies' lead, holding items to her body and looking at herself in the mirror. She purchased a flowing top in bright florals, and a pair of slender ankle pants that made her think of Chloe. At another booth, she held up a sleeveless tangerine colored dress. The woman working the street shop asked Jules for her shoe size then brought her a pair of pumps and a pretty baubled necklace that complimented the color of the dress. Jules slid her feet into the perfectly fitted shoes, then nodded her approval.

The woman handed Jules a handwritten receipt. "Carte bleue?" Jules knew that this woman who sold French clothes for a living, knew more about fashion than she ever would and happily handed her the payment.

By the time she left *la marché,* her new basket was overflowing with colorful produce, plants for her balcony garden, and fresh flowers for her table. She would need to empty her purchases in the apartment before shopping for groceries.

***

Jules filled the tiny refrigerator with her purchases then looked around the apartment for something to hold the cut flowers. A stoneware pitcher would have to do. She was pleased with how they looked on the petite bistro table.

Before leaving for the grocery store, she tried on her new clothes and decided to wear the floral shirt, ankle slacks, and pumps. She pulled her hair back into a sleek ponytail, grabbed her basket and was gone again.

***

After last night's dinner at La Pluie and today's trip to the market, Jules realized that she could easily spend too much money in Paris if she wasn't careful, so she would need to prepare most of her meals in the apartment. She took her time perusing the aisles of the Monoprix, choosing a few nouveau items along with some familiar staples. By the time she filled her basket, her feet were starting to ache in her pretty shoes.

***

As soon as she was inside the apartment, Jules kicked off the new pumps before unloading the groceries. After the wonderfully exhausting day, she catnapped in the cozy side chair.

Jules felt happy and refreshed when she woke up and was eager to prepare her first meal in her tiny kitchen. The velvety goat cheese spread like butter on the French waffle crackers. She topped the cheese with fig jam as the farmer had suggested and snacked on them while she cooked.

Juice poured onto the wood board when Jules cut into the heirloom tomato. The intense smells of diced red onion, the smashed clove of garlic, and freshly pulled basil leaves filled the apartment. After draining the noodles, she tossed them in walnut oil, pinched in some salt and pepper, then added the chopped ingredients. She sawed a couple of slices from the market baguette and slathered them in French butter. She was beginning to see what all the fuss was regarding the French way of eating. The simple meal was both satisfying and delicious. But when Jules looked at the empty chair, she realized that all her new experiences were a bit hollow, not having someone to share them with, someone to talk to about them. Her heart ached for Will.

After washing the dishes, she planted flowers in the balcony basket and gave it a good soak. She was relieved that her unfriendly neighbor, Estelle, wasn't out. Most of the other neighbors had their windows open. Their patterned curtains flapped in the wind and soft music wafted through the evening air. Looking down into the courtyard, she saw that someone had pulled weeds that had sprung up through the stones, leaving tiny piles along the way.

Jules left the window open to enjoy the music and then wiggled into the overstuffed chair and pulled her computer into her lap. Jules was anxious to share the exciting events of the day with Will. She detailed the various kinds of cheeses and the wooden bowls holding every kind of olive imaginable. She described how hundreds of baguettes were stacked high in patterns, left unwrapped on tabletops. She went on and on about the variety of fruits and homegrown vegetables, the bolts of Provencal fabrics, streets lined with buckets of freshly picked flowers, and booth after booth of ancient antiques.

She chose not to mention her new clothes and the fact that she'd stopped in a salon to make an appointment to have her hair cut and her nails done. Jules jokingly questioned herself about becoming a diva after only a couple of days in Paris.

A perfect end to this dreamy day would have been to soak in a hot bath. Instead, she lingered in the shower until the water ran cold. She stood messing with her hair in the mirror, wondering how she should have it cut, then decided to leave it up to the stylist.

She wrote a quick email to Chloe, copying and pasting most of what she had sent to Will, but left out the part about how she could love it there so much, but still miss him more.

When she finished writing the email, Jules lay back on the bed and closed her eyes. *Why do I feel such an unfamiliar contentment here? Can I possibly make peace with my past and take it back home with me?* For the first time in years, she felt hope that she could, and she lay there contemplating what that could mean for her future. She even made the decision to call her mother on her birthday.

As she was drifting off to sleep, her eyes shot open. "Chocolate! I forgot to tell Will and Chloe about the chocolate."

18

Joëlle
Baran, France 1685

A week later, Grand-père walked into the kitchen for breakfast with a handful of ripe tomatoes. "Looks like the fun and games will have to be put aside for the next few weeks. The garden is full of vegetables ready for picking. Since this year's garden is so large, it will take all of us to accomplish this."

Joëlle and Henri didn't mind at all. They both loved the work of life on the farm. It was a welcome change for children to be needed. "We can start right after breakfast," Joëlle said, passing a plate of warm bread to Grand-père, trying to stay on his good side.

In the field, Joëlle showed Henri how to pull the tomatoes without breaking the vine.

"Twist gently," she heard him whisper as she walked to the other side of the row.

Odette and Marguerite stayed inside the house preparing the containers, measuring out salt and sugar; vinegar and spices, all to be used for preserving the vegetables, while Grand-père shepherded the children in the field and hauled basketsful of artichokes, asparagus, cucumbers, spinach, and tomatoes to the house, one basket after the other.

Each day for weeks, excluding Sundays, the family worked exhaustively preserving the produce from three large gardens. Some vegetables were soaked in a salt brine, others layered in dry salt, and some were dried on screens in the sunshine. Then the vegetables were stored in earthenware crocks.

After all that was completed, the containers had to be hauled to the underground wine cave that Grand-père had told them had been there for centuries. The old wooden door, swollen over time, creaked and moaned when it was forced to be moved. Inside the cellar was cold, damp and dark. Joëlle believed it to be full of centuries of ghosts, so she saw to it that she never went in alone.

After weeks of constant garden work, Marguerite sat the children down at the kitchen table. "Your grandfather has learned about a festival happening in Sarlat this week. He thought we could all use a bit of fun. He says there are children's games, shopping and exhibits for everyone. It is a day's journey, so we will need to spend a night outdoors. It will be quite an adventure! How does that sound?"

"That sounds fun!" and an excited, "Oui!" came from the children.

"Well then, run along and pack an overnight bag."

Grand-père had already loaded the wagon with all they would need for the journey. Grand-mère had packed a few extra days' worth of food, just in case.

As they neared the town of Sarlat, they met traveler after traveler on the road who all seemed happy and refreshed after leaving the fête. This made the Reynauds even more anxious to get there.

When they arrived, they were shocked at the number of campers filling up the hillsides surrounding the medieval town. Grand-père chose a spot on the outer edge of the crowd.

"Can't we get closer?" Joëlle questioned. "I can't see anything."

"This will do nicely, Joëlle. Don't worry. We will see everything tomorrow. It will soon be dark, and we need to get the camp set up and take some time to eat and relax," Marguerite explained while looking at Louis and Odette's exhausted faces.

Joëlle heard lively music playing and watched smiling children return to their tents carrying trinkets and poles with twirling ribbons. "Henri, this is going to be our dreams come true." Morning couldn't come quickly enough.

Just as the sun was peeking over the horizon, Joëlle and Henri were awakened to quieted but serious voices. "Guy, what are you doing here? How did you know where to find us?" Marguerite asked her obviously upset husband.

"When I agreed for you and the children to stay in the countryside this summer, it was because I wanted you away from the danger of the crowds, certainly not right in the middle of thousands of strangers in a city where we don't know who we can trust," Guy said sternly. "I had hoped to surprise you and the children with my visit, but when I arrived in Baran yesterday afternoon, you were nowhere to be found. You can imagine my fear. I asked several of the neighbors who had no idea where you were. Thankfully Joëlle had told the Martin girl. That's how I knew where to find you."

Marguerite shot scolding eyes to Joëlle, who had been instructed not to tell anyone.

Once again, Joëlle found herself in hot water.

"I had to ride through the night, after riding all day, to find you and bring you home."

Marguerite watched her husband scanning the hillside with concern. "Why must we go home? What danger are we in?"

"Never mind that. Children, get dressed. We will leave after we have something to eat."

Joëlle pleaded with her father, "No! PaPa, no! Why must we leave? We haven't done any of the fun things yet."

"I know you are disappointed, but I am not the one who put you in this position." Guy looked toward his father.

By this time Grand-père was just catching up on the conversation, "What position are they in, my son?"

"I thought I had made it clear that you were to be diligent in looking after them. You and I will have this conversation later, not in front of the women and children."

Marguerite led her crying children to gather their things. On the long journey home, Joëlle sat with her arms crossed and didn't speak a word. She made a silent vow never to speak to her father again.

Later that night, Joëlle purposefully stayed as quiet as a mouse so that no one would suspect she was still awake. She knew that PaPa would wait until Maman and Grand-mère had gone to bed to speak freely to Grand-père.

"You must tell me the full truth of what is going on, Guy. I have never seen you this concerned. Has something happened in Bordeaux that has made you feel the need to be this cautious?"

Her grandfather was speaking so softly that Joëlle needed to move closer. As soon as she transferred her weight onto her feet, the floor squeaked, and the talking downstairs stopped.

After a few seconds of silence, her father answered, "For the last few months…the rumors have increased…at a fête outside Paris…You must be vigilant…"

Joëlle could not hear most of what he was saying and needed to move closer to the steps. She tried once more, and the floor did not move beneath her. Just as she got close enough to hear, the conversation was ending.

"You'll need to inform the other men, but again, no dinner on the grounds, no outdoor singing. Do you understand? Just the worship service, with the doors closed and that is all. Everyone must go straight home. I hope I am making myself perfectly clear about the danger."

Joëlle's stomach tightened. She couldn't believe what her father was saying.

"I understand and will never let anything happen to them."

She heard the men scoot their chairs away from the table, so she tiptoed quietly back to bed. When her head hit the pillow, she tried to imagine what could make her father this fearful. She was more determined than ever to find out what it was.

19

Jules
Paris, France

Jules arrived at the salon for her early morning appointment. She had been surprised that there had been a chair available on short notice but assumed it was because French choose not to forgo their beauty sleep. Jules told the stylist she wanted a new hairstyle but nothing too drastic. The French woman was serious as she walked around Jules and looked at her features while running her hands along Jules' jawline.

"You have the most unique eyes I have ever seen," the stylist said.

"Merci. I've always been self-conscious about them."

"Nonsense! They are unique, and unique is beautiful."

She ran her fingers through Jules' hair and tossed it from one side to the other. Once she was satisfied, she turned the chair to face the interior of the salon, dampened her hair and started cutting. Jules crossed her fingers beneath the smock.

After chopping, moussing, drying, and styling her hair, the stylist nodded her head in approval, then slowly spun her around. Jules stared at herself in the mirror. She could hardly believe she was seeing her own reflection. Her hair fell along her jaw line, with side swept bangs and long layers that made the natural wave of her hair curl up and stand out. Jules wanted to exclaim, "Oh, I love it!" but having learned more about French culture, simply said, "Merci, madame." Once her *cheveux* was finished, she had her nails painted a rosy pink, both fingers and toes.

***

There was a noticeable bounce in Jules' step as she walked out of the salon and into *la pharmacie* to purchase the hair products that the stylist suggested.

***

Notre-Dame Cathédrale was the next attraction on her sightseeing list. It was a long walk, so Jules stopped at the apartment to change into her walking shoes. While she was there, she made a last-minute decision to hand wash the new sheets she'd purchased at the market. She'd bought them to take back to the states but decided to enjoy them while she was in France. She wrung them out as best as she could in the shower stall then hung them on the retractable clothesline that stretched from the bathroom into the kitchen. She opened the small window over the sink and the window to the balcony, hoping the breeze would dry the sheets before bedtime.

***

Jules stood outside the massive Notre-Dame Cathédrale taking pictures of the French Gothic architecture, moving around the double towered entrance to capture every detail. Out of the corner of her eye, she noticed a constant flow of people, who did not appear to be tourists, entering the cathedral then exiting only a few minutes later. She wasn't familiar with the Catholic church and wondered what they were doing.

Eventually curiosity got the best of her, so she inched herself inside to find out. When the door closed behind her, Jules felt as though she'd stepped through a portal into a different time and place. Soft organ music quieted the outside world. The darkened chapel was lit with double layered chandeliers. Jules studied how the glow of the lights illuminated the circular gold rings that held them, making them look truly divine. She took a seat in the back then watched the French souls stroll in, their heels clickety clacking on the old stone floor. One by one they knelt on the altar. Some humbly bowed their heads, saying silent prayers. Others looked up, so sincerely whispering mumbled yearnings. Only moments later, they were up again, crossing their hearts and heading back out into the noisy world. She imagined them stopping here every day after work, before heading to a local shop to pick up their daily bread.

When she felt like she had snooped long enough, she stood and turned to leave, but bumped into a young woman who was visibly pregnant. "Pardon, madame," Jules whispered. The woman said nothing as their eyes met but Jules noticed a tear on her cheek and stepped back into the row of chairs, permitting her to pass. Jules sat back down and pretended not to watch her. The woman didn't go to the altar. Instead, she waddled toward a candlestand filled with twinkling votives then lit a candle for her prayer. Jules felt guilty about witnessing this intimate encounter but could not stop herself. The mother-to-be placed her left hand on her full belly and crossed her heart with her right. The flickering light of the candles illuminated an ancient statue of Mary, who stood watch over this prayer-sayer, a literal concrete proof of God, assuring the woman that her prayer would be answered. This made Jules feel something she had never felt before, a yearning, a draw toward God welling up inside her. Though she didn't actively participate, Jules felt closer to Him through this prayer by proxy.

Jules waited for the woman to leave before she stood to go. Something was pulling her here, and she wanted to know more. She would find a way to stop by again. On the way out, she saw a sign that read *Vespers, Daily 18:00* She didn't know what vespers were, but she would be here to find out.

***

While the microwave warmed leftover pasta, Jules watered the new plants and was surprised to see that Estelle had planted a couple of flowers in her basket. Jules smiled at the thought that she may have encouraged her neighbor.

After a nap, she wrote her daily emails to Will and Chloe. Outing, nap, emails, preparing for class, then dinner. Jules liked this routine.

Then once again, wearing her walking shoes, she made the trek through the busy streets, back to Notre Dame. As she neared the historic church, the ethereal sounds of the pipe organ and harmonious choral singing flowed through the opened doors into the street, drawing her in. This time the chapel was filled with seated parishioners. Jules felt like an intruder but took a seat in the back.

Once she was settled, she closed her eyes and breathed in as the glorious music filled her ears. But it did not stop there. She felt the music begin to overwhelm her. It felt as though her heart wanted to be released from her chest and float up into the rafters. She swallowed hard to suppress her emotions and wiped away the tears being drawn from her eyes. The old Jules would have bolted by now out of fear and discomfort, but Parisian Jules, wanting to know more, made herself stay. Something was happening to her. *Maybe there are answers here, inside this church.* For the rest of the service, she let herself drift where the vespers took her. Jules was experiencing yet another fully alive moment in France. After the service ended, she stayed to watch the parishioners leave. *What do they know that I don't?*

***

It was dark by the time Jules arrived back at the apartment. She checked the sheets, but they weren't quite dry, so she opened the double doors that faced the street, creating a strong cross breeze. The sheets responded wildly by dancing the can-can. Jules moved quickly to grab the pitcher of flowers on her table to keep it from being whipped across the room.

While the sheets dried, Jules made a few crackers with goat cheese and jam and poured a glass of wine. She pulled a chair up to the window to see what her neighbors were up to while she had her snack for dinner. Their lights were on, making it easy to see into several of the apartments. A well-dressed couple enjoyed a candlelit dinner, holding hands across the table. In another apartment, a mother tried to calm her crying baby by pacing back and forth while her husband obliviously read the paper. In a street-level apartment, an old man napped in his easy chair while his plump wife chatted with their cat. In the apartment a floor below and opposite hers, a large man with a beard, whom Jules imagined to be an opera singer, sat by his window, smoking a pipe while reading a thick book. The gentleman looked up from his reading to blow a pungent puff out into the courtyard. He caught Jules looking and nodded to her. She held up her glass of wine in response but didn't smile. Then Estelle walked over to the window for a smoke. She struck the match, placed the flame on the end of her cigarette then took a long drag, as she swayed to someone's music that filled the courtyard. Jules liked this community scene and would be sure to tell Will about it in tomorrow's email.

After finishing the glass, she readied herself for bed, then tucked the oversized sheets into the daybed. She closed the doors and windows and slid between the silky cotton. The sheets felt so wonderful on her skin that she tossed off her gown. Sheets this luxurious were meant to be felt all over.

20

Jules
Paris, France

Jules opened the curtains to brilliant sun on Whit Monday, a perfect day to spend outdoors. This was her last free day before starting the teaching position, but Jules was in no rush. She liked the fact that she had no one to consult with or to answer to. She set the coffee to brew and filled a glass with water, then went to check on her tiny garden. She was surprised at how it seemed to have grown overnight. The vine was already beginning to trail over the railing. As she dribbled the water in, movement across the way diverted her attention. Jules decided to try her American charm once more, "Bonjour, madame." Estelle glanced in Jules' general direction while fumbling for her matches. Though she didn't speak, she acknowledged Jules by nodding, her gray bun bobbing forward then back. *Progress*, Jules smirked. *This is going to be a great day.*

***

Out in the sunshine, Jules' floral sundress danced to her stride as she began the uphill climb toward Montmartre. She knew the painters would be setting up their easels in the Place du Tertre and she was hoping to find just the right painting to surprise Will with when he arrived in France. She wanted to show her appreciation for his encouragement to take this opportunity and for understanding her need to have this time by herself. Strangely, this time apart made her feel closer to him.

When she reached the summit of three hundred steps, she sat on a stone half-wall, rubbing her cramping calves while watching the locals pass by, their legs seemingly unaffected. She imagined they must be exercising them this morning to shop for art in the charming town square but noticed a steady flow of them heading into Sacre Cœur, the multi-domed, white stone church that overlooked the city. She had intended to tour the church after she found a painting for Will. Instead, she followed her instinct and the crowd through the massive, tarnished doors.

After taking a seat in the chandelier-lit sanctuary, she marveled at the mosaic ceiling and brilliant bronze altar. The sound of people talking quietly as they walked into the chapel echoed in the domes. Jules was admiring the stained-glass windows when the grand organ began to play. The crowd instantly quieted. It was such a lovely thing to watch them participating in Mass and to witness this often-unseen side of the French people, as they knelt, recited, and worshiped.

She wasn't sure if it was the organ music or the Gregorian chanting that made her feel the same feeling she'd felt in Notre Dame. It was an overwhelming emotion that she had never experienced in all the time she'd sat in pews as a child. She felt something deeply, but what? She allowed herself to begin an unspoken conversation with God. *What is this I'm feeling? Why are You pulling me here? Are You trying to tell me something?* Today, Jules chose to follow whatever was calling her. *I'm listening.*

After the morning mass, the crowd meandered from the church into the Place du Tertre. The petite square was filled with French artists, each with their own curated area. Many had umbrellas to protect their works from the elements. Several artists stood at French easels, painting a *scène typique* of Paris, which always included the Eiffel Tower. She surmised that while this might be a favorite of the average tourist, it was not at all what she was shopping for.

She passed several portrait artists sketching the innocent faces of gap-toothed children while their proud parents looked on. Jules quickly moved past.

She appreciated each artist's interpretation of the scenes they painted, some abstract, some impressionistic, some incredibly life-like. But this still wasn't what she had in mind for Will.

A booth in the center caught her attention when she spied an oil painting of a boat on the Seine. It had thick paint in muted colors applied with a pallet knife. It fell somewhere between abstract and impressionistic.

Though she admired the work, it still wasn't what she had hoped to find. She liked this artist's style, so she thumbed through his print rack. Still, nothing felt right. Just as she was about to walk away, an old painting in a chipped gold frame lying on the ground caught her eye. She asked the artist to see it. He shrugged his shoulders, "Non, madame." He told her that he had not painted that one and guided her back to his print rack, but Jules persisted. "I'd like to look at that one," she insisted pointing back to the painting under his easel. He explained to her that he had purchased the painting at a *brocante* for next to nothing. He picked it up and assured her that it was worthless, pointing out a tiny hole in the center of the painted wood board. He told her that he intended to use it simply for inspiration.

She reached for it, and he reluctantly handed it to her. She was instantly in love with the faded oil landscape of a shepherdess sitting on a hillside, watching her fold in the open field ahead of her. A distant castle stood on the horizon. This! This was exactly what she was hoping to find.

"Combien?" She asked, her eyes still fixed on the painting.

"Non, madame," he shook his head. "Ce n'est pas à vendre. It is not for sale."

Jules clutched the painting to her chest and pleaded with her eyes.

Defeated, he replied, "D'accord, cinq euros."

"Merci, monsieur! Merci." She could not hide her American enthusiasm.

He kindly wrapped her treasure in white paper and taped it closed. There was no need to continue looking. She could not have hoped to find a painting that suited her and Will any better.

The smell of fresh crêpes in the air made her hungry. The tables at the street side cafés were taken, so Jules took her place in the long line at the crêperie window. She didn't mind. How could she? The weather was near perfection. She was in Paris. She had found the perfect piece of art for Will. And surprisingly her anxieties seemed to have disappeared here. While she waited, she counted her blessings, including the Nutella banana crêpe being made fresh for her. Her arms full, she found a bit of grass and laid out her sweater as a blanket. While she enjoyed the crêpe, Jules listened to the conversations of families as they passed by. It pleased her that she understood what was being said and that felt like a comforting hug to her.

After she finished eating and was gathering her things, she heard a distant roar of thunder and looked up to see that a dark cloud had moved overhead. She tucked the painting under her sweater and hustled homeward. She had barely entered the building when she heard the downpour behind her. Inside the apartment, she unwrapped Will's painting and propped it up on the television. *I might as well enjoy it until he gets here.*

She cracked a window and settled in for a rainy afternoon *petite sieste.*

***

Whether it was the patter of the rain through the open window or exhaustion from the morning's climb, Jules slept for hours. When she woke up, she remembered she'd dreamed a dream in French. She recalled that a professor had once explained that this was a sign of truly knowing a language. She wasn't sure if this was true but thinking about it gave her an idea.

Since Jules had been in France, she had not experienced a single bout of anxiety. *Why do I feel so at ease here, alone in a foreign country?"* Though she didn't understand it, she felt stronger here and ready to face her issues.

She pulled the laptop from the desk into her lap, and then typed a short email to Dr. Gray.

Do you think you could find a therapist in Paris who would be willing to try hypnosis in French?"

Before she could change her mind, she hit the send button.

21

Jules
Paris, France

Jules' first few weeks of teaching in Paris had gone well. The class was made up of high school graduates from other countries that hadn't learned English as a second language. Most of the students had been in France for years and spoke French fluently but needed a basic course in the English language before starting university full time in the fall. When Mme Merritt had introduced herself on the first day of class, the students had a lot of questions about America, asked in French. She was surprised how interested they were in Kentucky Fried Chicken and the Kentucky Derby. She appreciated their enthusiasm and decided she would use it to teach them. It sparked an idea for a surprise she would plan for them.

***

Dr. Gray had emailed Jules to inform her of the appointment she'd arranged with Dr. John Louis LaRoche, a French psychologist who had been recommended to her through a trusted colleague. With Jules' permission, Dr. Gray had emailed the notes from her sessions to Dr. LaRoche.

***

After the introductions were made, Dr. LaRoche began, "Please tell me why you're here."

During the hour-long session, Jules did most of the talking. She replayed her life for him, beginning to feel like a broken record. She began with how she knew that her family loved her but also that they made sure that she knew how different she was from them.

"Can you tell me how they felt you were different?"

"A lot of little things that added up from the very beginning. Apparently, I screamed hysterically for hours after I was born. It was so unusual that it alarmed the doctor and nurses. For weeks afterward, my parents thought something must have been wrong with me. The only time I wasn't crying was when my mother rocked me or when I was sleeping."

"Did they have you examined medically?"

"I really don't know. They never mentioned it. I was born into a farm family. We didn't see the doctor much."

"I see. Please go on."

Jules recited the things that she had been told about her early years. She told him about the incidents with the creek when she was a baby and how fearful she was of large bodies of water, even as an adult.

Jules noticed that he did not take notes, as Dr. Gray had. He rarely even spoke. But he listened. She watched the intensity in his eyes as they moved back and forth and around, as he both gathered and processed what she was telling him. Dr. LaRoche really listened.

She told him how she would become physically ill whenever her mother burned something on the stove and how even now, she retches at the smell of smoke. She described how her anxiety level rapidly increases to the point that she wants to jump out of her skin. "It's completely irrational."

She described the dream that has haunted her for so many years, and the anxiety that it causes in her life.

"Is there anything else that you feel is important to share with me today?"

If Dr. LaRoche was going to help her, he needed to know about the middle school incident and how it completely changed her life. She paused and took a deep breath then recounted the details of that life-altering day but did so with no feeling.

"Have you ever directly faced what happened?"

"Faced it?" she asked. "I've lived with it every day since."

"As an adult, have you ever confronted them about how they made you feel?"

"I try not to think about it."

"Before our next session, I would like for you to do just that. You might even write it down as if you were writing each of them a letter, though I highly recommend that you do not send them. Whatever they did, knowingly, or most likely not, is their issue. My concern is for you, as my patient. Processing what happened and forgiving someone is for your healing, not for theirs. Then I want you to gather the letters and destroy them however you choose. This will serve as a visual reminder that you have chosen to put this trauma behind you. Do you feel comfortable with that?"

"Yes. At least, I'll try."

"If you feel this would be too difficult to do alone, we can do it together in our next session. Otherwise, I'll see you again once you've completed this."

Jules liked Dr. LaRoche and for a reason that she didn't understand, she trusted him. Knowing that her time in France was limited, before leaving his office, she scheduled her next appointment with him for the following week.

***

Walking home, Jules believed that Dr. LaRoche was going to help her. Though she dreaded his assignment, at least he'd given her something concrete to do.

Back in the apartment, she opened her computer to write her nightly emails to Will and Chloe and was disappointed to see there wasn't an email from Will. Jules had made a point of emailing him every evening, as they'd promised. But his emails had gotten fewer and farther between. A tinge of worry bubbled up within her. But she consoled herself. *This is Will we're talking about. Everything is fine.* She sent him a brief note telling him that she had a surprise for him. Then she wrote a lengthy letter to Chloe.

Bonjour, mon amie,
Hope today finds you well. How are things between you and Josh? You haven't mentioned him lately. Let's see, maybe I can guess. It's baseball season, right?
Maybe he has seen my husband who seems to have gone missing. I'm not serious, of course. It's just that Will is writing less and less but I know he's busy building the deck. I'm looking forward to your visit. I think you will find your friend much changed by then. And I am not just talking about my haircut. I feel like a different person here, and I'm learning so many new things about myself.
For instance, I now find myself brave. At home, I was scared of my own shadow. When I first arrived in Paris, I closed and locked the windows at night before going to sleep even though I'm on the fourth floor. Now, I find myself falling asleep to the lullaby of clicking heels, honking horns, and late-night laughter. In the beginning, I thought it was rude, but I now see that the French live life to the fullest and do not expect anyone to be offended by it.
At the same time, I've found life to be slower here. Simple things, like the French people do not rush their meals. They take a two-hour lunch every day! They sit and talk before they order. They don't seem to mind that their meal isn't served right away. They laugh and talk over a glass of wine. (Yes, at lunch!) Then they sit, talk, and laugh some more until they've had their dessert, more times than not, leaving half on their plate. Then and only then, they have a café, served as a course of its own. They don't expect the waitress

to bring the check the second that they've finished. And that's just for lunch. Did you know that when you reserve a table in a nice restaurant in Paris for dinner, you reserve it for the entire evening? I just love that.

Another thing that I've learned from the French is that they aren't afraid to feel. At home, we set our thermostats to a perfect 70 degrees year around and complain that we are "freezing" or "burning up" if it's just one or two degrees off. Here, they don't use air conditioning that I can tell. Everyone leaves their windows open. I have come to love the feel of the cool night air. It makes warm blankets that much cozier. I feel more alive living this way. All my senses are heightened, instead of being leveled to the point of numbness. Could it be that I am just noticing these things and appreciating them more? Possibly, but I think there's more to it than that. The French truly know how to appreciate the little things in life. As do I. I find myself closing my eyes to enjoy the sound of church bells or a smoker's gravelly voice.

I don't think I've ever seen a television turned on in any of my neighbor's houses at night through their windows. They seem content simply living their own lives. In so many of these ways, I think I am just naturally more like them.

I feel at home here, Chloe, and honestly, it scares me a little. I wonder if I can be this happy back home. I do miss Will but I'm not ready to come back home yet. If I'm being completely honest, I'm not even ready for Will to join me here. I feel like I'm making real progress and want to feel confident that I won't revert to my old anxious self. Does that make sense or am I being selfish? Sorry to rattle on and on about myself. Let me know if you find my husband.

Until tomorrow,

Jules

***

When Chloe read the message, she felt sick to her stomach. She felt certain she knew why Will had not written as he had promised. She'd seen Will walking with Laura Harris, whom she'd met in college, in the park that afternoon, appearing to be in a serious conversation. They were so engaged with each other that neither of them noticed her watching. She slid behind a tree and watched Will walk the woman to her car. He put his hands on her shoulders and looked directly into her eyes. He was speaking passionately and then he hugged her. It was a long intimate hug that made Chloe feel so uncomfortable that she had to turn away. She wanted to tell Jules but didn't have the heart to destroy the progress she had been making. She wrote Jules a brief note praising her friend's hard work, ignoring the comments about Will.

***

The sun sent beams through her windows, warming the silky linens. She happily tossed them aside. Finally, the day of Jules' surprise for her students had arrived. She left the apartment early to have everything set up by the time the students got to class. From the very first day, they had been constantly asking questions about American culture. Today, she would see that they got plenty of it.

She wore a cheeky grin as she greeted each student when they entered the classroom, "Bonjour! Good morning!" They greeted back the same. When all the students arrived, she asked them to follow her outside, saying only, "If America is what you want, then an all-American picnic is what you'll get. "Un pique-nique américain," she said while sweeping her hand across the yard. The teenaged students were wowed at the sight of red and white checkered tablecloths spread out on the lawn, each with a wooden basket in its center. Jules pushed the button on the portable CD player. Don McLean's *American Pie* covered the lawn. She was surprised to see a couple of students singing some of the words. They chose their spots and opened the baskets, filled with hotdogs, chips, and canned sodas, the best she could do on short notice. While they ate, Jules delivered watermelon slices to each plate. As she walked, she quizzed the students on the names of each of the items they were eating, then one of the students asked, "What is dessert for?"

"What is for dessert?" she corrected.

"De tarte aux pommes, bien sûr. Apple pie, of course."

When they finished their picnic, she dismissed them early from class. A few of the students asked to assist in cleaning up. Mme Merritt thanked them but declined. She wanted this to be a class they would always fondly remember.

As she was loading the last of the baskets onto the cart she had borrowed from the cafeteria, Margeau, her student aide, called to her from just inside the classroom. "You have an urgent call, madame, from your husband. I will finish."

"Merci, Margeau." Jules froze, unable to move. She knew that it had to be something bad. *Could Dad have had a tractor accident or a heart attack?*

"Madame?" Margeau directed her inside.

Jules rushed to the phone. "Hello?"

Will said in a soft voice, "I'm sorry to scare you like this…"

"What!?"

"Your mother had some sort of episode early this morning. She couldn't talk or get out of bed. Your father called an ambulance. They suspect it was a stroke. I am so sorry to do this to you, but I thought you would want to know. I tried several times to reach you on your cell phone."

"Do I get a flight home right away? Do I quit the job? Will, what do I do?" Jules rapid-fired the questions as they flooded her mind.

"No, no. Don't do any of that right now. We should wait to see what the doctors say. There's nothing you can do for her right now. Just hang tight. I'm on the way to the hospital now and will let you know as soon as I find out anything at all."

"Ok, I guess," she took a breath. "Will?"

"Yes?"

"I love you. Thank you for being there."

"Love you, too. Try not to worry. I'll talk to you soon."

She shakily gathered up her things and knocked on Mme Fornier's office door. Speaking in French, Jules informed the department chair that she had received a phone call from her husband saying that her mother had likely suffered a stroke. Jules wanted the university to be prepared if she had to fly home.

"I'm sorry to hear this. We would certainly hate to lose you. I hear the students are very fond of your class. Please keep me advised. I wish your mother well."

"Merci," Jules turned to walk out.

"Mme Merritt? Would you know anyone from your university who would consider taking over the position for you should you need to leave? They would need to apply for a visa right away."

Jules thought of Chloe, "Possibly I do. I will look into it this evening. Au revoir."

She made a mental note to email Chloe, but for now, all she could think about was getting to the church to pray.

***

Until now, Jules had only watched as others lit a candle to pray for someone. Though she had been feeling increasingly more connected to God through her visits to the churches in Paris, she had yet to pray. Today would be different. The church was her first thought after hanging up the phone with Will. She walked briskly to the church without thinking to pray on the way.

As she neared the cathedral, Jules slowed herself and took a deep breath before entering. In the early afternoon, the sanctuary was practically empty. She was grateful for that. She chose an imperfect candle, and lit it from the flame of another, conscious of the connection with another seeking soul. She placed it in the stand and for the first time in her life, she knelt to pray.

"Please forgive me for coming to you now, when I am desperate, when I'm in need. I pray that you will be with my mother. Please save her. I have wronged her. I have hurt her. I want to be able to tell her that I'm sorry and that I know she was the best mother she knew how to be."

Jules went on and on, years of neglect and regret poured out. She asked forgiveness for putting her faith on the back burner. She asked forgiveness for how she had treated Will and prayed for God's guidance in helping her to be more like her husband, always thinking more of others than of himself.

Jules had no idea how long she had been there pleading for her mother's healing and her own, when she heard footsteps behind her. She wiped her tears with her hand and rose, crisscrossing her heart, though she didn't know what it meant. Her mind a blur, she walked home.

***

It felt comforting to be back at home in the apartment. She sat in the tattered chair and opened her laptop, hoping to see an email from Will. There was. Her breathing stopped as she opened it.

> *J,*
> *I wanted to let you know that they do think it was a mild stroke. She seems to be doing ok, though. There is no paralysis at all! She said to tell you that there's no need to make a fuss. I've called in to school for tomorrow and Friday so that I can be here to help. Your father and brothers need to harvest the winter wheat as rain will be setting in early next week. It looks like everything is going to be ok. I'll let you know how things progress here. Try not to worry.*
> *W*

She could barely see through her tears as she typed the reply.

W,
I am so relieved! I have thought of nothing else. I stopped to pray on the way back to the apartment this afternoon. It seemed like the right thing to do, and it sounds like my prayer was answered. I think I will be able to sleep tonight, knowing that you are there for my family. I can't tell you what that means to me, Will. I've done a lot of thinking since I've been here, and I have a lot to apologize for. You are such a wonderful man, and I am so lucky, no, I am very blessed to have you.
So much love for you right now,
J

But sleep did not come easily. She lay on her pillow facing the ceiling. Even though Will had good news, she felt guilty about not returning her mother's phone calls.

"Oh!" She sat up in her bed, remembering that she needed to email Chloe about the possibility of replacing her. Jules was sure Chloe would love the opportunity to come earlier than planned, as she had already received her passport and purchased the plane ticket.

Hi, Chloe,
I know this is the second email today, but I wanted to let you know that my mother suffered a light stroke today. Will is there with her now and said for me to hang tight until we know more, but I need to have a backup plan in case I have to fly home. The department chair, Mme. Fournier, asked if I knew anyone who would want to replace me. Of course, I thought of you. You would need to apply for a work visa right away, just in case. Let me know what you think, but for now it's a wait and see. Say a prayer for my mom if you

feel so inclined. That is yet another new thing for me here,
but that is a story for another time.
Jules

22

Joëlle
Baran, France 1685

The following morning, Guy woke his children with gifts he had brought from Bordeaux for them. He sat on the edge of the bed and tried to explain why he couldn't allow them to stay at the festival. "There are things in this life that you are too young to understand, but you must know that I would never hurt you intentionally. It is my job to keep you safe from harm."

"What kind of harm, PaPa?" Henri asked, while opening his gift.

"I will not concern you with that, but you are safe here in the hamlet and at the church, and that is where you're expected to stay. Do you both understand that?

"Oui, PaPa." Her father's gift and his words had softened her heart. "Thank you for the ragdoll. She's lovely." Joëlle wanted to be too old for dolls but couldn't help herself from hugging it.

"I have other news for you. I must go to London on business and will be away for many weeks, but you will be fine here with your mother and grandparents as long as you stay close to home. I need your word on that."

"We will, PaPa." Joëlle spoke for them both, while Henri petted his new wooden horse.

"Joëlle, I know you have a birthday coming up and I'm sorry that I will not be back in time for it."

"It's okay, PaPa, as long as you bring home a special gift from London for me."

Guy smiled, "I love the way you live your life in color, ma fille, though I worry it might not serve you so well in society."

***

The day Joëlle had waited for finally arrived. Henri rolled over and whispered to her, "*Joyeux Anniversaire*, JoVee."

Joëlle smiled from her pillow, "Merci, Henri."

Birthdays on the farm were celebrated simply. There was only a cake and a small, usually handmade gift. But Joëlle would not have it any other place, even if she could.

"Get dressed, let's get to the barn."

They found their grandfather already hard at work, assembling a barrel. "Can you teach us?" Joëlle asked.

"Did I hear you correctly? You want to learn about barrel-making on your birthday?"

"You remembered?" Joëlle smiled.

"You haven't let us forget, ma chérie. I seemed to have heard it mentioned a dozen times this week."

"I'm sorry. I just really love birthdays…everyone's birthday," Joëlle was slightly embarrassed.

"No need to explain. I do, too." Her grandfather handed a short-handled hammer to her, an adze to Henri, then began explaining the basic tools used in the cooperage. They spent the morning learning about the family trade from Grand-père.

After lunch, Marguerite suggested that the children go back to the barn with their grandfather, "Your grandmother and I have work to complete in the house and don't need the two of you underfoot."

Grand-père was happy to teach a new generation about the family business and proud that Joëlle was content to spend her birthday doing so. "We shall be back in the house by dinner time," he promised the women.

"Or possibly sooner," Grand-mère teased.

A little more than an hour had passed when Marguerite called the children from the back door. "Joëlle, Henri, can you take a break from helping Grand-père and come to the house?"

"Yes, Maman?" Joëlle questioned as they entered the kitchen.

"Follow me." Marguerite led them through the house and out the front door, oddly ringing the string of doorbells when she passed.

"Surprise!" came from a half dozen children from the village.

Joëlle's face lit up when she saw the lane to their house from the village center was decorated with handmade banners hanging back and forth to their door.

Louis heard the ruckus from the shop and went running through the house. He pulled Odette back inside. "What have you done?"

"Marguerite planned a small gathering of children for Joëlle's birthday. What harm is there in that?"

He didn't answer. Instead, he spent the next hour patrolling the outskirts of the hamlet while watching the children have their fun.

"Grand-mère and I have created our own versions of the games they may have played at the fête in Sarlat."

She led the children around the courtyard and explained the games to them. There was a soap bubble table with rings to blow them through. A table full of hoops and ribbons attached to sticks for twirling. There was an area marked out for leapfrog relay races and a game of trying to kick a ball through a hoop. Joëlle was floating on a cloud of pride and happiness. But the cherry on top of the party was the dancing. The hamlet was mostly inhabited by Protestants who did not approve of dancing among adults. Marguerite was possibly crossing a line but convinced Odette there was no harm in children dancing. Together, the women began humming a happy tune and danced around with the children.

There was a moment when time stopped, and Joëlle felt as if everything around her ceased to exist except the sight of Maman happily dancing with Henri. Her mother's face was animated and her smile bright as she twirled around him, her dress flowing outward in slow motion. Henri laughed out loud, something he rarely did. Somehow, she knew this memory would stay with her for the rest of her life.

Grand-père interrupted her dream-like state, "Grand-mère, Marguerite, the children have had their fun and now it is time to send them back to their homes." The party was suddenly over, but Joëlle was happy as a lark as she helped clean up.

"Merci, Maman et Grand-mère. It was simply perfect." She hugged them both then danced her way into the house.

After dinner outdoors, Marguerite brought out a honeyed sweetbread cake and gave Joëlle the first piece.

When dessert was over, they gathered around Grand-mère in anticipation of Joëlle's birth story which she told every year. Joëlle loved the way her grandmother spun a tale, using hand motions and facial expressions, whispers and shouts.

Grand-mère leaned forward and spoke softly, "Your mother thought she had time. She thought she would spend a week on the farm and would be back in Bordeaux weeks before you were to be born." She pointed her finger and shook it back and forth. "But Joëlle," Grand-mère paused and drew back her finger then pointed it toward the sky, "It seems that you and God had other plans."

Joëlle clasped her hands together at her chin and rolled her shoulders forward, wide-eyed and hanging on her grandmother's every word.

"It was to be your mother's last day in Baran," Grand-mère picked up her pace and increased the tension in her voice. "But she woke me before dawn to tell me that you were coming early and that we needed to get a midwife right away. While I helped her into bed, Grand-père went to fetch my friend, Simone, who assisted in all the births in the hamlet. Then he galloped away, as fast as his old mare would run." Grand-mère patted her hands on her lap to the pace of his trot. "He had hoped to meet your father somewhere along the route, who was due to arrive that very day to take your mother home to Bordeaux. As it turned out, they missed each other, but Grand-père said he had to try."

Joëlle turned her eyes to her grandfather and smiled a sweet smile at him, acknowledging his part in her birth. Then she turned her attention back to her grandmother's words.

"The sun was just coming up, but the birds were already singing loud and happy." She flittered her fingers in the air. "The restless wind made the candles flicker this way and that." She blew the sound of the wind and swayed her hands back and forth. Joëlle and Henri sat staring at their grandmother, mesmerized.

Her grandmother then returned to speaking calmly. "Simone, who is your friend Amelie's grandmother, attended to your mother's needs, cooling her face with a cloth and giving her sips of water while she hummed softly to keep your mother calm." Grand-mère hummed a few bars of a lullaby. "And calm she was, she didn't scream or toss to and fro as some women do."

There was a pause as her grandmother went silent and looked down at the floor, remembering, before beginning again in almost a whisper. "Yours was the most peaceful birth I had ever witnessed, and still is to this day.

Grand-mère brought both her hands to her chest, "*I* was the one to deliver you, ma chérie. *Mine* was the first face you saw." Her grandmother smiled, looking directly into those same eyes. "You didn't cry as other babies do. We should have been concerned, but your eyes were bright and wide, searching the new world around you, as if you were ready to begin your life. You are the same child today. *Joie de vivre* should have been your middle name."

A tear rolled down Joëlle's face as she got up to hug her, "Thank you, Grand-mère. This is the best part of my birthday, even better than the cake."

23

Jules
Paris, France

The clomping of horse hooves grew closer, but the sound of barking dogs had stopped. She hunched over, cramped into an opening in the rock with a hand on her back to keep her still. Her breathing halted when she saw the horse blow a breath of fog into the night air. When she heard the familiar whistle, she knew it was safe to come out of hiding but her relief was short-lived as he rushed them both onto his horse. "Quick, they're close."

The fear that woke Jules out of her sleep was instantly replaced by an overwhelming sadness. Just when she thought her troubles hadn't followed her here, she'd had the dream again. Compounding that disappointment was her concern for her mother and the guilt she felt for never having reconciled with her.

While the morning coffee brewed, she opened her laptop and was disappointed that once again, there wasn't an email from Will.

Jules pulled a bowl from the cabinet but realized she couldn't possibly eat. Also weighing on her was the fact that after class, she would have to relive, in detail, what happened to her in middle school. *It's no wonder I had the dream again.*

She walked to class in a fog, her emotions a cocktail of sadness, guilt, and dread.

***

After class, Jules took the long route home, passing Notre Dame, this time without stopping. She took her time walking the street along the Seine, acutely aware that she was delaying the inevitable.

She came to the carousel that she had seen on her first day in Paris and took a seat on a bench across from it. Jules watched the happy children float up and down and around without a care in the world. She thought about Will and his desire for children. She felt guilty for not allowing him to have the experience of being a father. Then, for the first time in her life, Jules allowed herself to admit that she wanted to have children. But felt that she couldn't, she shouldn't. Sitting there in public, she ached for the children she would never have. She didn't stop herself from feeling the pain. She let her heart release its anguish through her eyes and down her cheeks. She didn't care who saw her.

***

As soon as she got back to the apartment, Jules checked her email. She immediately opened the one from Will and began nervously twirling the opal ring on her right hand.

J,
Just a quick note to let you know that your mother is doing okay. She is sleeping a lot but the doctors say that's normal. No word yet on when she can go home. They are still running some tests. I'll let you know when we have the results.
Your Aunt Rachel stayed with your mom today, so I was able to get most of the deck finished. You're going to love it.
Talk soon,
W

There was no need to water the flowers today. It had begun to rain. "Of course," she mumbled. "How fitting."

She poured herself a glass of courage and stared at the blank paper she'd torn out of a school notepad.

When she finished the glass, she drew the curtains closed and turned on the lamp beside the bed. She propped up the pillows and made herself comfortable. Breathing in deeply, she relaxed her body from her feet upward. When she felt tension fall from her face, she let her mind go back to the darkest time in her life.

She replayed the details in her head, allowing herself to feel the emotions again as if it were the first time.

She began with feeling the apprehension she'd felt about asking her mother to seek help for her anxiety and troublesome dreams. 'Our class has been studying psychology so I think that if I could just talk to a psychologist, he could get rid of my phobias and nightmares. I really don't want to have it happen when my friends spend the night, Don't you think that's a good idea, Mother?' she'd asked with the innocent hopefulness of a child.

Then Jules let herself feel the disappointment of her mother's rebuke. 'A psychologist? Absolutely not! They cannot do anything to make nightmares go away. They'd just want to label you. No, and that's the end of this discussion.' Even as a child, Jules remembered thinking that her mother's response seemed to have gone a bit overboard.

Next, she remembered defying her mother and summoning the courage to walk into the school psychologist's office and the hopefulness she'd felt that she would be able to help her. After all, Mrs. Morgan was the mother of her best friend, Sarah.

Then Jules remembered the look of confusion on Mrs. Morgan's face as she offered no real words of advice. She had only asked her pointed questions that seemed focused on her friendship with Sarah. As a child, she never considered that this woman whom she trusted would betray her by telling Sarah about their confidential conversation.

She took a few minutes before letting herself remember what happened next. She tried to remain relaxed but couldn't stop her stomach from knotting.

She thought back to the excitement she felt when her mother finally agreed to let her have her first real birthday party with friends. Every year before, her mother would bake a birthday cake and she would receive only one gift. Her family would sing to her at the table after supper and let her blow out the candles. That was the extent of celebrating birthdays in her family. Farm life was practical. Money and time were not spent on unnecessary things.

Her brothers had never gone to birthday parties, so her parents didn't understand Jules' desire to have one. As she'd grown older, she was allowed to attend her friend's parties and had begged year after year to have one of her own. Finally, her parents gave in and even the boys got in on the party planning. Jules wanted a pool party but the only water on the farm was a spring fed pond. She begged her father to build a jumping board and he got to work making her dream come true. The boys weeded and mowed around the crystal blue pond. Her father had even surprised her by moving a large pile of sand that had been at the back of the tobacco barn for years to create a sandy beach.

Jules handmade the invitations, drawing different colorful beach towels on each one. When her eight friends received their invitations, they were impressed with Jules' creativity. The party was all they talked about during that week of school.

Feeling optimistic, and not wanting to have the nightmare during her sleepover, she made the decision to talk to Mrs. Morgan early in the week. It was a fateful decision she would forever live to regret.

She had asked her mother for a new swimming suit instead of a birthday present and Jules was pleased that her mother took her to the mall to let her pick it out. She chose a navy and white striped one piece with a ruffle at the scooped neck.

The morning of the party, Jules had woken up early to make sure everything was in place. The sun was bright and hot, a perfect day for a swimming party. She helped her mother assemble the sandwiches and stuff them into plastic bags. She iced down the Coca-Colas in a tin tub and James hauled it to the pond in a wheelbarrow.

When everything was in place, Jules excitedly put on her new suit under denim shorts and a peace sign t-shirt. She sat, dancing her legs, on the empty hay wagon that her father had hooked to the tractor to haul the excited girls back to the pond. She waited and waited. She went inside to double check the time. Her mother told her that two of the girls' mothers had called saying they were not feeling well. Jules was disappointed but went back out to wait for the others. But the others never came. No one came.

Jules pleaded with her mother to call her friends' mothers to see if there had been some mistake. Jules needed to be helped. She needed to be comforted, but instead she heard the words she will never forget. "What in the world did you do?"

Jules tried to call Sarah but there was no answer. She cried in her room all afternoon, not understanding. Her brothers tried to get her to swim with them, but she couldn't bring herself to even look at the pond.

The following week at school, Jules found out what she had done. Her stomach sickened at the thought of facing her friends on that Monday morning, not knowing why none of them had shown up for the party. But she'd put on a fake smile and walked into the classroom. Her friends all stood in the back of the room around Sarah's desk. When they saw Jules in the doorway, they all turned their backs to her, except for Allison who gave her a half smile until Sarah pulled on her arm.

What is happening? Jules' face reddened as she took a seat in the front row. She didn't dare turn around, feeling their stares and hearing their sneering. At lunch, she sat alone until the new girl that she barely knew and who hadn't been invited to the party, sat down beside her, and told her what she'd overheard, "Sarah told the girls that you had gone to see her mother about some problem you have. They asked Sarah what kind of problem and she said that since her mother was a school psychologist, it must have been a mental problem and that since her mother wouldn't tell her what it was, it must be something really bad."

"That's not true. I do not have mental problems! I had a nightmare. That's all."

"Well, all I know is that Sarah told them she wasn't going to hang out with you anymore and they needed to decide where their friendship lies." Courtney picked up her tray and moved to the boy's table. Apparently even the new girl didn't want to be her friend.

Again, Jules felt the loneliness that came with losing all her friends at once. It all came back, all of it. She let herself cry, grieving each betrayal, one by one.

Exhausted from the emotional release, she poured another glass and began the process of writing the letters. First, she penned an angry letter to the Mrs. Morgan for her unprofessional behavior and her lack of understanding of how this would affect a child's life. She scrawled an angry letter to her classroom teacher, who'd witnessed the subtle bullying on a daily basis, but did nothing. She had to have noticed the change in the relationships between Jules and her friends.

She wrote individual letters to her closest friends, questioning how easily they had turned on her and demanded apologies for their herd-mentality meanness. With each letter came another hurtful memory. She remembered their whispers. Jules covered her ears. She could feel their piercing stares. She rubbed the imagined wounds on her arms. Then she remembered the next afternoon in the school gym when she had bravely tried to join their conversation. She'd watched Sarah look up at her mother for guidance. Mrs. Morgan gave

Jules a half-hearted smile, then turned away. All the girls followed, leaving her standing all alone. Jules, once again, felt the ache of alienation. She turned on her side and drew herself into the fetal position on her bed. These wounds were never going to heal.

Before she started the letter to her mother, she thought about her role in all of this. She hadn't given her the help she'd needed and had asked for, which is why she had gone to Mrs. Morgan in the first place. If her mother had taken her to a psychologist outside the school as Jules had requested, none of it would have ever happened. She would have gone to sleepovers in middle school. She would have hung out with friends in high school. She would have gone to parties and dated boys. She would have been asked to the prom, but instead she withdrew into herself and became a loner. She read books, watched movies, and her horse became her only friend. Those things could not hurt her.

Jules didn't think her mother ever knew exactly what had happened, but she knew that her daughter had lost all her friends. She had to notice the change in her behavior, yet she did nothing. She never even asked her what happened. Jules began to sob again. This loss was the hardest. *How could she do that to her own daughter?*

Jules cried herself to sleep. She never wrote the letter.

24

Jules
Paris, France

Jules was grateful she had canceled classes for this overcast Friday, as she lay in bed feeling the hangover of yesterday's emotions. But soon, an old saying came to mind, *You can sleep when you're dead...or back in Kentucky*, she added.

She forced herself from the comfort of her warm covers and made her morning coffee. Though she had learned to appreciate the French's espresso when she was out and about, she was thankful there was a Mr. Coffee in the apartment. It was a familiar comfort and today, she needed that. She opened the window, letting in a damp breeze. Most of the neighbors' windows were still closed this morning because of last night's rain. She looked around at the balconies and noticed that a few more neighbors had planted flowers in their metal baskets but realized she had not been the one who had inspired Estelle or any of the others to plant their flowers.

She noticed that the rain had sprouted more weeds in the gravel and decided then how she would spend her free morning. Dressed in jeans and a sweatshirt, she filled a small thermos with coffee, wrapped a croissant and an apple in a kitchen towel and placed them in her market basket, along with a throw from the desk chair.

The neighbors rarely took the elevator. They almost exclusively took the stairs, even to the fourth floor. Following their lead, she descended the steps to the courtyard. Jules sat on an iron bench to eat her croissant and drink from the steaming thermos while she watched the neighbors, one by one, as they started their days. They opened their windows. Some put on music. The smell of *jambon et œufs* frying and strong espresso hovered in the morning haze. Glorious.

When she finished the croissant, she set about to pull weeds from between the rocks. She realized she hadn't brought anything to put the weeds in and didn't want to dirty her new basket, so she put them in piles, as she had seen done, and made a plan to come back for them. She listened attentively to the sounds of morning as she weeded, rattling dishes, a man singing in his shower, the crunch of her own footsteps, and the differing songs of birds overhead. Estelle had opened her window, but Jules never saw her come out for a smoke.

After an hour, Jules stood appreciating the pristine courtyard when she heard footsteps making their way toward her. She was surprised to see Estelle holding a lit cigarette in one hand and a paper grocery bag in the other. "Madame?" she said, holding it out to her. Jules smiled and thanked her.

The woman quickly turned and left the courtyard. Jules gathered the weeds into the bag and placed it in her basket then sat on a bench to eat her apple. *What a lovely way to spend the morning.* Jules was beginning to feel a little better.

After showering, as Jules was leaving for her appointment with Dr. LaRoche, she saw the letters sitting by the bed. She'd fallen asleep before she could destroy them, and she still hadn't written the letter to her mother. Knowing that Lillie lay in a hospital bed, Jules didn't have the heart to write it now. She picked up the letters and chucked them into her bag and set about her hike. As she walked along the river, she wanted to throw her cares into the Seine. Instead, she carried them into the doctor's office.

***

Dr. LaRoche greeted her warmly, asking her to take a seat on the couch for this appointment. "Were you able to do as I suggested in the last appointment?"

"Yes, mostly."

"Très bien. In our last session, you said you felt betrayed by your mother. I'd like to explore this further." Dr. LaRoche was unaware of the stroke.

Jules felt guilty talking negatively about her mother but internally reasoned that she was here to get help and needed to be honest. "If my mother had helped me in the first place, none of it would have ever happened. This all started with her."

"Is that how you see it? From what you have told me, I would say that your mother's response was as a result of the situation presented to her. Have you ever thought of it in that way? That your mother did all she could with the resources she had, given her own life experiences. She was having to shepherd a situation that she was unfamiliar with. Yes, she hurt you. Yes, the school therapist betrayed your trust. Certainly, your friends let you down. But do you see that all this stems from something else? I am certainly not saying that you are at fault. You are not. These things happened *to* you. You did not create them."

"So, I am to just forgive them and forget the fact that my life was ruined?"

"Is that how you see it? Your life is in ruins?" he asked, drawing a distinction between her experience as a child with her life as an adult.

"No, not now, but it certainly was!" She paused, aware of her anger. "Maybe I should have destroyed the letters."

"Would you like to do that now? It will symbolically put the past where it belongs."

She pulled the letters out of her bag, aware that she still had not written the letter to her mother. "May I have a piece of paper?"

He handed her a notepad and a pen. She simply wrote, "You hurt me, Mother, but I forgive you."

He instructed her to begin tearing the letters over the trash can. As she shredded them, Dr. LaRoche spoke of forgiveness and healing. When she finished, he said, "Jules, you have now faced each hurt directly and can now put these feelings behind you. Let go of them, throw them in the Siene, then watch them float away. If you start to feel them again, remind yourself that you chose to rid yourself of the hurtful things in your past and are moving forward, extending grace where needed, choosing to live your life in a more positive way.

"Now, I'd like to spend some time getting to the root cause of the issues themselves." He asked her to lie back on the couch and coached her through the relaxation process. Because Dr. LaRoche's training was more Eastern influenced than Western, he had a different perspective than Dr. Gray. He had experience in all forms of hypnotherapy, including trance therapy. He had a lengthy career dealing with similar cases and had seen this sort of thing before.

He waited until he felt she was ready, then began. His monotone voice was deep yet calming as he spoke in velvety French. "*Je voudrais que tu retournes à ton rêve et dis-moi tout ce que tu vois.*"

The doctor watched her breathing as her eyes began to move. Subconsciously, his speaking in French comforted her. It felt natural and unforced as she responded, "*Ma mère et moi, nous sommes dans la forêt, chassés. Parfois nous courons. Parfois nous nous cachons. J'ai trop peur.*"

Jules body contorted and moved about uncomfortably.

Continuing in French, "We hide in a small cave and hear a horse approaching… But then I see it's my father, and he takes us with him. We ride away at a steady pace through the trees… We come to a river and need to cross, but my father can't tell how deep it is."

Dr. LaRoche frequently reassured her in his low and leveled voice.

"We hear dogs barking in the distance. We have no choice and start to cross. The horse fights my father, but finally it relents. We're in the middle of the river when the horse disappears from under us." Her voice intensifies. "It's too deep!" Jules slightly lifted her head off the couch and took a deep breath.

"You're safe. Please continue," he spoke in French.

"My father tells us to swim but he keeps his hand on me. It's freezing. His horse is swept away, and we don't see my mother. I start to scream for her, but my father covers my mouth. Then she comes to the surface and my father leads us both safely to the other side. He pulls us into the brush... I cry, begging them to go home. I want things to be the way they used to be, before."

There was a long silence as she thought about the before. A tear slid down Jules' cheek.

"My father leaves us to retrieve his horse... Then we ride again... Mother wakes me up when we reach the meadow. We made it," Jules said, relaxing her body.

The doctor watched her closed eyes searching. He remained silent, allowing his patient all the time she needed.

"It feels safe inside the church. Father shows us where to hide inside the altar.

Dr. LaRoche waited. Jules' breathing slowed and her eyes became still. She said nothing further for several minutes, so he called her back to the present.

Jules sat up, realizing that she didn't remember what had happened during the hypnosis. She felt groggy and confused. She waited as Dr. LaRoche was making detailed notes on this session this time.

Speaking in English, "Have you looked into your family's history?"

"Yes, I recently found out that I actually have French ancestors."

"I see."

Jules was curious by his question, but thankful that he didn't bring up reincarnation, as Dr. Gray had.

"Will you bring a copy of your genealogy in with you next session?"

"Yes, I can have my husband send it, but I don't see what that has to do with anything." she said, leading him to explain further.

"I will explain in due course," he said. "I'd like to see you again once you've received it."

***

Halfway home, Jules realized she should have asked him why she hadn't remembered what happened under hypnosis. The only difference from her session with Dr. Gray was that Dr. LaRoche had spoken to her in French. Whatever the reason, she still trusted Dr. LaRoche.

***

Back in the apartment, she was happy to see an email from Will in her inbox.

> *J,*
> *The tests all show no permanent damage. She may get released as early as tomorrow. Looks like I will be able to come to France, as planned.*
> *W*

She responded, *That's wonderful news,* at least about her mother. She was still not ready for Will to come to France yet.

25

Jules
Paris, France

Jules marked another Saturday off on her calendar. She couldn't believe how quickly the weeks were passing. She wanted it to slow down. She needed it to slow down.

Sitting at the bistro table in the apartment, she checked her email to see if Will had sent the genealogy as she was eager to schedule the next appointment with Dr. LaRoche. But there wasn't an email from Will or one from Chloe, which was unusual as she had never missed a day.

The dreary front had thankfully passed, and the sun beamed in from the courtyard window. Jules chose a sleeveless sundress and sandals then plopped on a floppy hat to protect her face from the summer sun that was growing hotter by the day.

***

Jules was pleased to see the familiar faces in their booths at the market. These vendors were the only people that she had regular conversations with other than her students. She visited the *fromager* who handed her a package of goat cheese without her having to ask. She purchased a couple of kinds of olives, dipped directly out of uncovered wooden bowls. The olive vendor was more reserved, but always acknowledged that he knew her.

This Saturday, Jules spent more time in the chocolate booth trying samples. She would never tire of watching the vendor run the wood handled knife through the large chunks. Years of experience showed as he always cut the exact amount she ordered. Her mouth watered as she watched him weigh and wrap her delectable slabs.

Jules spent the rest of the morning shopping for gifts for her nieces and nephews. She felt bad that she'd missed Ivy's birthday, so she chose a small oil paint set that included a desktop easel. She wanted to encourage Ivy's new-found interest in Will's paintings.

Her market basket was getting full. But there was one more item on her list. She'd been meaning to read a book written in French while she was in France, so she rummaged through a booth filled with vintage books. She came across a tall stack of books, all with similar binding, tied together with a heavy string. Upon closer inspection, she saw that they were the volumes of *In Search of Lost Time*, by Marcel Proust. Jules could not believe her luck. She had always wanted to read the series, and here it was, right in front of her, at a Paris *marché*. Her basket had now become unbearably heavy.

***

At home, Jules made a light lunch of a single crispy tartine with strawberry jam. She planned to eat dinner at La Pluie and wanted to arrive hungry. She took the first volume in the series, *Swann's Way,* and a blanket then descended the stairs to the courtyard. She lay on her stomach in the small grassy area, hiking her dress to bare her legs to the sun. She turned from time to time to keep from getting a sunburn. She soon became sleepy, gathered her things, and headed up the four flights of stairs.

When she walked back into the apartment, she heard the unfamiliar sound of her cell phone buzzing. *Mother!* She fumbled to find it and she was relieved to see that it was Chloe calling. "Hello! I can't believe it. Don't tell me you're calling to cancel on me."

"No, no, not at all. Only a few more days. I can hardly believe it's happening."

"I can't wait either but I'm curious why you've phoned."

Jules heard Chloe draw in a deep breath. "Chloe, is everything okay with you and Josh?"

"Better than okay. We're done. Through your emails, I've realized that I'd be settling with Josh. He doesn't make me happy. I've felt your enthusiasm for life, and I want that for myself."

"Well, then, I'm happy for you. Maybe you can change your flight and spend more time here. I would love that."

"That's actually why I'm calling…"

Jules interrupted, "Wonderful!"

"Okay, then I'll change my flight, but Jules, there's another reason that I called," she spilled before she had time to change her mind.

"What is it?"

"I've struggled with whether or not this is any of my business, but I know if things were reversed, I'd be furious if you didn't tell me."

"Chloe, tell me now. I'm serious!" Her tone grew urgent. "Is this about my job?"

"No. I wish it were just about a job. It's about Will." Chloe paused to swallow. "Jules, I saw him out with Laura Harris."

"Yes, they're co-teachers. I guess they have a project or something."

"Jules, school is out," Chloe responded, confused.

Jules felt embarrassed that she was so detached from Will's life at home that she hadn't even asked him about the end of school. She had been so wrapped up in herself and her mother that she'd once again taken her husband for granted.

"It hurts me to tell you this, but I can tell that it's not about school. Their conversation seemed intimate and serious."

"How can you be sure?"

"Jules, I'm sure. They walked closely and he had his arm around her. They were so involved in each other that they didn't even see me watching them. When he walked her to her car at the park, he hugged her, a long hug. It made me feel so uncomfortable that I couldn't watch."

Jules wanted to throw up. *This can't be true.* She couldn't think straight so, she said nothing.

"I'm changing my flight now, Jules. I'll be there as soon as I can. I'll email you as soon as I know when."

Jules hung up the phone without saying goodbye.

She paced the floor though her limbs were weak. She replayed Chloe's words, trying to make sense of what she had just heard. *We're fine. At least I thought we were fine. This is all my fault. I should never have taken this job. How could I jeopardize the best thing that ever happened to me?* She closed the windows to be alone in her grief.

It must be the baby thing. Of course, Laura can give him babies. She already has two little ones. Wait! What about her husband? Jules' mind was spinning. *How could she do this to her children, to her husband?* Then anger took over. *How could Will do this to me?*

Her phone rang again. This time it was Will. *Did Chloe tell him that she told me? Why is he calling?*

"Hello," she answered, agitated.

Will was confused. "Jules?"

"What is it, Will? Do you have something you need to tell me?"

He shrugged off his confusion and continued, "Jules, Honey, it's your mother. She's had another stroke and this time it's a bad one. I'm afraid you need to come home now."

"Oh, no." She took a moment to process what he had just told her and what it meant. "I'll call Chloe. I will be there as soon as I can. Will, please tell her that I'm sorry and that I love her and that I'm coming home." She didn't wait for a response. She hung up the phone and immediately called Chloe.

"I'll change my flight. I can be there late on Sunday. I just received my work visa this week, so you don't have to worry… at least about the class."

"I'll put together a detailed list of everything you'll need to know during my flight and will send the email as soon as I've landed." Will wasn't mentioned.

Jules held back her tears until she booked her flight. As she packed up her life in France, she let the flood gates open. She cried for her mother and prayed that she would get the chance to apologize. She needed her mother to know that she had forgiven her.

She grieved having to leave her dream job and felt bad that she wouldn't get to say goodbye to her students.

She regretted that she would never be able to finish the good work she had started with Dr. LaRoche. She had begun to make real progress in her healing journey. Now, she feared she'd start back at square one.

But most importantly, she grieved the probable loss of her marriage. Even if she could forgive him, she would no longer keep him in a marriage without the children he so desperately wanted.

26

Joëlle
Baran, France 1685

Joëlle's birthday had been the last day of normalcy in and around Baran. The following Sunday, it was clear how different everything had become. The world had changed to such a degree that it had somehow reached their remote country lives. At PaPa's insistence, Grand-père instructed the parishioners that they were to attend only the worship service, then they were to go straight home. They could no longer share a meal nor sing together in the afternoon. Sundays were no longer Joëlle's favorite day of the week, as they were now a reminder of the mysterious cloud hanging over their heads.

"I can't believe I am saying this, but I'm ready to go home. Are you?" Joëlle confessed to her brother.

Henri shrugged his shoulders.

"At least, in the city, we will be back to school with our friends and life will be normal again." Naivete is a child's best friend.

***

A few weeks later, Guy arrived at the farm, more tense than ever, to take his family home to Bordeaux. Before he entered the house, Joëlle witnessed her father yank down the string of doorbells.

"PaPa, what are you doing?" she asked, confused at the sight.

"Just making a few changes. Where is your grandfather?"

"In the barn. I'll fetch him." She ran toward the barn while calling out an alarm to her mother.

Grand-père and Maman met at the back of the house and rushed around to the front to find Guy removing the potted flowers from the stoop.

"Guy, what on earth are you doing?" Marguerite asked.

He ignored her question and motioned to his father, "Help me move these steps."

After the men moved the steps to the back of the house, Marguerite and Odette went inside, assuming the men would follow. Instead, Guy began moving brush from the fence row to disguise the front entrance of the house. His father followed his lead, curious though he was.

"Do you still have those old boards in the barn?" Guy asked his father while continuing to pull large branches to the front door.

"I do. What do you plan to use them for?"

"To board up the front windows and the door. Yes, I know it seems crazy, but I will explain everything when we've finished."

When the men began hammering boards onto the windows, Grand-mère peeked her head outside the top of the Dutch door. "What…"

Grand-père shook his head to stop her from finishing and waved her back into the house.

Once the task was complete, Guy wiped his brow, walked inside the house, and finally took time to greet his family.

Marguerite accepted his kisses but pulled back to look at her husband's haggard face.

"Guy, what is going on? You are scaring us all to death."

Joëlle had been intently watching everything unfold and was wide-eyed awaiting her father's answer.

"Ma fille, please go outside and play with your brother."

"But, PaPa."

"Joëlle!" Marguerite uncharacteristically raised her voice.

She knew better than to press any further and walked out the screen door. She heard her father close the wood door behind her.

Guy turned from his wife and spoke directly to his father, "Since the Revocation of the Edict of Nantes, the troubles in Paris have begun to move south. I believe you are safe here, away from any large city, but you should be sure you are doing all you can to minimize your risk. I want you to use the back door as your entrance, and only go off the farm when it is absolutely necessary. There are things going on in this country that I hope you never learn about, and it is just as well. I don't want you to live in fear, but you must take precautions and stay vigilant."

Odette took the doorbells from around her son's neck and placed them on the table where she sat down to steady herself.

Guy continued, "Once we have gone, if at any time you feel you are in danger, take the back roads to Bordeaux. Do not hesitate, as it could mean your very lives."

Joëlle's eyes bulged, and she bit her lip to stop herself from making a sound. She wobbled on the rain barrel she'd climbed onto to listen from underneath an open window. She steadied herself then slowly slid her head over to peek inside.

Joëlle saw her father pull out a stack of papers and an envelope overflowing with money from his satchel. "This is to go into the barrel labeled Chateau Violette 1673. You may use some of the money if you need it."

"My son!" Louis looked around to make sure no one was watching them through the windows.

Joëlle quickly ducked, causing her to fall off the barrel, but she could still faintly hear their conversation.

"Why?" Louis was beginning to panic at seeing his son had made such detailed plans on his fears.

"Pack two of the barrels with the dried meats and preserved vegetables from the cellar. I will help you pack the other barrels with the items I've brought with me today before we return to Bordeaux. If you are forced to leave here after we have gone, bring the barrels with you to Bordeaux, if you are able. If not, I will pick them up as soon as I can return."

Joëlle felt sick to her stomach. She'd never known her father to be fearful. She felt as if her legs had been kicked out from under her.

Joëlle waited until the kitchen had cleared then snatched the doorbells from the table and slid them under her shirt. She slowed her pace to quiet the bells as she creeped up the steps to the loft.

Thankful that Henri was still outside, she took the paperdolls from Grand-mere's box and pushed them deep into an open eave. She placed the bells inside the box and slid it back beneath the bed. Joëlle then sat on the floor, holding her stomach. She no longer wanted to know what it was that her father feared and now regretted her curiosity.

27

Jules
Paris, France

Leaving for the airport, Jules realized that she had no one to leave the key to the apartment with. It was too late to reach anyone at the university, so Jules wrote a note in French, explaining why she had to leave on short notice and asking Estelle to hold the key for Chloe. She put the oversized skeleton key and the note into an envelope and slid it under her neighbor's door.

As she was crossing the courtyard toward the street, Jules heard, "Madame?" from four floors above her. She looked up to see Estelle waving from her balcony, *"D'accord.* Safe travels." Jules had made a friend, just in time to leave.

On the nine-hour flight home into the headwinds, Jules tried to hold back her tears. She was thankful to fill the time making multiple lists for Chloe. The first list began with where to find Estelle then how to find the university's apartment. She detailed everything she would need to know about the apartment, including where to find the hidden clothesline and when to water the flowers.

The next list detailed everything Chloe would need to know about the teaching position, including where she had left the curriculum, grade books, and the keys to her office. She included the walking directions to the university and where to find the classroom. Then she made a list of the students in her class and what she had learned about each of them.

Jules made a list of her favorite places to eat and what to order, then another about the market and where to find the best cheese and chocolate. She told her that she'd left the *Michelin Travel Guide* with the best times to visit each place written on their pages.

When she finished making the lists for Chloe, Jules emailed Dr. Fournier at the university, introducing Chloe to her. She explained how quickly everything had happened and that she hoped she had done the right thing, then Jules thanked her for the opportunity she had been given.

Between the list making for Chloe, worrying about her mother and the reality that her marriage was likely over, Jules had forgotten to arrange for anyone to pick her up. When she landed, she opened her phone to call her brother and saw that she had a missed call and a voicemail message from Will asking whether she was flying into Louisville or Cincinnati, and what time she was scheduled to land.

She had flown into Louisville, which was an hour's drive for either of them. Jules felt her anxiety rising at the thought of having to face Will right now. Dealing with her mother's stroke was more than she could handle. Will would have to wait so she called Jasper to pick her up. She texted Will that she had a ride.

Will called her immediately after receiving the text. "Jules, why didn't you tell me when and where to pick you up? I've been waiting and wondering."

"Well, you'll have to excuse me. I wasn't really thinking clearly," she responded bitterly.

"I understand, honey. Do you want me to meet you at the farm?"

"There's no need. I'm going straight to the hospital."

"Okay, I'll meet you there."

"Will, no! I have a lot to deal with right now and can't get into this with you."

"You can't get into what?"

"I can't talk to you right now about this. I'm in the airport surrounded by people. But Will...I know." She hung up. She didn't care to listen to his explanation or excuses.

He tried to call her back, but she had silenced her phone. *She knows what? Why is she acting this way toward me?* Confused, he drove to the hospital and sat in the parking lot waiting for answers.

***

When he saw Jasper drop Jules off at the entrance, Will followed him and parked beside his truck.

"Will, I'm surprised to see you here," Jasper said.

"Why would you be surprised? My wife just got back from France. We haven't seen each other in weeks and her mother may be dying. Why in the world would that surprise you?" Will's confusion was becoming impatience.

"Look, Will. This is not the time or place. I don't know what is going on. It's frankly none of my business."

"Well, it certainly is *my* business and I'd sure like to know what is going on."

"All I know is that Jules is devastated about Mom and said she doesn't want to see you or discuss why with anyone. I am asking you, Will, to go home. I'm sure she'll see you tomorrow."

Will sat in his car, staring out the window. He sent Jules a text. *I don't know what's happening, but just know that I love you and want to be here with you to help you through this.* Jules didn't respond, so he drove home.

***

Jules held Jasper's arm as they walked down the cold corridor that led them into the Intensive Care Unit. He chose not to mention that he had seen Will.

It sickened Jules to see her mother through the glass, with tubes and wires attached to her. "She doesn't belong here. She should be at home on the farm," she told her brother.

Her father heard voices and looked up to see his children's concerned faces looking back at him. They watched him kiss his wife on the forehead before coming to speak with them.

It had been six months since she had seen her parents. Jules started to cry when she hugged her father, realizing how much she had missed them.

"How's she doing? What are they saying?" Jasper asked his father, while Jules gathered herself.

"Nothing new. They're still trying to determine the extent of the damage caused by the stroke. It doesn't look good, though. She hasn't woken up or responded in any way. But there's always hope. Praying is all we can do right now."

"It's the most we can do. I've been praying for her ever since I heard. I'm sorry, Dad. I am so sorry for everything." Jules began to sob again.

"Now, that's all just water under the bridge. Don't worry yourself one more minute about that. Why don't you go home and get some sleep and come back after you have rested? Where's Will?" He asked, looking around.

Jules ignored his question. She hated to leave but she knew her father was right. The truth was she had not slept or eaten. They said their goodbyes and Jasper drove her to the farm.

***

It felt good to be back in her childhood home. Her room was unchanged. She crawled into that familiar place and slept for hours.

When she woke up late in the morning, she walked into the farmhouse kitchen, which smelled of coffee and bacon, as always. She was irritated to see Will sitting at the table with her brother. He quickly pushed his chair back and went to Jules. He hugged her for a long time, and she let him. She needed him. No matter what had happened, it comforted her. He pulled back to look at her.

"Now, look at you, my beautiful Parisian wife. I love the new haircut."

"I'm sure I look awful." She rubbed her eyes and poured herself a cup from the percolator. "How long have you been here?"

"Hours. I could not sleep knowing you were on American soil. Here," he said, pulling out a chair for her, "Sit, eat."

Jasper scooted away from the table. "I'm going to the barn. I'll drive you to the hospital when you've finished eating."

"There's no need to leave." Jules widened her eyes, signaling to him that she wanted him to stay.

"I have chores I need to get done for Dad." He walked out the screen door and let it close on its own behind him. *Creak, whack.*

Jules closed her eyes and breathed in the sound. It was a small comfort to her hurting heart.

"Okay, Jules, we are finally alone. What is going on? Have I done something? Did something happen in France?"

"Will, no. You just need to go. I cannot do this right now. Can't you understand that? My mother is dying." She put down her fork and sobbed into her hands.

"But I want to help you."

"You can't help me. No one can help me." she said through tears. "Please just go. I'll come home when I can. I need to be alone."

Will stood behind her chair. He put his hands on her shoulders as she cried. "Please, let me know of anything at all that I can do" he said then turned and walked out the door. He sat in his car, staring out the window, trying to make sense of Jules' attitude toward him, before driving away from the farm.

Jules forced herself to eat a few bites of the scrambled eggs that Will had cooked for her. She picked up the toast and walked through the house. It felt strange to be in the house alone. Every day of her life, her mother had been inside this house, cooking or cleaning. She walked into her mother's room. She and her father slept in the big bedroom in the back of the house, but her mother had her own space in the "little room" off the kitchen where she sewed, read, and made jewelry. There was an antique half-bed pushed up against a wall with a small window that looked out onto one of the barns. Jules saw her brother through it, bent over repairing a tractor.

She took a close look at the things her mother had chosen to put on the walls. There were postcards tacked straight into the cedar paneling behind the bed. They had been there for as long as she could remember but she had never questioned them until now. She pulled one of the postcards of the Grand Canyon off the wall and read the note on the back from her Aunt Rachel. It was the basic, "Wish you were here" postcard. Jules pushed the tack back into its place in the wall, and read the others, all from her mother's side of the family. Above her mother's sewing machine, was a landscape scene of a large waterfall on a page torn out of a magazine. Beside it was another torn out page of a tropical scene of Hawaii.

She must have wanted to travel. Jules realized she was looking at what she thought were her mother's broken dreams. Her mother had come from an upper middle-class family. They always had the finest of cars. They had lived in a nice neighborhood and had taken lots of trips. Jules' family had never vacationed. Her mother had married into a farming family and on a farm, there was always work to be done.

Her mother's words replayed in her mind. *Sometimes in life, you choose to give up one thing for another.* Jules was seeing her mother through new eyes, and she hurt for her. She lay across the bed and cried.

28

Jules
Lexington, Kentucky

At the hospital, Joseph greeted them with a tired smile. Jasper went into his mother's room while Jules and her father talked in the corridor.

"Would you mind sitting with your mother for a while this morning so I can go home to get a little sleep?" Her father looked drained. Joseph was accustomed to working long, hard hours on the farm, but this was a different kind of exhaustion. Lillie's illness had visibly taken its toll on him.

"Of course not, I was going to suggest that myself."

"I'm sorry you had to cut your trip short. How was it?" Joseph was so distracted that's all he could think to ask.

Jules had her arm around her father's back as they both stood facing the window. She simply replied, "It's good to be home."

"I'll sleep for a few hours, then I'll be back to spend the night. James will be here soon." As he was hugging her, Jules realized that her father had not taken his eyes off her mother the entire time they were talking.

After her father left, Jules pulled the chair close to the bed and took her mother's limp hand into hers. "I'm here, Mother. I'm home." When Lillie did not respond, she could not control her emotions. She walked into the bathroom and leaned over the sink to cry. After a few minutes, Jules heard the nurse come into her mother's room. She wiped her face before going to speak to her. Jules introduced herself and asked the nurse about her mother's condition.

"She's holding her own. Time will tell. I've seen patients in similar situations go on to have a full recovery. Let's hold on to that hope." Jules followed closely behind the nurse as she walked around her mother's bed, pushing buttons and straightening tubes. She desperately wanted to do something, anything at all, to help her mother.

"Do you think she can hear me if I talk to her?" Jules asked, looking for hope.

"I don't know for certain, but it can't hurt. I always encourage people to say whatever they feel they need to, so they will not have any regrets," the nurse said as she made notes on the dry erase board.

'Regrets.' The word was a knife to her stomach.

"If you need anything, press the call button."

Jules straightened her mother's blankets and rearranged the pillow. She sat quietly with her for a while before beginning a one-sided conversation that would last off and on for hours.

She started by apologizing for her reaction at Christmas. "I know how you've always felt about me seeing a therapist, but Will just suggested it to see if she could help me." Jules wanted her mother to know that neither she nor Will were serious about reincarnation. "The therapist brought it up, but Will only said it to make everyone laugh. I am sorry, Mother." She told her that Will had seen how much it upset her and that he had felt awful about it ever since. Jules did not know that Will had called to apologize to Lillie the day after Christmas and had been in contact with her parents while she had been in France.

Jules was quiet for a while as she thought about her childhood, then apologized for being a troubled child and causing her mother stress. "I'm sorry I blamed you for everything wrong in my life. I know it was not your fault.

"I loved growing up on the farm." Jules talked to Lillie about some of her favorite childhood memories, one by one, as they came to mind, some made her cry, others made her smile. "I especially loved our Christmases. You always made them special. Thank you."

Jules explained what she had been learning about herself in France. "I recently discovered that I like feminine things, beaded necklaces and floral dresses. Just like you."

Then she talked to her mother about the thing she knew was most important to her. Jules told her about the churches in Paris and how drastically different they are from the churches she had grown up in. "The doors are always open to anyone, day or night. The sanctuaries are barely lit and there are always candles burning." Jules told her about the day she was photographing Notre Dame Cathedral and how she had felt pulled to go in. "My words will never be able to truly describe it, but the churches in France feel like such sacred places. Maybe it's the darkened rooms, the flickering candlelight or simply the fact that there aren't any distractions, but it's clear that you have entered His house, and the focus is directed solely at Him. It felt like praises were being pulled from my body. I had never experienced a connection to God like that. It encouraged me to begin a conversation with Him.

"Another difference I noticed in the churches there is that people don't just attend weekly services. They come to the church often, even daily to light a candle and say a prayer for someone they love. As soon as I heard about your stroke, the first thing I did was to go to church to pray. I lit a candle for you, Mother."

Just then, Jules thought she saw her mother's eye move. "Mom?"

She pushed the call button, and the nurse came right away. Jules told her what she had seen. The nurse checked her mother's vital signs and tried in vain to get a response from Lillie. "It's okay. Sometimes we see things we want to see," the nurse said lovingly while touching Jules' shoulder.

After the nurse left the room, Jules told her mother, "I don't care what she says, I know what I saw. I know you can hear me."

Knowing this, Jules took a moment to think about what she most wanted her mother to hear. "Mom, I want you to know that I love you and am so thankful for you and everything you've done for our family."

Jules saw her mother's eye flutter again beneath a closed lid.

She held her hand tighter and continued, "I saw the postcards and pictures on your walls and for the first time, I see how you sacrificed for us. I know that your hopes and dreams may not have been realized, yet you never complained about it."

She paused, watching her mother's face. She saw the muscles on one side of her face begin to move. It looked as if her mother wanted to wake up, as if she wanted to say something. Jules blinked her own eyes, wondering if she was indeed just seeing what she wanted to see.

Having Jules at her side, Lillie was trying her best to come to consciousness. Her mind a blur, only flashes of memory, Jules' traumatic birth, rocking her constantly to calm this baby who apparently did not want to be born, years of learning to manage the strange phobias of this otherwise happy child. Then a core memory surfaced, one that had haunted Lillie every day since.

Lillie's breath turned instantly to frost on the glass of the kitchen door. The bitter cold made her shiver. She pulled the dish towel from the pocket of her apron to wipe it away. In the glow of the security light, she watched the snow fall heavy and wet, silencing the night air and every sound with it. The farm had never felt so still.

Jasper and James were finally asleep in their bunk beds after a long day begrudgingly spent indoors. They'd fought over toys, argued over sports, and wrestled in the floor over absolutely nothing at all. Lillie sighed, remembering, as she walked through the house picking up a basketful of their toys.

Joseph, too, had gone to bed earlier than usual out of sheer boredom. Hard working farmers like her husband did not want to be sidelined by the weather. But the deep and drifted snow, accompanied by subzero temperatures and blizzard force winds, had forced him inside. She rolled up Joseph's scattered newspaper sections and stuffed them into the kindling box.

Lillie took her time finishing the daily chores, dreading what may come. Dishes washed, laundry folded, fire stoked, she treaded lightly down the hallway and listened at the door to be sure that Joseph was asleep. When she heard her husband snoring, she opened the hallway closet, careful to avoid the squeak, to retrieve the video camera.

After having a houseful of discontented people in foul moods at her heels all day, Lillie sat down in the rocking chair and closed her eyes. All was finally quiet inside the hundred-year-old farmhouse, save the crackling fire and whistling wind. She breathed in the stillness while she waited.

Every night for the last week and a half, Lillie had waited like this. Video camera at her side, power on, she'd waited. Night after night, she prayed she would not have to use it. Night after night, she prayed that it would never happen again and that she could forget that it ever had.

But tonight, it was not to be. Lillie was startled out of her prayers. It was happening again. Lillie knew she needed help, but first she would need proof. She grabbed the recorder and hurried down the hallway. She paused just before entering to take a steadying breath and to clear the blurring tears from her eyes.

Lillie opened the door and pressed the record button.

***

Jules felt her mother move her fingers and noticed her quickened breath. "Mom?"

She didn't bother to call the nurse this time. She saw her mother try to move her lips. "It's okay. Don't try to talk. You need to rest." Jules was reaching for her cell phone to call her father when she heard her mother mumble. She looked up to see her mother with one eye slightly open, smiling a one-sided smile at her. "Mother!" Jules smiled back. She thought her mother had never looked so beautiful but before Jules could say anything more, she watched the consciousness fall from her mother's face.

"Mom. Can you hear me? Open your eyes again. Please come back." Jules pleaded in a shaky voice.

Lillie didn't respond so Jules pushed the call button to let the nurse know.

She phoned her father and her Aunt Rachel to let them know that Lillie had responded for a few minutes. She sent a text to Will.

That is wonderful. Do you want me to come to the hospital? He responded immediately.

She explained that her father and Rachel were on their way and for him to stay home.

If that's what you want, but I will bring dinner to the farm later.

When Rachel arrived at the hospital, Jules met her at the door to invite her to the farm for dinner. After what Chloe had told her, she was not ready to be alone with Will.

***

Before leaving for the hospital, Joseph drug a kitchen chair over to the cabinets and hoisted himself up. He ran his hand along the top, searching until he felt it.

He blew the dust from it and looked at the sealed envelope, simply addressed, 'My dear, Jules.' He assumed that it was a letter apologizing for what had happened at Christmas.

After the first stroke, Lillie told Joseph that if anything happened to her, she wanted him to find the letter and give it to Jules. After today's news, Joseph wanted Jules to read it so that she and her mother could reconcile.

He laid it on the kitchen table and left for the hospital, with a renewed hope that Lillie was going to recover.

29

Jules
Midway, Kentucky

After a few hours with no further response from Lillie, Rachel drove Jules to the farm, questioning her nonstop about her time in France. Jules gave short answers while staring out the window, but she just wanted to talk about her mother.

"Something smells good," Rachel sniffed the air as she entered through the screen door. "Will, it's good to see you," she said, giving him a hug. "Thank you for inviting me to dinner. It looks delicious." Jules saw the questioning look on Rachel's face and knew she must be wondering why she had not greeted her husband.

Before Rachel had a chance to ask, Will picked up the conversation while adding another setting to the table, "Sit down, let's eat before everything gets cold," Will pulled out the chairs for both women.

As he began passing the food around, he kept the conversation going. "Did your mom regain consciousness again?" Rachel shook her head, but Will was looking at Jules. "What had you said to your mother just before she responded?"

Jules replayed the conversation in her mind. "Let me think, I had rattled on for hours, trying to see any sign that she was hearing me. I talked about things that I remember about our life on the farm. I told her that even though I was such an odd kid, so different from the boys, I loved growing up here."

Rachel looked up from her plate and set down her fork, reminded of Jules' childhood. "I had forgotten about the quirky things you used to do when you were a kid. I remember you used to say words in funny ways, like you had a foreign accent."

"I did? How so?"

"Well, I remember when you were learning to talk, and even for years later, you said your name with a Z instead of a J, like *Zules*." You even told your kindergarten teacher that it was the correct way to say it and that your mother was pronouncing it incorrectly. We all had a lot of laughs over that one." Rachel picked up her fork and began eating again.

"That's one I've never heard before. It is strange because that's how they pronounce my name in France. But it is more like 'Zhules'," Jules said in her full French accent.

"Yes! That's it!" Rachel said with her mouth half full. She was so surprised that she didn't take the time to swallow. "That is exactly how you said it. Wow, I cannot believe you remember that."

Jules did not remember it at all. She shook off her confusion and changed the subject back to her mother. "Then I talked about my time in France. I told her that it was strange that I could love it there so much yet truly ache for home. I was telling her how wonderful the churches are in France when she first responded. I really hope this is the first step to her recovery."

"I'm sure it is. Will, thank you again for dinner. It's late and I know you two would like to be alone after all the time apart. I'm sure I will see you at the hospital tomorrow. I am hoping Lillie will wake up again and talk to us." She hugged them both before making a quick exit.

Will watched through the window to be sure that Rachel had driven away before handing Jules the envelope with her name on it.

"What's this?"

"I don't know. It was on the table when I got here. I set it aside when I saw that Rachel was coming inside with you."

"This is Mom's handwriting. I wonder when she wrote it," she said, staring at it.

"Open it." Will, though he was curious, walked out of the kitchen to let her read it in private.

Jules sat down at the table, the same table where her mother sat to write it.

Jules,
First, I need for you to know that everything I've ever done, the decisions I made were done to protect you. Right or wrong, I acted out of love and concern, trying my best to give you as normal a life as possible.
Something started happening around the time you turned three that I've never told anyone about, not even your father.

Jules leaned in and blinked her eyes to convince herself that she was actually reading these words. *What started happening?*

I used to have to wake you up after you had been asleep for a couple of hours to take you to the bathroom so you would not wet the bed. That is when it started. The first night, I just thought it was funny, like you were having a bad dream, but then it kept happening night after night. I knew no one would believe me so I decided to record it on a videotape. I held on to that recording for a long time, watching it over and over, before I decided what I should do with it. Finally, I got up the courage to schedule an appointment with a psychologist in Louisville.

"What?!" Jules exclaimed aloud. Will looked in the direction of the kitchen but remained curious from the next room.

I told your father that I was taking you shopping for the day, which was unusual, but thankfully he did not ask why. I questioned myself during the entire drive, looking at your smiling face in the rearview mirror, but I needed answers in order to help you.

When the psychologist asked me why we were there, I did not know how to explain, so I just handed him the videotape. With you sitting in my lap, we watched the video together. The psychologist was just as astonished and confused as I was, asking a lot of questions I didn't know how to answer. I saw the way he looked at you and it scared me. He asked to keep the videotape to show his colleagues. He wanted to hospitalize you so that they could run tests on you. I was never going to let them make a guinea pig out of you, so I grabbed the videotape, left, and never went back. I hope you now understand that this was why I never wanted you to see another therapist.

Jules tossed the letter on the table and looked away from it. She pushed the chair back, physically distancing herself from the gut-punching revelation that her mother had kept something of such apparent significance, that she had secretly taken her to a psychologist. *What could it be?* Jules could barely make herself pick it back up to find out. Jules slowly reached for the letter as if it were a snake that was about to bite her.

I hope you can forgive me if that was the wrong decision. I have second-guessed myself many times over the years, especially after what happened at Christmas. I am so sorry, Jules. I now see that my keeping this from you has led to a lifetime of questions. I have kept the videotape in the back of my sewing drawer under a stack of fabric, knowing that no one would find it there. I hope it gives you some answers. Please forgive me.
Mother

Jules stared at the letter in shock, trying to comprehend what her mother was telling her. She was not sure at all if she wanted to watch whatever was on that videotape.

When Will saw Jules get up, he followed her into her mother's sewing room. He watched as she dug her hand down into the deep drawer, searching until she felt it.

"What's that?" Will asked.

"I have no idea. I guess we're about to find out. Here, you can read it," the letter was shaking as she handed it to him. He read it while she loaded the VHS cassette into the player.

"What in the world?" Will sat down on the couch, leaning forward in anticipation.

"I know, this is crazy. I'm honestly scared to watch it." Without thinking about what she was doing, Jules sat down close to her husband for comfort. She bit her nails, as anxious as she'd ever been in her life.

Together, they watched the short clip of three-year-old Jules sitting on a toilet. Her eyes were glazed over, yet very intent. Though her eyes were open, it was clear that she wasn't seeing her mother at all, rather something in her mind. She was speaking with urgency, her voice deeper and more mature than that of a three-year-old. It was a shocking thing to watch. It was not simply the ramblings of a toddler talking in her sleep.

Will and Jules looked at each other, eyebrows raised, mouths agape as confused looks overtook their faces. Jules shivered and wiped away chill bumps from her arms.

"What the…?"

"I know! She said I did this a lot! What is that? What was I saying?"

Jules and Will both moved onto their knees. "I don't know. Turn it up." They watched the video again and again, moving closer to the television with each rewind.

Jules turned the volume even higher and concentrated on her three-year-old lips, mouthing the words as she listened.

Then suddenly, Jules gasped and slammed her hand over her heart.

"What is it, Jules?"

"Will, I…I think I was speaking French."

"What? Are you sure? I didn't hear that." This time he pushed the rewind button.

As they watched it again, Jules explained what she heard. "It's hard to make out but it sounds like I'm saying, 'mon Dieu' and 'les enfants' and something else I can't understand."

Will asked, "Maybe. I can't tell but what does that mean?"

Jules' voice cracked, "My God…the children?"

They sat in silence, their minds searching to understand.

Will watched Jules as she played it over and over, with a look on his face that suggested he was not at all convinced that he was hearing what she thought she heard. "Are you sure?" Will asked sheepishly.

"Look, Will. There's no need for you to stay. We aren't going to figure this thing out tonight. You can go home."

"I brought my things to spend the night."

"Thanks, but that's not necessary." She absentmindedly waved him off, still looking in the direction of the television.

"I understand, but unless you insist otherwise, I'll sleep in your brothers' room. I won't bother you, but I'll be here if you need me, and I can take you to the hospital in the morning."

"Fine." She didn't look up as she, once again, pushed rewind.

Will washed up the dishes before retrieving his bag from the car then stood, curiously watching his wife before walking down the hallway to the bedroom.

Play…pause…rewind, she pushed repeatedly, trying desperately to be certain of what she thought she was hearing. Her words were slurred and muddy, but she believed she heard, "mon Dieu" and "les enfants." But there was something else she couldn't understand. She mouthed the sounds, "aw-ee." She couldn't think of a French word that sounded anything like what she heard. After watching a few more times, she resigned herself to the fact that she would never fully be sure. She sat in the recliner, staring at the frozen image of her three-year-old self. She was convinced that she was speaking French. Or was she? But how could she have been? She had not learned to speak French until college.

Maybe the nurse is right about me. Maybe I do see things I want to see and hear things I want to hear.

30

Joëlle
Bordeaux, France 1685

Back in Bordeaux, life was not as Joëlle had hoped. Though her mother tried her best to make life as it was before, it was clear to both Joëlle and Henri that she was keeping them from their father. He was no longer there for family meals. The only time they saw him was for their nightly Bible reading and prayers. But even that had changed. There was no longer a poetry reading or family singing. When Joëlle worked up the nerve to ask why things seemed different, her father simply said, "The world has changed. It is time to grow up a bit." Joëlle wanted to grow up, but his words seemed ominous.

After being back in Bordeaux for several weeks with no mention of the promised dance lessons, Joëlle's limited patience had run out. "Mother, when will my dance lessons start? I want to be ready for the Christmas party this year."

"I'm sorry, ma chèrie, but there won't be a party this year." Marguerite knew she was disappointing her daughter.

Joëlle did not bother to ask why anymore. That alone broke her mother's heart.

Joëlle and Henri were no longer allowed to visit their father in the cooperage. There were no shopping trips with their mother. Their father had uncharacteristically taken over shopping for only the essentials. They no longer attended Mass, much to the dismay of her paternal grandparents.

The biggest change of all was that they no longer attended school with their Catholic friends. Her father and a few men had quietly started a small school of sorts in a cellar room of the Protestant church. Their mother now walked them to school every day. There was only one teacher for a dozen students, ranging in age from six to sixteen. Joëlle and Henri were happy to at least be in class together. It went without saying that they were not allowed any activities after school.

Though their lives were much changed, Marguerite made sure their home was a happy one. She kept the children busy with music and painting lessons inside their home. Joëlle preferred music, but it was Henri who had inherited his mother's artistic talent. He excelled in it and was proud that he could finally do something better than his big sister. While Henri painted, Joëlle began writing her thoughts in a discarded notebook she had found in her father's study. She felt she could no longer share them with anyone, not even Henri. She did not want him to feel the dread that now never left her.

Time passed slowly after returning home to Bordeaux, but finally Christmas arrived.

Joëlle had known not to expect a party and had come to accept that there would likely be no presents either this year.

"No presents?" Henri questioned.

"Père Noël has more things to worry about this year." Joëlle chimed in before her mother had time to answer.

"Are we at least going to Christmas Mass, Maman?" Henri continued.

"No, I am afraid not. But we will celebrate Christmas, here at home, with each other. Your father and I have planned a special dinner and gifts."

"Gifts?" Joëlle and Henri's spirits rose.

"Yes, of course, there will be gifts. It's Christmas!"

For the first time in months, life seemed familiar. Father was relaxed as he read the Christmas story from Luke 2. Mother happily played Christmas tunes on the piano while the family sang along. The children went to bed filled with the Christmas spirit that their parents had purposefully gifted them. After Joëlle and Henri had gone to bed, Marguerite cried in her husband's arms, knowing how temporary it might be.

Christmas morning Henri opened his gift first. He tore open the wrapping to find an easel, a pallet and brushes. "I cannot wait to use these. Thank you, Maman, PaPa."

Before Joëlle opened her gift, Marguerite explained, "Your father and I have noticed that you are growing into quite a young lady. I hope you are not disappointed that you're not getting a toy this year."

Joëlle was thrilled when she opened a velvet box containing a gold locket. "Thank you, Maman! Thank you, PaPa. I love it. I may never take it off," she said as her mother fastened the clasp beneath her held up hair.

PaPa handed her an unwrapped present, "It's a journal that I picked out for you. You not only have a strong will, young lady, but an equally strong mind. I thought you might like to write down your many thoughts."

"I will, starting today! Thank you for making this Christmas special, Maman, Papa."

They spent the afternoon with her grandparents De la Croix, just as they did every year. Christmas Day seemed just as it ever was.

After dressing for bed, Joëlle stooped down and pulled Grand-mere's box that she'd taken from Baran from its hiding place. She took the string of doorbells from it and slid under the covers with them. She shook them gently under the covers, as she had done every night since she'd been back in Bordeaux. She clutched them to her chest with her left hand and with her right, she wrote the first line in her new journal, *'I miss the sound of doorbells.'*

31

Jules

Midway, Kentucky

Jules woke up early, eager to get to the hospital but first checked her email from her bed. She was glad to see that Chloe had arrived safely in Paris, had settled into the apartment, and experienced a great first day with the students.

The class sends their well wishes to your mother. They said to tell you that you made the class fun.

Jules smiled at their kindness and was genuinely happy that her friend was also getting to have this experience. Jules sent her reply,

Mother is making progress, but with her in this critical state, I have not addressed what you saw with Will yet. I want to know every detail about your daily life just as I did for you. I can't wait to see Paris through your eyes.

Jules walked into the unusually quiet kitchen, and wished her mother were here cooking for the family. The last time she had seen her in this kitchen was at Christmas. The sting of the memory filled her with regret but using the coping skill she had learned from Dr. LaRoche, she mentally tore up the hurtful memory and symbolically tossed it into the Seine.

Jules retrieved the ingredients out of the old refrigerator that had once belonged to her grandparents. She thought about how practical farm life was. Nothing was wasted, not even a sixty-year-old refrigerator.

Jules savored this time, cooking in her mother's kitchen. It was a comfort to use her mother's black iron skillet. While the bacon sizzled, she looked out the kitchen window at the lovely farm. She knew it would not have been beautiful in everyone's eyes. There were pieces of seldom used farm equipment scattered everywhere with grass growing tall around and under them. The century old barn had a rusty roof with warped boards pulling away on the west side. Jules pictured herself inside the barn, in its better days, grooming Honey and smiled at the memory.

When she heard Will coming down the hall, she took the biscuits from the oven and set them aside to cool while she scrambled the eggs. She and Will never ate like this at home, but granola did not belong in this country kitchen.

"Hope you were able to sleep. Did you figure anything out about the video?" Will asked while pouring himself a cup of coffee. There was a hopefulness in his voice, seeing that his wife had cooked for him.

She quickly stamped out his hope. "No and no," she answered, taking her biscuit and announcing that she was going to take a quick shower so they could leave for the hospital right away.

***

Will let Jules lead the conversation on the drive to the hospital. "I tossed and turned all night with questions. Did Mom know what I was saying? Did she think I was speaking French? Did the therapist? How long did I do that? What other things are there that I need to know?"

Just as they were pulling into the parking lot, her phone rang. Jules looked to see that it was her father. Her heart sank. "Dad?" Her voice was barely audible.

He did not know they had just arrived, "Jules, honey, I hate to tell you this but your mother…" There was a moment of silence before she heard her father's broken voice, "She's gone."

"No! Oh, Daddy," Jules dropped the phone and ran from the car.

She didn't wait for Will as she ran to the elevator. She fidgeted nervously until the doors opened. She rushed inside and pushed the third-floor button before the people inside the elevator could exit. They looked at her with sympathy, seeing her urgency and the tears streaming down her face.

When the elevator doors opened, her father was standing there with Jasper and James. Jules fell into her daddy's arms then felt her brothers' arms tight around them. "Can I see her?"

Jasper went to ask at the nurses' station.

Jules walked into her mother's room, her father and her brothers trailed behind. She noticed the silence. There was no noise, no beeping, no clicking. All the machines had been turned off. She laid her head on her mother's chest and cried, her father's hand upon her back. This happened too fast. Jules was not ready to lose her mother.

"May I have a moment alone?" Jules asked.

After the men left the room, Jules touched her mother's face. "I'm sorry, Mother. I am so sorry for everything. I read your letter and there is nothing to forgive you for. I found the video," she paused, broken. "What did you know, Mother? What does it mean?"

32

Jules
Lexington, Kentucky

Will was standing with her family outside her mother's hospital room. Joseph informed them that they would not be able to meet with the funeral home until the following day and that he wanted to go back to the farm to be by himself for a while.

Jules understood her father's need to be alone. "Of course, but promise you'll call me if you need anything at all." Joseph nodded an agreement. The family said their broken-hearted goodbyes, realizing that their lives were forever changed.

Jules turned to her husband, "Will, could you take me home?"

"Of course." He put his arm around her waist and together, they walked out of the hospital.

Jules stared out the window, speechless, on the sad drive home.

***

Jules barely recognized the house when they turned into the driveway. The red brick had been painted with a fresh coat of alabaster. Will had added new shutters and a flower box under the double window, which he had planted with crimson geraniums and trailing vinca vines.

"It's lovely, Will. Thank you. This must have taken forever," she said emotionlessly.

"I had a lot of free time."

Will's words unintentionally stung. *What else did you do with your free time?* The thought went through her head, but today she simply could not bring herself to care.

Jules was drained and wanted to sleep away her heartache but when she walked back to the bedroom, she realized that her luggage was still at the farm.

Outside the kitchen, she heard Will calling from the deck, "Okay, it's ready." He had turned on the string lights and opened the umbrella.

Jules could not believe her eyes when she walked out the kitchen door. Not only was the deck built, but it was also stained and finished. He had added built-in seating with tall corner posts that held dangling party lights. He had purchased a round patio table and chairs with an umbrella that matched the shutters. He had even scattered potted plants around the space. "I can't believe you did all this. I love it, Will." She hugged him, which made her weep again, thinking about what she had just lost and what she was about to lose.

"You sit here and enjoy our new spot. I'll pour us a drink."

By the time he came back with the drinks, Jules had decided that there would never be a good time to talk to him about her conversation with Chloe and she was tired of holding her feelings in.

"Will, first of all, I don't want to argue. I…I can't. But I must get this off my chest so we can move on." She paused, then added, "Whatever that means." She took a sip of her iced tea to brace herself for the bridge she was about to cross. "You asked me over the phone what I know. Well, I'm just going to say it. Right before you called me in Paris to tell me about Mom's second stroke, Chloe had called me. She hated to be the one to tell me, but she felt guilty for keeping it from me. Will, she saw you with Laura."

Will sat stunned, trying to process what Jules was insinuating.

"When she first saw the two of you, she thought nothing of it. But when she walked closer to say 'hello,' she could tell that you were having an intimate conversation with her." Jules put her face in her hands and sobbed.

"She misunderstood what she saw."

"Stop, Will. Let me finish. I know I have not been a perfect wife. I know now that I should have never accepted the position in France. Maybe I was running away from something I couldn't face."

"What are you talking about, Jules?"

"That you'd be better off without me," she couldn't look at her husband.

"No, Jules. Don't be ridiculous."

"I just thought you should know that I know, but I cannot begin to process this right now. Can we wait until after the funeral to talk about how to move forward? Please, Will."

"No, Jules. You have to know the truth. Chloe was wrong about what she saw. Let me explain." He reached for her hand, but she drew it to her chest to protect her heart. "Laura came to me back in the fall. She needed a friend. We work together every day, and she knew she was going to need my help over the next few months."

Jules interrupted, "What could she be going through that she needed *my* husband. Why couldn't she go to her own?"

"Because he is dying, Jules. He has stage four pancreatic cancer. Laura asked me not to tell anyone because she didn't want it to get out before she could tell their daughters. I hated keeping it from you. I'm sorry, I should have told you."

Jules sat frozen, taking a moment to process what Will had just told her. This changed everything she'd been feeling toward Will for the last few days. In fact, it made her love him even more. She closed her eyes as they began to tear again. She felt guilty for how she had felt about Laura and sick for what she must be going through. And worst of all, she felt like a fool for assuming the worst in her husband.

Will continued, "He doesn't have much longer, and she finally had to tell her girls. They knew he was sick, but they didn't know how bad it was. She wanted to meet with me at the park that day to discuss how she should tell them. They are so young, and she doesn't have any family. That is all it was, Jules. That is the only time I ever saw her outside of school. I am sorry you had to go through this, especially now."

Jules got up and sat in his lap. "Oh, Will. I hurt for Laura. Their poor children, what will they do?"

"I don't know. I haven't known what to say or how to help her, except to just be there to listen."

"I am sure you've been more help than you know. You are such a wonderful man. How could I have ever believed that of you? Please forgive me, Will."

"There's nothing to forgive you for. You were going through something very difficult, and Chloe misread the situation. Let's forget it ever happened. I am just happy to have you home and back in my arms."

33

Jules
Midway, Kentucky

Will and Jules stayed at the farm for the next couple of days to help Joseph with funeral planning and preparations. Jules had intended to cook for the family but instead found herself managing the incoming food brought in by neighbors and the church family. Dish after dish arrived, delivered by the hands that prepared them. Vegetable casseroles, meat casseroles, pots of fresh-out-of-the-garden green beans and fried corn. The homemade breads smelled as good as the fruit pies and tiered cakes. Pitchers of sweet tea and fresh squeezed lemonade lined the countertops. Each of these people had taken the time and effort to prepare food for a hurting family. *How lovely*, Jules thought. *I wish Mother could be here to see this*, but then realized that her mother had not only seen it but had most likely participated in this thoughtful farming community tradition.

When she wasn't in the kitchen, Jules walked through the house, room by room, seeing it with fresh eyes. She had been young and immature when she left home for college at the age of eighteen. She and Will had gotten married only a few weeks after graduation. When she had come home for holidays, the house was filled with siblings, spouses, and excited children. For the first time in her life, Jules was noticing how her mother had made the old farmhouse a home.

She saw the things that had been important to her. They were literally hanging on the walls. Room after room, family pictures hung in mismatched frames or were simply tacked into the walls, gallery style. The oldest photos were in the center and Jules could see that with each passing year, her mother simply added new ones to the ever-expanding collection. She hadn't bothered to rearrange them. She never rearranged anything.

The house had remained unchanged for as long as Jules could remember. There wasn't a new piece of furniture in the house. Most of the pieces had been handed down. She thought about how these things, this farm, represented the continuation of life. Generation after generation had lived similar lives on this same piece of land. A tinge of regret hit her when she again realized that the line would not continue with her, but she was thankful that it would go on through her brothers' families. They would keep the family traditions. They would tell the family stories.

 She replayed in her mind the story told over and over by her grandfather of the Jackson Press. He loved to tell about how he and his brother had pulled the piece in disrepair out of an abandoned house and how his brother had complained about it with every step. Her grandfather had been so proud of how the restoration had turned out and never let his brother forget it. As she exited the room, she ran her hand across his smooth finish, past and present connected.

Jules had washed a load of her father's clothes and when she opened the dryer, she found a load of laundry that had been inside for weeks. A wave of grief once again rolled over her as she pulled out her mother's everyday dresses. She sat in the floor of the laundry room and sobbed, holding them tight to her chest.

Later that evening, Jules asked her father if she could have one of the dresses and one of the necklaces her mother had made.

"Take them all, honey. Your mother would love for you to have them."

Jules picked a favorite necklace for herself and laid it on top of her dress for the funeral. She let Nichole, Scarlette, and Ivy each pick a favorite piece. She even saved one back for Caroline to have one day. It made her sad to think that little Caroline would not remember her grandmother. Before she closed the jewelry box, Jules decided to bury Lillie wearing her grandmother's pearls. They had meant so much to her.

***

The funeral for Lillie James Laurent was simple and beautiful. *Just like Mom*, Jules thought. She was buried in the ancient cemetery behind the church. After everyone left, Jules asked Will to wait in the car while she went back to place a rose on her mother's casket. "Until I see you again."

***

On the drive back to the farm, Will asked, "Who were those two women that you were talking to, the ones about our age?"

Jules had been surprised to see two of her best friends from elementary school. At least, they had been her friends up until the middle school incident. They had barely spoken to her in high school. But Jules thought it was sweet of them to come and took it as an apology, thanks to Dr. LaRoche. In this moment, she was glad she had not sent them one of her therapy letters. "Just some old friends," is all she said.

***

When they arrived back at the farm, the rest of the family was already seated at the table. Members of the church had cooked and were serving the family a hot meal. As they ate together, the family wanted to know about Jules' trip. She told them all about the cheeses and chocolates, the artists and the antiques and the churches. She went on and on, describing the churches in elaborate detail.

While the others cleaned up, Joseph asked his family to come into the living room. He wanted each of them to tell a cherished memory of Lillie and asked Jules to write them down so that he would never forget. They took turns as one memory led to another. They cried a little but laughed a lot. The grandsons grew tired of all the talking and went outside to play. Ivy took Caroline's hand and followed the boys. Joseph was glad for the time alone with Jasper, James and Jules. He wanted to tell them about something special that Lillie had done for them.

Joseph explained that during her time in the hospital after the first stroke, Lillie had asked him to do something for her. Joseph told them about the inheritance that she had received years earlier from her parents' estate and that together, they had agreed to put the money into savings for their children since they already had everything they needed. "This is a final gift from your mother." Joseph walked around and handed each of his three children an envelope. There were separate envelopes for each of the grandchildren which he handed to Jasper and James. No one chose to open their envelopes there.

After James and Jasper had packed up their families and left, Jules asked her father, "Would you like for Will and me to stay a few more nights? We'd be happy to."

"No, no. You have been gone from home for far too long and I'll be fine. How could I feel alone in a house so full of memories?"

***

After a hot bath, Jules crawled into bed. She stared at the envelope and paused to think about what might be inside before she opened it. She hoped it might contain another letter explaining more about the video but there was only a note written by her father that read, *From Mother. She loves you.* Jules was disappointed, but realized her father had written it after the second stroke when he knew that his wife was not coming home. Behind the note was a folded check. When she opened it, her jaw dropped in surprise. She thought about the postcards on the wall and could now see that her mother certainly could have afforded to go any place she had wanted to. She could have bought new furniture and replaced the ancient refrigerator. But she had *chosen* not to spend it. Her mother had wanted to be with her husband on the farm more. She had wanted to share this gift with her children even more. Jules grieved for a while, holding her mother's sacrifice to her chest, before going to tell Will.

She found him in the office going through a stack of mail that had piled up after a few days away. "Would you like to go to France as we had planned?" she asked, waving the check in the air.

"You want to go back? Yes, of course, I do!"

"Paris, it is then."

"How would you feel about Bordeaux?" he asked, waving a paper of his own.

Will filled Jules in on the details of the research he had been doing on her genealogy during the time she'd been away. It had taken him weeks of working late into the night to go through it all. He handed her a computer printout that he had made of her lineage, starting with Jules, then her father, Joseph and so on, all the way back for twelve generations to France in the early 1600s. He told her how they had come to be in America. It had not been by choice. Will told her that her ancestors had been forced to leave France, just after the Edict of Nantes was revoked by King Louis XIV. Jules' ancestors were Protestants who had chosen to flee to London and were later sent to colonize America.

"Huguenots? My ancestors were Huguenots?"

Jules listened intently as Will detailed her family's life in London and their harrowing journey to Virginia, which had taken thirteen weeks at sea. He told her that they had to make their own roads along the James River to get to their granted lands and how the French and Native Americans had lived side by side in harmony. He explained the conditions of poverty that they had to live in after living a prosperous life in Bordeaux. He showed her a copy of a letter written back to England, reporting on the French settlers' progress, stating that the French were "poor, but happy."

He went on to tell her how her family had been tobacco farmers for over three hundred years. He described their American journey and how they came to be in Kentucky. Jules listened in awe to all the information he had discovered.

Then he told her that he had located a Huguenot Museum in North Carolina and that he had written to inquire if they had any information on Jules' family. The museum had responded that it was not likely that they would have any specific information on her family, but that they would continue their search.

When Will finished, Jules thanked him and for the first time in months, she kissed her husband goodnight. "Will you make the travel plans? I think I am going to sleep for days."

34

Jules
Lexington, Kentucky

Will planned every detail of their trip to France, occasionally calling on Jules for her travel experience. He scheduled their trip for a week after the funeral, allowing Jules to spend more time with her father, helping him to adjust to his new life alone on the farm. Jules used the week to give the farmhouse a thorough cleaning while Will prepared freezer meals for Joseph to eat while they were away. Jules gathered her mother's personal items from around the house and placed them in her sewing room. She was not ready to part with them yet but wanted them out of sight so her father wouldn't have to see them at every turn. Both of her brothers lived close by and were on the farm daily, so Jules felt comfortable leaving her father while she and Will took their long-awaited honeymoon.

***

After the week of preparations at the farm, Jules was happy to be going back to France. She was excited to show Will her home away from home and to give him a glimpse into her French world.

Chloe met them at Charles De Gaulle airport when they landed. The friends were happy to be together, although it felt strange to see each other somewhere other than campus. When they exchanged hugs, Chloe said to Will, "I want to personally apologize…"

He stopped her, "There's no need. I'm happy she has a friend that looks out for her."

In the car, Chloe filled Jules in on the students' progress. Will smiled, listening to them move seamlessly between English and French. The taxi dropped the three of them off at the Haussman-style hotel that Will had booked for the night. Jules pointed out its mansard roof. "You're going to see a lot of these."

They placed their luggage in the tiny room then walked the short distance to the university's apartment. Jules was almost giddy as she pulled her husband down the sidewalk toward her home in Paris. As they approached the building, Chloe told Jules, "You're in for a big surprise."

When they got into the glass elevator, Jules saw what Chloe was referring to. Every balcony, all forty-eight of them, was overflowing with flowers. Jules laughed aloud at the most satisfying sight.

She gave Will the five-minute tour of the apartment, then the three of them stood out on the street balcony catching up over the sounds of honking horns and flittering Parisians.

"Do you mind if I pick the restaurant for dinner tonight?" Jules asked Chloe.

"Of course not."

"La Pluie?" I can't wait to take Will there. I've missed it."

"Perfect. I eat there all the time but have not gotten tired of it yet and I don't suspect I will anytime soon."

***

They arrived for their early dinner and Jules requested her favorite table in the raised area at the back of the restaurant. She would never tire of watching the way Parisians celebrate every meal. Over dinner, Jules subconsciously noticed that the service had been excellent and the waiter especially attentive. After they had eaten their meal and had dessert, the restaurant manager, in lieu of the waiter, delivered a tray of four *cafés*. "Do you mind if I join?" he asked in his deep voice and thick French accent. Jules and Will looked momentarily confused when he sat down beside Chloe and planted a soft kiss on her cheek. Chloe smiled slyly then introduced him to her American friends. When the men were talking, Chloe leaned in close to Jules and whispered in her ear, "I told you I'd find myself a Frenchman." While they savored their *cafés*, Jules and Chloe made plans for the places they wanted to show Will when they returned to Paris from Bordeaux. They made an early evening of it as the Merritts had to catch the sunrise train to Bordeaux.

***

During the high-speed train ride from Paris to Bordeaux, Will and Jules were awed by the unending hillside vineyards with row after row of staked vines. They imagined aloud how this harvest of plump grapes would one day be wine in someone's glass, perhaps their own. "There was nothing like this in Paris. I'm happy we get to experience the countryside of France together," Jules said, taking his hand in hers.

After the train ride into Bordeaux, they took a taxi to the boutique hotel Will had reserved for them on the outskirts of the city. The hotel sat at the end of a long gravel drive which was lined with grapevines from horizon to horizon. The lane ended at the circular driveway to the vineyard *château*. They were greeted by a teenage boy with curled up hair sticking out from under a worn, maroon bellhop's cap. He was still tucking in his shirt as he reached for their luggage. As soon as the young man closed the trunk, the driver of the taxi sped off, hurling a plume of dust at the three of them. Monsieur Fenelon, the proprietor of the hotel, came running from the side of the building, shaking his fist in the air and cursing insults in French toward the taxi. He dusted off his clothes, while introducing himself and apologizing to his guests. M. Fenelon guided them inside to check them in then instructed his son to take the Merritt's luggage up the staircase to their suite.

After they were settled, the hotel's driver took them back into Bordeaux for their early afternoon appointment with a professional genealogist, Monsieur Robert Cellier, whom Will had hired to search through various government archives, libraries, and church records that might provide additional information about Jules' ancestors.

After exchanging pleasantries, M. Cellier got straight to his findings. He handed Will a copy of the research report that he had compiled and explained to them that Protestant church records, which would have been a more detailed source of births, marriages, and deaths, had been destroyed in fires during the religious wars and therefore, he was unable to provide any information prior to 1600. "I also searched the archives of the city of Bordeaux and found some interesting information about Mme Merritt's nine times great-grandfather, Louis Guy Reynaud, III." He handed Will a copy of the record he had located. "M. Reynaud owned a cooperage in the city center of Bordeaux from 1672 until the time that he sold it to a Catholic vineyard owner from London in 1686. The fact that he owned a cooperage in the city of Bordeaux during a time of great wine expansion, probably meant he was wealthy, which most likely facilitated your ancestors' escape out of France. Many others would not have been so lucky."

"Do you have any information about the specific location of the cooperage or where they lived?" Will asked.

"It is in an area that has greatly changed and of course is no longer there. But I will be happy to show you the location." He motioned them to a large map on the wall of his office. He placed one finger on the map to indicate where his office was located then ran it along the path to where the cooperage had been located centuries before.

"Merci, Monsieur," Will and Jules said in unison, appreciative of his efforts.

"There is one more piece of information that I came across. It seems that M. Reynaud inherited property from his father, in the Dordogne region. I do have the address of that property.

If you are going to be here for a length of time, I would highly recommend visiting the area. It is a two-hour drive by car, but I can assure you it will be worth your time. The area is full of rivers, and therefore is overflowing with castles. My family and I often spend our holidays in the region. It is not a tourist location. It is quiet and lovely, the opposite of Paris, I am afraid."

"We would actually love that." Jules added, looking at Will for confirmation.

After the appointment, the Merritts walked the streets of Bordeaux trying to find the location of the cooperage, though there was no way to be sure.

As they sat on a nearby bench trying to imagine life during those times, Jules noticed the clock and realized that it was just a couple of minutes until two o'clock, when French restaurants close until dinner. They dashed into a nearby boulangerie, which had only one sandwich left. They shared it back and forth standing near the bridge over the river, Garonne.

Before heading back to the hotel, Will rented a sporty Peugeot for the next day's adventure.

35

Jules
Bordeaux, France

Will was smiling his toothy grin when they pulled off the main road onto the vineyard property. "What's that about?" Jules asked.

"I guess I'm falling in love with France, too." Will said convincingly, reaching for her hand. Jules looked at her husband with a loving smile.

"That, and I *love* driving this car!"

"Will!" She snickered and flicked his hand.

"Seriously, though, France is a special place. It seems like we're in another world."

When they entered the hotel, M. Fenelon informed them that dinner would be served at 8pm.

***

After dressing for dinner, the Merritts descended the spiral stairs. The Fenelon's daughter greeted them and led them outside to a terrace that ran the length of the hotel. They were seated under a wide umbrella at a table for eight.

Will and Jules were offered an aperitif but were not given a menu. Soon, other hotel guests began filling the terrace and eventually their table. As each of the couples were seated, they ordered drinks then turned their chairs toward the vineyard. Will and Jules followed their lead while questioning each other with their eyes. Their confusion was short lived as the focus on the grapes rose upward to the colorful play the sun began to perform for them. As they sipped their drinks, the gorgeous blues turned to ever intensifying pinks, marbled with streaks of vibrant orange. Slow swirling clouds moved in recognizable shapes along the horizon. As the guests were served more drinks, the *oohs* and *aahs* became more exaggerated. Then everyone became suddenly quiet as the sun made its descent, sinking slowly into the vines.

When the last sliver of the glowing orb disappeared, the guests broke into applause, then noisily moved their chairs back to the table. The staff, dressed in white shirts and black slacks, left the line where they had stood together, hands behind their backs as part of the nightly ceremony. They lit gaslights and a myriad of tiered candles on the tables. While Will and Jules were getting to know the other guests seated at their table, couples from Australia, England, and California, they were served course after course of beautifully plated, delicious seasonal foods.

Will and Jules politely excused themselves after more than two hours of lively conversation, dinner, dessert, and coffees. The Merritts had expected to have a great dinner in the hotel, but what they experienced was so much more.

***

The Merritts woke with the sun, eager to begin the day's journey. As they drove, they passed vineyard after vineyard, many with posted signs offering vineyard tours.

"Should we?" Will asked Jules, knowing this an important day for her.

"Yes, I'd love to. We have all day."

They stopped at the next vineyard along the route but found that they had arrived too early for a tour. The owner was already outside working and was kind enough to allow them to walk around the property on their own. He kept his eye on them as he readied the tractor and wagon for the day's vineyard tours. When he noticed them walking toward their car, he motioned them into a large barn that had a display of the chateau's wines sitting on top of upright oak barrels. He led them to a small tasting station and poured a sample for them, even though the day had barely begun. Will asked the vineyard owner to recommend a couple of wines. Since they would be in France for another week, they purchased a box set for themselves and another for Chloe.

***

On the two-hour drive away from the city, Will and Jules watched through the open car windows as wine country turned slowly into castle country. "M. Cellier didn't exaggerate the number of castles we'd pass." There seemed to be a centuries old *château* around every bend. "I wish we'd kept a count."

The sputtering Peugeot carried them along lush green valleys, hugging the meandering curves of the riverbank. Then narrow roads sent them skyward, winding up steep hillsides that provided grand vistas of the grid-like farmlands below. The fields and their tree-lined fence rows were so perfectly laid out, they were surely designed to please the birds and God, Himself.

The GPS eventually led them to a gravel road, marked only by a small wooden plank attached to a stake which was nearly hidden in the weeds left unmown on the side of the road. The make-shift sign read simply 'Baran.'

"I can't believe we're really here." Jules said as they made the turn onto a one lane, crumbling paved road that wound around climbing its way to a plateaued summit. At the top, they came to a small hamlet of around a dozen homes that radiated out from a circular graveled courtyard. An olive tree stood in its center, protected by a half stone wall that surrounded it. Chickens and cats wandered everywhere. The entire hamlet appeared ancient.

"It must have looked this way for centuries," Jules remarked after they parked the Peugeot in the courtyard.

The homes were built with honey-colored stones that changed with the light. Faded blue shutters sat ready to protect wavy glassed windows that opened outward. Smaller windows were guarded by forged iron bars. Stone drains poured water into gravel pathways, creating a soothing trickle. Each of the houses had a barn behind with sloping fields that encircled the picturesque hamlet. Colorfully painted, but sun-bleached iron gates separated yards from fields, while tall stone walls separated neighbor from neighbor.

"You're right. It feels like we've stepped back in time," Will agreed.

The doorways were surrounded by climbing roses or trailing grapevines. Overflowing flower boxes sat on stone stoops everywhere.

"Listen," Jules said, lifting her eyes, "I've never heard so many birds singing. They must know how lucky they are to live here."

Jules supposed that most of the homes had been passed down through the generations and wondered if everyone in the hamlet knew everyone else. She imagined they knew intimate details of each other's lives. She hoped they deeply cared for one another. *What a beautiful way to live,* she thought, letting herself believe it.

From behind them, a man called, "Puis-je vous aider?"

"Oui, monsieur. Merci."

Will smiled, watching his wife converse in French with the old man. She was clearly in her element. Jules handed the helpful gentleman the address of her ancestors' home. Though Will could not understand what the man was saying, he watched Jules' face light up. The gentleman pointed then motioned for them to follow him.

"It is still here, Will! The house is still standing."

They followed him down a narrow lane, the three of them crunching gravel underfoot. When they reached the *maison,* the man jiggled a string of rusty doorbells. Each new sound was a delight.

A flood of peace waved over Jules as she studied this quaint home of her ancestors. The grapevine trailed the trellis along the front of the yellowed limestone. A discolored streak of gray fell to the gravel underneath an ancient stone sink drain. Moss grew here and there on the chipped stone steps which held mismatched pots of flowers in varying sizes. These worn details were lovely in Jules' eyes.

A middle-aged woman, wearing a tattered dress and a well-worn apron, rested her arms on the half-opened Dutch door.

"Bonjour," the neighbors happily sang to each other.

Jules sang it, too. Will nodded and smiled.

The gentleman made the introductions in French, explaining that Mme Merritt's ancestors had once lived in the home.

"Enchanté." Mme Bisset and Jules greeted each other.

Jules asked in French if the woman spoke English, and Will smiled with comprehension when she answered, "Oui, madame, I do."

Madame Bisset kindly invited them into her home, explaining in broken English that she knew little of the house's history, other than it was nearly four-hundred years old.

"I wonder if my ancestors may have built it."

Mme Bisset told them that the small pebbles that made up the patterned floor of the kitchen were one of the many details original to the house.

Jules realized that her ancestors had walked on these very stones. She stooped down to run her fingers across their worn-smooth surface. Again, past and present connected.

Mme Bisset explained that when she and her husband purchased the home forty years before, the bathroom had then been a chicken coop. Though the house had been updated with necessary conveniences, it still retained its historical beauty. The fireplace opening was tall enough to walk into, its mantle blackened with centuries of smoke. Rough-hewn beams held up the low ceiling. The stone steps of the staircase were dipped from hundreds of years of use.

In the kitchen, a multitude of cutting boards were stacked on the kitchen counter. An exposed wooden slat ran the length of the kitchen wall with cast iron cookware in varying shapes and sizes hanging from it on rusty nails.

Though the windows did not have screens, they were left open, letting the melodies of the birds float through the house with the breeze.

After touring the inside of the house, Mme Bisset asked, "Would you like to see the garden?"

"We would, if we aren't taking up too much of your time."

She led them out the glass door through the back yard to the barn which was built from the same golden stones as the house and had an attached rustic covered porch that looked out across the farmer's fields.

Mme Bisset spoke in hushed tones as she told them that silence was revered in their tiny village. "Would you like to go inside?"

"Oui, merci," Jules explained that she had grown up on a farm and loved playing in the barn as a child.

Mme Bisset used her strength to lift and open one side of the faded wooden door. Will and Jules walked into the dark space to find it surprisingly barren. There were only a few stacks of lumber, stones and roofing tiles. Will walked deeper into the space to peer around a walled opening where he noticed a gathering of old barrels with a small pile of junk on top.

"May I?" He asked Mme Bisset, who nodded her approval.

"What's this?" Will picked up a frame that held a colorful landscape painting. He blew off the dust and turned it toward the sunshine streaming in from the opened door. "What a beautiful work of art! Just look at the light painted on the flowers!" He spun it around to show Jules. "It's practically glowing."

"And those roses! So many gorgeous roses." Jules walked over to take a closer look.

"You may have it if you like," Mme Bisset generously offered.

"We couldn't possibly. Will is an oil landscape painter and it simply caught his eye."

"I insist. It came with the house, and I have no need of it."

"We would love to have it then if you're sure." Jules watched Will run his finger across the signature, simply marked with a fancy cursive *M*.

"It is yours then."

"Merci. Merci infiniment!" Will and Jules looked at each other in utter surprise, not believing their luck.

An enormous tree at the edge of the yard bordered the wheat field beyond, its limbs outstretched as if to protect the property. One of the thick branches held a weathered porch swing. Jules asked Mme Bissett if she would mind if she sat in it for a moment alone.

As she sat gliding in the swing, looking toward the home of her ancestors, Jules felt the same feeling she had felt in the churches of Paris. This all seemed surreal. It felt like a dream. It felt like *her* dream. Her lineage was so far removed from France, yet she felt at home here. She stared at the house, wishing she could understand, but felt disappointed knowing that she never would.

Jules walked back toward the porch with her head down and her hands in her pockets. The remarkable tree stood in the background. Will snapped a picture of the unforgettable scene from his phone, capturing an image that he knew Jules would want to remember.

As Jules walked closer, she noticed Will listening carefully as Mme Bisset was giving her husband instructions, both shaking their heads and pointing in the same direction.

"I would like to invite you to come back for dinner this evening," Mme Bisset offered.

Jules looked questioningly at her husband. Then Will surprised them both by saying, "Oui, madame. Merci."

He took Jules' hand and pulled her toward the rental car.

"Where are we going?" Jules asked, pleased at seeing her husband giddy and carefree.

"Mme Bisset told me about a church of legend that is a special place to the local people. She said it is not often visited by tourists but that she would not want us to miss it, *since we belong here.*" He dragged out the words, causing Jules to smile from ear to ear.

"There isn't a road in. We have to walk through the woods to find it.

"Do you think we can?"

"It will be fun to try. She also said that the village is filled with meandering paths that are begging to be explored, and that people walk here without regard to property lines, which makes for a feeling of community living. Isn't that wonderful?"

"It is. Will, can you believe this day?" Jules asked while tying the laces on her walking shoes. As they walked toward the outskirts of the village, they noted aloud the quaint things they saw along the way, bedding hung from upper windows to dry, old barrels used to collect rainwater from roofs, small but full garden plots, rounded stone walls, ornate fountains on the sides of houses with watering buckets stacked underneath. Jules pointed out an old woman who was bent over picking vegetables. They watched as she placed the harvest into her upturned apron. There was no lack of charm, no matter which direction they looked.

***

Walking through tall trees and emerald-colored moss, they navigated the nearly nonexistent paths for an hour. Finally, they came out of the trees into a large meadow, filled with a sea of wildflowers.

They were admiring the sheer size of the field, scanning from left to right along the horizon when Jules stopped in her tracks and gasped.

"What is it?" Will asked. He turned to see both her hands over her heart. "Jules, what's the matter?"

It took a moment for her to be able to speak, her eyes moved back and forth as she searched her memory. "That cross. I have seen that cross before," she pointed to a tall, yellowed stone cross on a rock wall at the edge of the wood. Part of her session with Dr. LaRoche was coming back to her.

"Yes, it's wonderful, isn't it?" Will took Jules' hand that had remained on her heart and held it to continue walking but felt it shaking.

She did not budge. "Will, listen to me. There is something I haven't told you."

"What is it?" He asked, witnessing her shock and confusion. "Tell me."

"We may need to find a place to sit. There is a lot to say."

Will watched his wife staring at the cross as they walked through the clearing, leaving rippling wildflowers in their wake.

When they entered the trees on the other side of the meadow, they saw the ancient church, sitting in seclusion from the accessible world. Will turned to look at Jules when he heard her mumble. "Oh," she exhaled, her expression trance-like.

Jules noticed a door propped open at the back. As they walked along the side of the church, Will pointed out the exterior stone staircase, but Jules did not see it. She was laser-focused on the entrance to the church.

Though Jules had been moved by the churches in Paris, she became completely overwhelmed when she stood at the back entrance and looked into the one room chapel. Her knees became weak, and she doubled over and started to cry.

Will rushed to her side and lifted her. "Jules, are you okay? What is it that is making you so emotional?"

She didn't look at him. Her focus remained solely inside the church. Jules was mesmerized at how the flaxen walls cast a golden glow through the chapel. There were no electric lights inside the church, only a few distinct rays of sunlight coming from three inset lancet windows, their beams landing directly on the ancient altar. "I don't know how to explain it. It feels like I've come home, like my soul belongs here." She wiped her tears and stepped across the threshold.

Jules ran her hand along the cold walls as they walked past dark wooden pews toward the front of the church.

It seemed such a sacred place that neither of them spoke as they walked past the altar. Jules felt pulled and turned back to look at it. She ran her hand across the scripture engraved along its edge, Psalms 32:7. She committed it to memory so she could look it up later. Will watched her eyes narrow as she concentrated on it.

He followed his wife as she walked on toward a delicate three-legged metal stand. A single candle stood flickering in the pronged metal plate. A wooden box sat beside it, stacked to the top with new and previously lit tapers.

The side wall of the chapel was covered to the ceiling with marble plaques, in varying sizes, engraved with gold letters, all reading 'Merci.'

Jules' voice cracked as she broke the silence, "Will, I saw these, too."

They instantly looked up as her voice resonated through the church, up and around the barreled ceiling and back. Her echoed words were both beautiful and haunting.

Will watched his wife, deep in thought, glance her fingers over the gold letters set into the marble.

"Mrs. Bisset told me about those," Will's voice thundered through the chapel, shaking Jules out of her concentration. He quieted his voice to almost a whisper, "She said that the local people write their prayers on tiny pieces of paper and stick them in the gaps between the stones on the wall, and when their prayers are answered, they have these plaques made. The small date in the corner marks the day the prayers were answered. Isn't that an incredibly beautiful thing?"

"It is. It truly is," she said, lost in wonderment.

Past the candlestand, a partially painted statue of Mary stood in the front corner of the chapel. A tall crown, elaborately decorated with stone roses, surrounded her angelic yet modest face. She wore a flowing robe, the color of the sea. Her hands were folded in prayer and a white shawl draped her shoulders. A necklace hung around her neck, with an image of her son, Christ, on the cross. The statue defied time and beauty.

When they finished walking through the chapel, they took a seat on a bench in the back. Will had not experienced the churches in Paris as Jules had. She watched her husband as he sat mesmerized, watching the candlelight create flickering shadows of Mary on the wall.

Every sound that was made reverberated through the chapel. "I cannot imagine how beautiful singing must sound in here. It is such a special place, it feels as though God, Himself, could reside here."

"I'm certain He does," Jules said, believing it.

Jules then turned to face her husband, wrapping his hands with hers. "While I was away, I had time to think about my life. I have always tried to be the daughter my parents expected. I did my best to be the wife you deserve. But being alone in Paris, I was free to discover who *I* am, away from everyone's expectations, even my own.

"Part of what I learned, I discovered through my experiences here. Seemingly insignificant things, like taking time to enjoy the individual moments that make up a life, the smell of freshly baked bread, the joy of growing flowers, the sound of rain through an open window; these things seem to ease my anxiety.

"I found that it's okay to let myself feel things, both good and bad. I have lived such a guarded life, trying to protect my heart. I've learned so much about myself and the way I want to live my life going forward. I want to live a more authentic life, and I know you'll be surprised to hear it, but I want to live a more connected life."

Will listened, searching her eyes.

"Part of my growth was due to Dr. LaRoche, a therapist I saw just twice in Paris." Then for the first time, Jules told Will about the middle school incident that changed the course of her life.

Tears fell from his eyes, a witness that he now understood her brokenness and personally felt her hurt. It explained so much; why she had closed herself off to relationships, why she was afraid to trust potential friends with her heart and, most importantly, her precarious relationship with Lillie.

Jules explained how she had blamed her mother, and that Dr. LaRoche helped her to realize that Lillie had done the best she could, given a situation she did not know how to manage.

Will gently slid his hands out of his wife's and took them into his, showing his support.

"Dr. LaRoche encouraged me to forgive my mom and the others for my own healing. He showed me how to put it in the past. I've done that."

She went on to explain that for her to be able to fully move forward, Dr. LaRoche wanted to help her with the issue that had started the downhill spiral. "He hoped to accomplish it through hypnotherapy but after only one session, I had to go home." She told Will that it was strange that she had not remembered the hypnosis with Dr. LaRoche, as she had with Dr. Gray.

"But Will, I remembered some of it today. I remember that cross. I remember those plaques. I remember them so clearly from my hypnosis with Dr. LaRoche. And the altar. There's something about that altar."

"Could you have seen something similar in the churches in Paris?"

"No, I saw lots of crosses but none like that one. I know this sounds crazy, but I saw *that* cross! How could that be possible, Will?"

"I don't know. But I believe you."

"That means a lot to me. It's hard to understand it myself."

"What I'm trying to say is that I have learned so much here, some on my own and some with the help of Dr. LaRoche, but there's something else. It is the most important change.

"On one of my first days in Paris, I was taking pictures of Notre Dame Cathedral when something happened. It started as curiosity when I saw the French people, not tourists, going in and out, one after the other. I wanted to know what they were doing, so I walked into the back of the church and watched as they strolled in, prayed, crossed their hearts, then walked back out, all in a matter of just a few minutes.

"Anyway, what I want to tell you is not about them, it's about me. I felt something, Will. I can't really describe it. At first, it was a draw into the church, but soon I became overwhelmed with emotion at the intense yearning I felt. It was as if I'd found something I didn't know I'd lost. I felt the same thing when I went into Sacre Cœur. It felt like God was pulling me in. I've felt Him near to me here. In my entire upbringing I never experienced anything like that. When I found out that Mom had her stroke, a church was the first place I thought to go, to pray for her."

"I prayed for her, too."

"Will, that means a lot to me. I've done a lot of soul searching here and have come to see what is truly important in life. Can you understand that?"

Will shook his head and she continued, "Maybe we can find our way together when we get back home. How would you feel about that?"

"Let's go light a candle and pray for Laura and her husband." Jules knew this was his answer.

***

Sitting at the rustic table under the covered porch, Jules was keenly aware of the fact that she was having dinner, watching the same sun setting behind the same hillside that her ancestors once had. She tried to picture the scene, baking bread in the outdoor bread oven, washing dishes in the stone sink, sleeping inside this very house after an exhausting day of hand-crafting barrels that would carry wines on horse-pulled wagons throughout France.

"Jules?" Will gently nudged his wife.

"Je suis désolé, forgive me. I let my mind wander back a few centuries. I've just noticed the small window," Jules said pointing up toward the house. "I remember seeing stairs inside the house but didn't think to ask where they led. May I ask, is it just an attic?"

"It leads to an upper bedroom. Would you like to see it?"

"Merci, no. We have troubled you quite enough,"

"I would like to show you after dinner. I've just remembered something."

"We'd love to then."

The Merritts and the Bissets learned about each other's families while sharing an authentic French supper of duck confit, served with roasted summer vegetables from the Bisset's own garden.

After they'd savored the apple tarte and *cafés*, Mme Bisset led them up the dipped stone steps to a single room that ran the length of the house. The ceilings were low with wooden support beams hanging even lower. One by one, they ducked underneath. Mme Bisset asked them to sit on the bed while she went deeper into the space.

"Now, where did I put it?" Jules heard her mumble in French.

While Mme Bisset searched the eaves, Jules became aware of her escalating feelings. "Will, I'm not feeling quite right."

"What is it? Do we need to leave?"

"I'm not sure. I feel disoriented."

"I understand. This is a lot to take in."

"I think we should go now."

Will stood and reached for Jules hand.

"Aah. There you are." Mme Bisset reached her arm deep into the eave and pulled out a rusty metal box. She dusted it off with her apron while walking back toward them then handed it to Jules.

"We found this just after we moved in when we were storing boxes up here. There are initials carved on the underside."

Jules turned the box over and saw the initials JVR scratched into it, apparently by a child. The box was so lightweight that Jules assumed it to be empty, but when she turned it back over, she heard a rattling inside. "Do you know what's inside?"

"Oui, we opened it once, but it is just some papers and a few worthless trinkets. What did you say was the name of your ancestors?"

"Reynaud. It does have the initial R."

"Reynaud. That sounds familiar. It's been a long time since we moved here. We thought about throwing it away, but figured it belonged with the house. Now it belongs to you. Would you like to open it?"

"Merci, but it is getting late, and we have a long drive ahead of us," Will spoke for Jules.

Will and Jules expressed their sincere gratitude for the kindness they had been shown.

As they walked toward the rental car, Jules stopped and turned back for one last look at the house, "I really don't want to leave."

On the long drive back to the hotel, Jules sat with the box in her lap, silently trying to comprehend the incomprehensible and reliving the surreal experiences of the day. Will concentrated on navigating the winding roads back to Bordeaux.

36

Joëlle
Bordeaux, France 1686

On New Year's Day, Henri called Joëlle into his room.

"What's behind your back?" she asked while trying to peer around him.

"I've made a late Christmas present for you." He pulled the painting he had made of their tree swing from behind his back.

"Henri! This is wonderful! Did Maman help you paint it?" Joëlle was in awe of the detailed likeness to their Bordeaux swinging tree. She noticed the contrast of the dark wood branches set against the lightness of the sky, the whisp in the clouds and the empty swing, set askew in the wind.

"No, Joëlle. I did it myself," he said proudly.

Joëlle concentrated on the details of the painting. "I am impressed. I'm going to hang it in my room. Then she looked up at Henri, her mood changed, "I'm sorry, Henri, but I didn't make anything for you."

"So, it seems you owe me a favor," he said with a mischievous look on his face.

Joëlle smiled at her clever brother. "I see that you are finally growing up. Oh, the trouble we are going to get into together."

***

The following week, Joëlle and Henri were to start back to school in their new makeshift classroom.

"Awake, Mademoiselle. Your dreams shall have to wait," Marguerite sang as she pulled the rose-printed door drape aside. She held the candle high to awaken her daughter's room. Joëlle willed her heavy eyelids open but said nothing.

"Your brother is already down to breakfast. You shall have to scurry."

When Joëlle had not come down to breakfast by the time Henri sat down to eat, her mother had suspected something was awry.

Joëlle begrudgingly forced one foot, then the other, over the side of the low mattress. A feather tip scratched her leg. She groaned as she tried to rise to her feet but became light-headed and fell backward toward her bed. Marguerite dropped the candle as she lunged for her daughter, catching her just in time to soften the fall.

"Chérie, are you quite alright?" Marguerite picked up the still-burning candle and stamped out a spark on the wood floor. She placed the candle in the candlestick on Joëlle's bedside table, then knelt beside her daughter.

Joëlle put her hand to her throat as she pushed the words from her mouth, "No, Maman, I fear that I am not," then leaned into her mother. Marguerite put her cheek to Joëlle's forehead, "Indeed, you do feel warm. I think you should stay in from school today." Marguerite steadied her daughter's back and gently guided her onto the pillow. "If you're not better by the time Henri gets home from school, we shall send for the doctor." She tucked her child's limp legs beneath the thick quilt that Grand-mère Reynaud had made her for Christmas then pulled it up and tucked her in tight. While she was still on the floor, Marguerite scooted over to pile a few more logs on the fire.

"Lie there and rest. I shall be back up as soon as I see your brother to school."

No sooner than she heard her mother descend the stairs, Joëlle was back to her dreams.

Downstairs, Marguerite called for Henri as she slipped her woolen-socked feet into her boots.

It had been snowing for days. The snow was deep and drifted. This wintry morning called for the heaviest protection against the elements. She held open the sheep's wool coat as Henri wiggled into it. He had already put his gloves on, so Marguerite bent down in front of him. She buttoned his coat and cinched his hood tight to keep out the bitter wind. He was his usual quiet self this morning, but she noticed a sweet smile on his face and got momentarily lost in his eyes.

"Maman! We shall be late," Henri said and brought her back to the present. She gave him a pat on the cheek, rose from her knees, and slipped on her gloves and hat.

Marguerite looked carefully in both directions before descending the back stoop. She had overheard rumors of Dragoons heading south out of Paris, going into large cities, raiding homes, scaring children, forcing them to give up their faith or face unthinkable consequences. The revocation of the Edict of Nantes had already wreaked havoc in the lives of Protestant French citizens in the northern cities. The people of Bordeaux hoped to escape their fate.

Seeing nothing out of the ordinary, Marguerite put her fear aside. Guy had assured her that the hostilities had calmed and that he felt that their family was safe in Bordeaux for now. She reached for Henri's gloved hand and pulled him close to her as they walked briskly to school. He was still young enough that he didn't mind. She knew it would not last much longer, so Marguerite savored it.

As they arrived at school, she wished Henri a good day and nodded a smile to him. Henri waved back before climbing down the cellar steps of the half-timbered building. Marguerite shoved her hands deep into her warm pockets. Head down into the wind, she hurried on.

***

Back at home, Marguerite pulled off her snow-covered boots and with quiet feet, she headed up the stairs to peek in on her deep-sleeping daughter. She placed first a kiss, then a damp cloth on Joëlle's forehead then went about her chores for the day. Marguerite busied herself with cooking and keeping logs on the fires while Joëlle slept and hours passed.

Joëlle awoke late morning to the startling sound of her father bursting open the heavy wooden door, slamming the stone wall behind. "Marguerite!" His voice was loud and forceful. Joëlle shot up in her bed, chills running down her limbs. She could hear her father's boots strike the stone floor as he ran from this room to that, desperately looking for his wife. Joëlle sat frozen, afraid to breathe. The footsteps halted, but only for a second. The moment of silence was broken by her mother's shrill scream, "No!"

The running started again. Joëlle listened intently, this time as two sets of footsteps ran through the entry hall. She heard her father's urging as he helped her mother into her boots.

Joëlle ran to the window in Henri's room which faced the street in front of the house, trying to catch a glimpse of the drama that was unfolding. Then she saw it in the distance. Thick black smoke rolling up to the heavens. Her brain raced. Where was it coming from? It was not coming from the direction of her father's cooperage. It was not coming from the Catholic church tower.

Joëlle spotted her parents as they joined a street full of frantic people running in all directions. She saw that her mother had not taken the time to put on a coat. She gasped as she saw the military men, on their muscular horses, swinging swords, trying to keep the people from running toward the smoke. Her parents would not be redirected. She watched as they evaded the swinging blades. Holding hands, they raced on.

Where are they going? Joëlle traced the streets in her mind. Then it hit her. Her parents were running toward the church school. "Henri!"

37

Jules
Bordeaux, France

Will and Jules arrived back at the hotel close to midnight. The crunch of the tires pulling onto the gravel drive and the amber glow of the gas lights coloring the limestone exterior made Jules feel like she was in one of her beloved vintage movies.

In the room, Jules said, "I'd like to soak in that luxurious tub if you don't mind."

"Would you like for me to open a bottle of the wine we bought this morning?"

"That sounds perfect."

After the emotional day, Jules took the hotel's monogrammed robe from the hook on the double door entrance into the bathroom. The marble floor felt cool under her feet as she sat on the edge of the deep tub and turned the squeaking handles on the porcelain cradled hand shower. She noticed that attention to detail in the suite's décor had not stopped in the bedroom. The cabinetry, as well as the paneled walls, were painted a dusty cornflower blue. An ornate gilded mirror hung above the stone sink that held fresh flowers, thirsty towels, and decadent bath supplies. She savored the experience, soaking in the silky bubbled water.

When Jules came out of the bathroom, she saw a note from Will lying on the bed that simply read, "Be right back." She guessed that he had gone to the dining room to look for wine glasses, so she went back into the bathroom to dry her hair. Just as she finished, Will walked in with wine glasses in one hand and a small stack of papers in the other.

"I thought that's where you went," she asked while taking the glasses. "But what's with the papers?"

Will pulled a corkscrew from his pocket. "While you were in the bath, I checked my email and was surprised to see I'd received one from The Huguenot Museum in Charlotte. I thought about waiting to let you open it, but I didn't want you to be disappointed if it wasn't anything important. After reading it, I wanted you to have it in your hands, rather than read it on a screen. When I was in the kitchen, I ran into Mr. Fenelon's son, who helped me print these from the printer in his father's office."

"Really? It must be something interesting. Let me see." Jules made herself comfortable, sitting cross-legged on the bed.

Will handed her a glass of wine and a copy of a ship's log from 1688, listing the passengers that were traveling from London to Virginia. He retrieved the copy of Jules' lineage from his suitcase then sat down beside her. Together they scanned the pages in search of the name Reynaud.

"Look, Will, there they are! Louis Guy Reynaud, his wife, Marguerite De LaCroix Reynaud, and a daughter, Joëlle Violette." Jules paused in thought. "Joëlle Violette Reynaud, JVR! Could that box truly belong to her? Could it have been up there for all those years?"

"Let's open it and find out." Will used the corkscrew to pry open the bent lid.

Jules peered into the box and saw an ancient notebook. She tried to pull it out, but the cover came off in her hands. Will pulled out the loose pages which all appeared blank. He turned them over to place them on the bed and saw writing. "Jules, what does this say? It seems to be the only entry."

"It says, 'I miss the sound of doorbells.'"

"Well, here are the doorbells," he said while pulling out the tattered string.

"That's strange. I wonder why anyone would want to save those. What else is in there?"

Jules picked at a piece of wood in the bottom of the box. She tried to remove it, but it was wedged in tight.

Will turned the box over and gave it a thump, releasing the wood board.

"It's a child's painting, Will!" She ran her fingers over the oil painting of a tree swing. "It's so sweet. It's signed, 'Henri.' I wonder who Henri is."

"There's more, Jules. Their daughter, Joëlle, kept a journal. The museum has the original, but they sent copies of a few of the pages." He handed her an entry dated just one week after they had arrived in America. "This one's written in French, so you'll have to translate it to me."

Jules read it to Will, slowly translating one line at a time.

October 21, 1688
Today is just like every other day since we arrived. We move very slowly as the men are clearing trees and brush, to make the horse path into a road wide enough to accommodate the buggies carrying our rations. Mother tries to be brave but she is still so sad. I guess we always will be. The women and children stay in the camp while the men clear out a few days of road, then we move the camp again. The women prepare food, and the children gather wood for the fires. I am one of the oldest so I am in charge of keeping them close and safe. I do not like being around them. I miss my brother.

Jules looked up, "Her brother? Oh, no! Where is her brother?" Jules hurt for Joëlle.

"I think you'll find the answer here." Will handed her the last piece of paper.

38

Joëlle
Bordeaux, France 1686

Joëlle pushed herself away from the window. She yanked her boots over her bare feet, under her floor-length gown. She grabbed a wool scarf at the end of her bed and ran down the stairs to find that the door had been left wide open. In her rushing, she slipped on snow that had blown in and melted, causing her to stumble through the opened front door, and onto the stone porch, cutting both her knees open. She barely noticed as she stood, looking for a path free of the chaos unfolding in the streets. There was none. She ran back inside and closed the front door, locking its thick wooden bolt. She grabbed her mother's coat and headed for the back of the house. Joëlle ran out the glass kitchen door. Her hands stuck to the frozen railing as she slid down the icy steps. She ran through her mother's snowy garden and out the iron gate. Joëlle ran as fast as her freezing feet would carry her.

As she neared the school, she heard the screams; screams of children inside the school and the screams of the parents trying to get to them. She heard windows being blown out and the banging of people trying to get in. She heard the whinnying of the horses and the deep shouts of the Dragoons telling them all to, "Get back!" She scanned the crowd for her parents. Joëlle weaved in and out of a sea of people, looking upward at horrified faces. As she heard their cries of, "mon fils," "ma fille," "mon Dieu!," a realization set in…no one was getting into the church…and no one was getting out. "Henri," she whispered as she grabbed her sickened stomach.

'This is all my fault. I was not at school to protect you when you needed me most. I am so sorry, Henri.'

She spotted her parents just in time to see her mother collapse in slow motion into the snow. Joëlle ran to her and dropped to her bloody knees. She placed the scarf around her mother's neck, the coat over her mother's shoulders and her head into her mother's heaving chest. She felt her father's arms envelop them both. His unfamiliar sobs joined theirs.

39

Jules
Bordeaux, France

Will handed Jules the paper. "It's a poem."
In English, the description read:

Written for my brother Henri Guy Reynaud, age nine, who was killed in a fire in our church school in Bordeaux, France, in 1686. I was twelve at the time of his death. The fire was intentionally set by Dragoons after the Revocation of the Edict of Nantes.
Rather than denounce our Protestant faith, my family chose to flee under cover of night, being hunted like animals, from our life in Bordeaux to my grandparents' house in Baran, where we stayed in hiding until Father arranged our secret passage to London.

"Henri? Henri is Joëlle's brother?! Will, they hid in Baran, in that house! They grieved there." Jules broke into sobs, her heart still tender from the loss of her mother. "Will you read the poem to me? I can't."

Will read the poem, written in English, as his wife sat weeping on the bed.

Ever, A Poem for Henri
By Joëlle Violette (JoVee) Reynaud 1692

Ever in childhood
Just you and me
Though separated by death
Separated by sea

Ever singing, ever swinging
Flying high, feeling free
Taking turns pushing, soaring
The wood swing in our tree

Through Maman's garden
Ever run, ever twirl
Climbing rocks with her roses
Just her boy and her girl

In PaPa's study, by candle
When day is done
Ever listening to poetry
Read for daughter and son

Ever worshiping together
Our Christ, our King
With hands joined in prayer
With joined hearts, we sing

Ever present, ever with me
Whether drought or life's flood
Christ's comfort, Henri's memory
France, flowing ever my blood

When Will finished reading, he put his hand under her chin and raised her face to look at him. "Jules, this is proof that your ancestors never wanted to leave France. Maybe that's why you feel such a pull to be here, toward all things French. I guess it really is that French blood running through your veins."

Wiping tears, Jules looked back down at the floor, deep in thought, trying desperately to hone in on the connection being made in her head. She whispered, "Henri." She mumbled, "Henri."

And then the connection was made. Her voice grew louder, "Aw-ee, On-ree?" She looked up. "Will! That's it! That is the other word I was saying on the video. Mon Dieu, les enfants, Henri. My God, the children, Henri!"

She stopped breathing and turned her wide eyes to Will's, searching for an explanation. He stared back, as bewildered as his wife.

Jules sat on the bed, staring at the poem. Her voice was shaking, but determined, "All my life, I thought something was wrong with me. But this." She shook the poem, "This is confirmation that I have not imagined any of this. Will, how? How could this be? How in the world is this possible?"

"I have no idea," Will responded, shaking his head.

Her mind still searching for an explanation, "I don't guess I'll ever know."

Will stopped her. "There's your answer, Jules."

She looked up at him, questioning.

"You said you won't *ever* know for sure. *Ever*. It all makes sense now. Henri, the fire, the way the smell of smoke sickens you, les enfants, the children in the school, your dreams of being chased through the woods. These are the things that are *ever* in *Joëlle's* blood, *ever* in *your* blood." He took the page from her hands and read the last line of the poem again, "France, flowing ever my blood."

Jules looked at Will with a smile on her face and peace in her watery eyes. She could not speak but laughed through her tears. Although she did not understand it, Jules felt justified. She felt released.

She was so incredibly thankful and overwhelmed by her love for Will. They drank their glasses empty and held each other for the first time in months. Will had never seen her so free.

They opened the second bottle and drank it slowly while sitting on the bed, talking about their unbelievable day. Jules picked up Henri's painting and held it to her chest. "What a precious treasure Mme Bisset has given us. She stared at the painting for a while before placing it back into the painting box. "I can't wait to find a special place for it at home."

They fell asleep in each other's arms just as the sun was rising over the vineyards.

***

They slept most of their third day in Bordeaux, ordering room service for dinner, prepared by Mme Fenelon. After they finished, they climbed back into bed. In the morning, they would catch the train back to Paris, where they would spend the remainder of their trip seeing the tourist attractions of Paris with Chloe and her Frenchman.

40

Joëlle
Bordeaux, France 1686

For the next few days, Joëlle and her mother grieved alone in a hidden room in the basement of the cooperage, sick to their stomachs in shock and disbelief, while her father made the final arrangements for their escape out of Bordeaux.

Marguerite pleaded with Guy to fetch her parents, but he would not risk it. "I am sorry, Marguerite. I will not. I was not able to protect Henri, and I will not risk your lives or theirs. We will write them a letter once we are settled."

Marguerite sobbed into her husband's shoulder. She needed her mother. He pulled away from her then left the cooperage to retrieve more items from their home. His own grief was overwhelming, but he could not bear the cries of his wife and daughter.

"But, Maman, we cannot leave Henri. I do not want to go to Baran without him," she pleaded. The happy home of their childhood was no longer. The thought of being inside that house without Henri sickened her.

"Neither do I, Joëlle. We have no choice. But we will not be leaving him. Henri is with us. He will always be with us."

Her mother's words were meant to soothe, but Joëlle knew that none of their lives would ever be the same. Her mother would never dance again. There would be no joy in her mother's eyes.

Her father would no longer be the man she had known, confident, proud, and at ease in the world.

Joëlle knew that her life might be the most changed of all. She did not remember a life without Henri. He was her everyday companion. Her life was *full up* because of him. She had always seen herself as his protector. Her life was now empty of purpose. *No one will ever call me JoVee again.*

"Can we please go home? I want to get the painting that Henri made for me. Please, Maman?"

Marguerite rose to her feet and went to a bag of items that Guy had already retrieved from the house. She pulled out a metal box containing the painting and handed it to her daughter, along with the string of doorbells that Guy had found under her blanket. Joëlle grabbed the items and held them tight to her chest, doubled over with grief.

***

Guy had been following what was happening in northern France and, for months, had been actively making escape plans should the violence move south. He had gone across the ocean to London to arrange for the future sale of the cooperage. He had supplies and money stored at their country house in Baran. He had planned for every contingency, except the devastating loss of his son. He blamed himself for not having done enough to protect his family, though he had been consumed with nothing else for the last eight months.

Their treacherous week-long journey from Bordeaux to Baran was brutal, inching slowly at night, as they lived in constant fear of being discovered.

After six harrowing days and nights of travel, Guy halted his horse when they reached the winter-barren meadow. Marguerite gently woke Joëlle and pointed to the familiar yellow cross on the stone wall near Baran.

When they arrived at her grandparent's maison, Joëlle could not make herself enter through the beloved dutch-door, not without Henri. She stood outside, her body shaking to its core, while her parents went inside to inform her grandparents. Only seconds later, she heard the grief-stricken scream of Grand-mère and the cries of her parents. Joëlle fell to her knees and heaved, though she hadn't eaten in days. Her grief was too much.

From that day forward, for the next two years, Joëlle did not speak a word.

It was not until she arrived in Virginia that she was able to put her fear aside and allow herself to see a way forward into a different life, but the trauma she'd experienced would always be present in her life. She would forever heave at the smell of smoke. She would never be able to cross another large body of water. For the rest of her life, her dreams would be haunted by the fear she suffered on their final trip to Baran. She would forever long for her old life in France.

Only Joëlle's faith sustained her. It was only in Him that she was able to live at all.

Ever present, ever with me
Whether drought or life's flood
Christ's comfort, Henri's memory
France, flowing ever my blood.

41

Jules
Lexington, Kentucky

For the next few months, Will and Jules enjoyed their free time together as they had in their early marriage. When the sun was shining, they went antiquing on the weekends. They watched movie marathons on rainy Saturdays. They attended different churches on Sundays, knowing that they would never find a church that came close to the one in France. But they would keep searching until they found one where they felt at home and where they could serve.

Will built a bread oven in the back yard just off their deck and added a pea gravel patio around it like the house in Baran. They held small dinner parties with family and friends. Their lives were good, and they felt blessed.

The new school year was going well for both of them, and things seemed back on track with one exception. Chloe had received an extension on her position with the university in Paris and decided to prolong her stay. Jules missed her friend but enjoyed the daily letter writing through email.

***

In October, Jules received a call from Dr. Gray's office informing Jules that she'd received a letter from Dr. LaRoche. She wanted Jules to schedule an appointment to go over his notes.

Dr. Gray raised her eyebrows when her patient entered the office. The haircut and the change in her dress were new, but the most notable difference was the lightness of being in Jules' demeanor. "It's good to see you again. You are looking well. How are you doing?"

"I'm great. The time away was just what I needed to give me clarity in my life. Away from the stresses of daily routines and relationships, I was able to let down my walls. I discovered things about myself that I would not have had the opportunity to otherwise. But there is so much more to it than that. I got answers there. Some questions remain, but I've put away past hurts and can move forward with my life. I no longer wonder what is wrong with me. In fact, I now see those things as beautiful in my life. I feel blessed because of them."

"That's good to hear. I was sorry to hear about your mother."

"Thank you. I was able to spend some time with her before she passed. Maybe I can make an appointment with you to talk more about that sometime."

"That would be a good thing. I would be happy to listen. As I said on the phone, I received the notes from your sessions with Dr. LaRoche."

"I appreciate your help in setting that up for me. In just those two visits, he really helped me. I regret that we did not get to continue."

"I was happy to do it and glad he was able to help you. In his letter, Dr. LaRoche wanted to address two issues. The first was your initial trance therapy session with me. Would you like for me to explain?"

"Yes, please do." Jules was eager to hear what Dr. LaRoche had to say.

"Dr. LaRoche, as you know, comes at this with a unique perspective. He has had a lengthy career of using hypnosis with his patients to great success. He cites a specific case that he feels is similar to yours. His patient presented to him with severe sleep anxiety after being troubled by a dream of two drastically different scenes of birth. The dream always began in a candlelit room, where the mother-to-be was surrounded by the calming hums of the women attending her. The baby came quietly into the world and was placed on the mother. During this part of the dream, his patient had remained calm and asleep.

"This woman, his patient, was from an Eastern culture that believes people are closely tied to their ancestors. This birth, having apparently taken place long ago, caused her to wonder if she was dreaming about the birth of one of her ancestors. Of course, Dr. LaRoche had no way to prove or disprove that assumption.

"The dream then always took a turn, ending with a modern-day birth. In a sterile hospital room, the masked doctor yelled, 'Push!' The frightened woman giving birth, screamed hysterically. When the baby came, she was slapped on the bottom until she cried, then was quickly whisked away from her mother, and placed under bright lights, naked on a cold metal table. The baby screamed in fear of falling, lying on her back with her arms flailing. During this part of the dream, the woman grew increasingly upset and would wake up terrified and screaming. His patient felt she may have been remembering her own birth. Again, Dr. LaRoche had no way of knowing if that were indeed the case.

"Since your hypnosis with me ended similarly, while you were remembering back as far as your mind could subconsciously go, Dr. LaRoche considered the possibility that you were experiencing trauma related to your birth or even that of an ancestor. He stated in his notes that he would have liked to have had more time with you to explore it further."

"This may surprise you, but none of that comes as a shock to me," Jules replied.

Dr. Gray continued, "The second issue Dr. LaRoche wanted to address has to do with transgenerational epigenetics, specifically genetic memory, which is a memory present at birth that exists in the absence of a person's own experience and is incorporated into the genome. He cited a specific study by Emory University. In this study, scientists performed an experiment, during which they shocked mice each time they encountered a cherry blossom. For many generations, fourteen if I am remembering correctly, their offspring exhibited a fear response at simply the smell of a cherry blossom, though those specific mice had never been shocked, potentially proving that the severe traumas of our ancestors can be responsible for the phobias we experience today."

Jules leaned in toward Dr. Gray. "Would you say that again?" *Did she just give me scientific proof of what Will and I discovered in France?*

"This study suggests that the effects of severe trauma can be seen generation after generation," Dr. Gray answered.

Hand on her heart, Jules breathed in the peace brought in those words. "Joëlle," she whispered.

"Pardon?"

"Nevermind, please go on."

Dr. Gray continued, "I would be happy to provide you with a copy of the published study if you'd like."

Neither Dr. Gray, nor Dr. LaRoche knew about the videotape and what all she'd discovered in France, but for now, Jules felt the need to keep it just between Will and herself.

"Yes, I want to share it with Will. What I have learned is that we are all a result of the experiences of our parents and our ancestors. In my case, it isn't reincarnation, it's biology. I'm happy now and free from all the things that troubled me in the past."

Dr. Gray smiled, obviously impressed by her very changed patient.

42

Jules
Midway, Kentucky

Sunbeams of auburn and amber warmed the car as Jules and Will drove out into the countryside on a late October Sunday.

Since Lillie's passing, the families had gotten together for a meal once a week. Joseph relished the new time he was spending in each of his children's homes. When Lillie was alive, the family had always gathered at the farm and Joseph had missed that, so he invited them all to go to church with him, then have a meal in the old farmhouse like they used to. Scarlette and Nichole had prepared Sunday lunch for them to eat after the service.

When it came time for dessert, Will went around the table refilling everyone's glass with more iced tea.

He remained standing. "This has been a difficult year. Losing Lillie changed everything. But it has taught us not to take each other for granted and made us all a little closer as a family. She would have loved our Sundays together.

"As you all know, Jules and I had some growing pains early in the year and spending time apart this summer certainly did not help our marriage, but Lillie's generous gift helped to get us back on track during our trip."

Then Will lifted his hand for a toast. So, will you all join me in raising our glasses to Lillie?"

"To Lillie." The boys thought it was fun to clink their glasses, but Ivy's tender heart made her cry. Jules leaned over to give her a side hug.

Then Will took Jules' hand and pulled her to stand beside him. Everyone looked on curiously.

"Now, don't put your glasses down just yet. We have another reason to celebrate. Jules?"

"Will and I are so glad we can all be together here at the farm today. I just wish that Mother was here with us. She would be so happy for me to announce that Will and I are expecting a baby!"

There was a moment of quiet shock before the cheers of congratulations. The women and children jumped up to hug Jules while the men excitedly patted Will on the back.

Ivy surprised them all by saying, "If it's a girl, we can name her Lillie!"

Jules loved that their baby was already part of the family.

When everyone was preparing to leave, Joseph asked Will and Jules if they would stay a little longer after the others left.

"I think your mother would like for you to have her rocker if you want it."

"Oh, yes, Daddy. We would love to have it. Being rocked by her is one of my favorite memories."

"How can you remember that?"

"I remember a lot of things." Jules winked at Will. She had never explained what she had discovered to her family, and she never would.

"Oh," Joseph suddenly remembered, "There's something else." He went to retrieve an envelope from his dresser drawer, then handed it to Jules.

"What's this?"

"It's from your mother, for the baby. It is the same small inheritance that she left her other grandchildren. She always hoped, Jules."

Happy tears fell as she hugged her father's neck.

***

On a windy spring morning, with the windows open, just as the sun was dawning, Jules was surrounded by flickering candlelight and the songs of happy birds. The landscape painting of roses they had been given in Baran hung above their bed. Lillie's rocker sat waiting in the corner with Henri's painting of the tree swing hung low beside it.

Above the crib, a simple frame held the words of Psalm 32:7:

"Thou art my hiding place; thou shalt preserve me from trouble; thou shalt compass me about with songs of deliverance."

While the midwife went quietly about her business, Scarlette and Nichole attended Jules while softly humming Lillie's favorite hymn, *It Is Well With My Soul.*

Jules had told Will that in France she learned that to fully live life, one must experience all of it, the good with the bad, the highs with the lows. She told him that experiencing the pain of childbirth would make the birth that much sweeter. In lieu of medication, Jules practiced the relaxation and focus techniques that she had learned for hypnosis to help her through labor.

Will gently coached his wife's breathing. He watched with pride how Jules managed each contraction. He watched in awe at how she remained calm yet determined through each push.

There was no screaming, no chaos of activity. The baby came quietly and was placed on Jules' chest. Will laid a warmed blanket over his child and looked at Jules, both crying tears of overwhelming joy.

The painting box that had kept Henri's painting safe for centuries, now thousands of miles from his home and across an ocean, sits on the small side table in the nursery, waiting to hold the trinkets and toys of another Henri, Henri Ever Merritt.

The End

AUTHOR'S NOTE

The Painting Box is a story of bones.

I once witnessed my adult son walk into the ocean with his grandfather while on a vacation together. I watched as the two of them walked in unison. Their rolled shoulders, the tilt of their heads, the position of their wrists, even the way they turned their bodies to the waves were identical.

We had lived away, so my son had not been around his grandfather enough to have picked up his mannerisms. I commented on this to my great-aunt who was sitting beside me. I'll never forget her quick response.

"It's the way our bones are strung together, Child," she said so matter-of-factly.

Nature, not nurture. But it isn't simply our outward physical characteristics, such as the color of our eyes or the curl in our hair that are passed from generation to generation. Recent epigenetic research is proving that trauma related to one's experiences, such as famine or tragedy, can be imprinted on our genes. Thus, we are born a culmination of our ancestors' physical traits as well as their life experiences.

I'd never considered such a connection to our ancestors before. Now, I can't unsee it in everyone I know.

The Painting Box is a story of bones, and so much more.

Julia R. Cooper

ACKNOWLEDGMENTS

A special thank you to those who have helped me along my journey in writing *The Painting Box.*

Christine Rockwell, my editor and book coach;
Amy Tylicki and her daughter, Shelby Tylicki, my first proofreaders;
Jon Winn and his father, Larry Winn for their professional and experienced opinions;
Suki Tutthill at French Vacation Rentals for providing the place that inspired it all;
Kathy Herm and Lori Hanson, my first fans and biggest cheerleaders;
A special thank you to Ashley Winn for the original painting for the cover and to Chelsea Wells Photo for the author photo;
And to my family, who put up with me while writing *The Painting Box* for the last few years, thank you to my mother, Joan Smith, my father, Jimmy Reneau, and my sisters, Tina Page, Kathy Herm and Melissa DeVries;
And to my husband, Jeff, and my children, Kurt and Natalie, Ashley and Jon, and Chelsea and Carter who have made my life happy and full. And to my grandchildren, Lila, Isaiah, Wallace, Sylvie, Ada, Eleanor and Lucy who have made my life complete.

Thank you, God.

ABOUT THE AUTHOR

A summer spent in the French countryside and a love of historical fiction came together to birth the story of *The Painting Box*.

Julia R. Cooper, mylittlefrenchfarm.com, lives in Kentucky with her husband.

The Painting Box is her first novel.

Made in the USA
Columbia, SC
23 October 2024

a1bfdcb1-f717-4ce7-9980-5b913acc46e2R01